JUST
SA

M000073241

"LAMB TO THE SLAUGHTER"
by Roald Dahl

This tale of the best way to get rid of a husband—
and a murder weapon—is a chilling example of
domestic violence served up with a twist.

"IN VINO VERITAS" by A. A. Milne

When a butler didn't do it, but had it done to him,
a mystery writer helps a police superintendent
solve a case involving poisoned wine—and a
diabolical mind.

"JUST DESSERTS" by Stanley Ellin

A Texas oil man takes private lessons from a
French chef so he can impress his gourmand
friends with the perfect dessert. And indeed the
meal may end with quite a bang!

"EXOTIC CUISINE" by George Baxt

An aging television chef has popularized such
rare dishes as leg of llama and reindeer tongue
braised with Welsh leeks, but now she is planning
to cook up a legacy no one will ever forget.

And over 15 more well-done
and juicy tales of mayhem and
murder ...

MYSTERY ANTHOLOGIES

Crime
à la Carte

EDITED BY

Cynthia Manson

A SIGNET BOOK

SIGNET
Published by the Penguin Group
Penguin Books USA Inc., 375 Hudson Street
New York, New York 10014, U.S.A.
Penguin Books Ltd, 27 Wrights Lane,
London W8 5TZ, England
Penguin Books Australia Ltd, Ringwood,
Victoria, Australia
Penguin Books Canada Ltd, 10 Alcorn Avenue,
Toronto, Ontario, Canada M4V 3B2
Penguin Books (N.Z.) Ltd, 182–190 Wairau Road,
Auckland 10, New Zealand

Penguin Books Ltd, Registered Offices:
Harmondsworth, Middlesex, England

First published by Signet,
an imprint of Dutton Signet,
a division of Penguin Books USA Inc.

First printing, December, 1994
10 9 8 7 6 5 4 3 2 1

We are grateful to the following for permission to reprint their
copyrighted material:

"A Dry Manhattan Story" by Alan Gordon, copyright © 1991 by Davis Publications, Inc., reprinted by permission of the author; "If Cooks Could Kill" by Robert
Gray, copyright © 1985 by Davis Publications, Inc., reprinted by permission of the
author; "The Maggody Files: Spiced Rhubarb" by Joan Hess, copyright © 1991 by
Davis Publications, Inc., reprinted by permission of the author; "A Coffin of Rice"
by Martin Limon, copyright © 1990 by Davis Publications, Inc., reprinted by permission of the author; "The Case of the Amateur Detective and the Chicken" by
James A. Noble, copyright © 1983 by Davis Publications, Inc., reprinted by permission of the author; all stories previously appeared in *Alfred Hitchcock Mystery
Magazine*, published by Bantam Doubleday Dell Magazines.

"Alfred Karns, Accessory" by T.M. Adams, copyright © 1977 by Davis Publications, Inc., reprinted by permission of the author; "Blown Up" by Robert Barnard,
copyright © 1986 by Davis Publications, Inc., reprinted by permission of the author; "Exotic Cuisine" by George Baxt, copyright © 1992 by Bantam Doubleday
Dell Magazines, reprinted by permission of the author; "My Compliments to the
Chef" by Marge Blaine, copyright © 1981 by Davis Publications, Inc., reprinted
by permission of the author; "The Avenging Chance" by Anthony Berkeley, copyright © 1929 by A.B. Cox, reprinted by permission of the author; "Food for
Thought" copyright © 1953 by Victor Canning, reprinted by permission of Curtis
Brown, Ltd.; "The Herb of Death" from "The Tuesday Club Murders," copyright

The following page constitutes an extension of this copyright page.

REGISTERED TRADEMARK—MARCA REGISTRADA

Printed in the United States of America

PUBLISHER'S NOTE
These stories are works of fiction. Names, characters, places, and incidents either are the product of the authors' imaginations or are used fictitiously, and any resemblance to actual persons, living or dead, events, or locales is entirely coincidental.

Contents

Introduction

If you have an appetite for murder mysteries where the key ingredient to murder is food, then you most certainly will enjoy this anthology *Crime à la Carte*. The stories in this collection are from *Ellery Queen's Mystery Magazine* and *Alfred Hitchcock Mystery Magazine,* and feature food and wine as either a purveyor of death or a backdrop for crime. The variety of selections should delight the most discriminating literary palates. In addition, we have a lineup of authors who are the "crème de la crème" such as Agatha Christie, Victor Canning, Stanley Ellin, Roald Dahl, and A.A. Milne. The international flavor of their stories should appeal to mystery connoisseurs everywhere.

The writers have chosen greed, hate, jealousy, and revenge as the ingredients used to cook up these delicious *Crimes à la Carte*. Samplings from the menu offer concoctions dished up by sinister master chefs and devilish gourmets. There are also carefully prepared desserts of "bittersweet" flavors which give new meaning to the "final" course.

I have included four "specials of the day," recipes from four of the authors whose stories are featured in this book. I am grateful to Joan Hess, George Baxt, Robert Barnard, and the Estate of M.F.K. Fisher for permitting me to include their delightful recipes. Contrary to the mood of this book, you will note that none of these recipes include a single poisonous ingredient.

Now that I have awakened your taste buds for reading *Crime à la Carte*, all that remains is to wish you "bon appétit!"

—Cynthia Manson

Exotic Cuisine
by George Baxt

"I am quite aware of my terrible reputation," stated the septuagenarian Theresa Camus. "I am incredibly rude, incredibly nasty, and incredibly unpleasant. Therefore, I must be incredibly rich. I am." She was addressing Andre du Blancmange, proprietor of Le Gourmet Deluxe, who was incredibly greedy.

"Madam does herself a disservice," said Andre, a certified servile toady, as he rubbed his itching palms together. "Would madam care to examine my fresh shipment of grouse? I also have some very rare ortolan bred in the Forbidden City of China. Ortolan is not easy to come by these days." When he smiled his obsequious little smile, his ears wiggled and his nose wigwagged, and the old lady restrained an urge to punch him in the jaw.

"You said you'd have rhinoceros steaks today. Well?" Her hands on her hips, her eyes narrowed into dangerous slits.

"Madam did not forget."

"I never forget. Have you got them?"

"I most certainly do. I also have fresh breast of tapir and roast leg of llama. I have a marvelous recipe for that, handed down to me from my great-grandmother, who was born in the Peruvian Andes. She was the one who was afraid of heights. It's a very special recipe requiring marinating the llama's leg for seventy-two hours in a marinade consisting of ..." He looked about him to make sure they were out of earshot of eavesdroppers, and then as a further precaution, leaned forward and whispered in her ear.

The old lady digested the information and said, "Interesting. Very interesting. So it requires edelweiss. Do you have edelweiss?"

"Indeed I do, madam. Three Swiss mountain climbers gave their lives to procure these edelweiss. Fortunately, one of them had placed his crop in a knapsack which survived the fall intact."

"Du Blancmange, you are a gustatory scoundrel." She rattled off her order and instructed him to have it delivered to her mansion within the next two hours. Later, he padded the amount he entered into her account, payable monthly, and then went to his office in the rear of his establishment to polish off his lunch of the burrito special from the fast-food Tex-Mex diner down the street.

Theresa Camus was a large woman. She stood five feet nine inches in her stocking feet, and weighed over two hundred and sixty pounds. Her grandson Chester had compared her to a Sherman tank. Now she was barreling along the main street of Mayflower, New Hampshire, an exclusive enclave created some fifty years ago by her late and unlamented husband Vernon. Thanks to Vernon and the village's charter, you had to be incredibly rich to own property, build, and reside in Mayflower. Several Rockefellers, Astors, and Vanderbilts did not qualify, and it was rumored that a certain Mellon had defenestrated from the Chrysler Building upon being notified of his rejection. As she made her way to her next port of call, Theresa paused briefly to confront a baby in its carriage and it took the tyke and its mother five minutes before they realized Theresa had stolen the tot's lollipop.

Theresa Camus. Tessie. Little Tess. Seventy years ago, at the age of five, Little Tessie Farina was one of the most adorable children to be found in the Bensonhurst section of Brooklyn. She was the youngest of eight of poor but dishonest parents who ran a numbers racket. Soon they were poor no longer and the Farinas moved to the Washington Heights section of Manhattan where Theresa blossomed into a tall, stately beauty, who at Vassar majored in wealthy husband. When not busy weaving in and out of the Vassar daisy chain, Theresa had her good eyes out for a likely prospect. When she was introduced to Vernon Camus at the annual Harvest Moon Ball and Supper sponsored by an organization known as G. and G., Theresa knew she had found her man. G. and G. stood for Gourmands and Gluttons. Like his exclusive fellow members, Vernon loved to eat. He ate anything and everything. Later there would be nasty rumors as to how he had survived an expedition into the Brazilian jungles, when he and only he of a party of ten had survived a plane crash that stranded them for over three months. When he emerged from the jungle he was forty pounds heavier.

Theresa loved to cook. She got that from her father's mother, who was born to the celebrated Ballabusta restaurant family. And like her grandmother, Theresa was on her way to becoming a brilliant gourmet cook. Before meeting Vernon, she had planned on opening a restaurant after graduation. But when she learned that Vernon was the heir to a monumental fortune, she concentrated on winning his love. After they were married, Theresa cooked and Vernon ate. Their first child was prematurely born four months after they were married. It was a girl and they named her Rose. Two years later, they were blessed with a son, Norton. Shortly after, Theresa published the first of her many cookbooks. This led to a syndicated newspaper column that was published around the world, and now in her seventies, Theresa was gathering in even more millions with her syndicated television program. At the beginning of the eleventh year of their tumultuous marriage (there were arguments about sauces, cuts of meat, savory aspics, and not too savory chateaubriands that were occasionally overcooked), Theresa began to suspect Vernon of trying to manipulate her personal wealth. Shortly after, Vernon was dead of a suspected heart attack brought on by acute indigestion. The village of

Mayflower that Vernon had founded was only two
years in existence, but Theresa took over its steward-
ship with a firm hand, and over the years, she single-
handedly converted Mayflower's Gourmands and
Gluttons into glorious gourmets. Mayflower's fame
spread across the world and Theresa Camus was a
household name.

Fame and wealth did not bring happiness, sadly
enough. The Camus daughter Rose married Dr. Oliver
Folger, a dietician whom Theresa loathed instantly.
He harped on cholesterol, and fatty substances and
heart disease and strokes, and was soon not welcome
in Theresa's house. He didn't dare let her know he
was a closet glutton, taking trips abroad on his own to
Paris and Rome where he could gorge to his heart's
content. When Rose found out about his secret vice,
she scolded him severely and mercilessly, and then
joined him on his international eating binges. Norton
Camus, the son, proved to have evolved into a wast-
rel, a liar, a womanizer, and a cardsharp. His wife, Titania, designed high-style clothing for women and
was somewhat successful at it. But unlike her mother-
in-law, she couldn't cook worth a damn, though she
loved her food. Norton prevailed upon Theresa to invite them more often for a meal, but Theresa couldn't
stand Titania because although she respected and enjoyed food, she was very careful about her diet in fear
of gaining weight and being an adverse advertisement
for her line of clothing. It was about this time that the
family began to realize that Theresa talked to herself
a lot, muttered dire imprecations under her breath,
and hoarded her splendid gastronomical concoctions
in the gargantuan walk-in freezer she had constructed
in her ample basement.

The freezer became as famous as its mistress.
There were speculations as to what fabulous culinary
creations it contained. Geraldo Rivera tried to make a
deal with Theresa to open the freezer for a one-hour
television special, much as he had done years earlier
with Al Capone's secret basement (which revealed

nothing). If she were to be a party to such a tasteless spectacle, Theresa privately opined to her housekeeper, Nellie Baker, she preferred Oprah Winfrey to Geraldo, as Oprah had such a terrible weight problem.

Rose and Oliver Folger had no children as, tragically, Rose was barren. Titania and Norton, however, had one child, a son. They named him Chester and briefly, Theresa thawed towards them. She adored Chester, who was the apple of her eye until his tenth year she realized that like many apples, he was rotten to the core. Chester was indeed a chip off the old block. Like his father, he lied and cheated and stole money from his grandmother's handbag. Nellie Baker caught him at it several times, and she would never forget the day she caught him attacking the fabulous freezer with a crowbar.

Theresa was unhappy. She was lonely. She wouldn't permit a replacement for Vernon because she was positive every man who showed an interest in her was actually interested in her vast wealth. Her books, her columns, her TV shows occupied most of her time, but she usually ate alone, occasionally asking Nellie to join her. During one such meal, Nellie, who was gently outspoken and genuinely fond of her employer, said to Theresa, "Mrs. Camus, you're over seventy now."

"I can count," snapped Theresa.

"Your family is all you've got."

"I've got my money and I've got my freezer."

"But they're cold comfort. Don't you think you should consider making peace with your loved ones?"

"Loved ones, ha! They don't love me and I don't love them."

"They always call to ask after you."

"And I can tell you why," roared Theresa, "it's the money they're after! I know about Norton's gambling debts! I know Chester can't cut it trying to write articles for the newspapers and the magazines. You think I don't know he's been trying to sell exposés about me

to *New York* magazine and *Vanity Fair*?" She pushed
her chair back and began circling the table, building up
a head of steam. "You think I don't know he sold that
article to the *Enquirer* calling my husband a cannibal!
Just because he survived that South American expedition. The very idea of his eating human flesh! All that
gristle." She shuddered. "The truth is, he was rescued
by a tribe of cannibals who worshiped him as a god because there was an epidemic in the village and he had
a bag of medicine with him and saved the lives of the
chief and his family. So they looked after him. They
housed him and they fed him. Lots of meat soups and
meat pies, and a polite guest doesn't ask what kind of
meat they're using, right?"

"Right," agreed Nellie as she repressed a wave of
nausea and pushed aside her plate of woodchuck liver
en gelee, a new Theresa Camus creation inspired by a
wildlife series she watched on PBS.

"My son Norton is a bum! They'll be writing books
about him and his Mafia friends one day and then he'll
be played in the movies by Joe Pesci. And that wife of
his, that Titania. All she wants is for me to back her in
a chain of dress shops!"

"They could be highly profitable," Nellie suggested.

"Woman, haven't you heard there's a recession?
Dress shops and department stores are going bankrupt
all over the world. I read in the papers that in Bali
they're selling sarongs for dust cloths. Bah!" Her eyes
were misting. "And my Rose. I really expected a lot
from her. So she marries a doctor who tells everybody
not to eat my wonderful gourmet food."

"No he doesn't!"

"Yes he does! No cholesterol, he yells. No fats! My
dishes are loaded with them."

"Your dishes are delicious."

"Delicious? They're masterpieces! They shouldn't
be eaten! They should be framed and hung in muse-
ums!" She clasped her hands together. "Delicious is
what you die from and what a way to die! Oh . . .
oh . . ." she was clutching her breast.

"What's wrong? What is it?" Nellie leapt to her feet and assisted Theresa into a chair.

"It's nothing," gasped Theresa, "it's just a spasm."

"I'll call a doctor."

"No, no! He'll want something to eat."

"Mrs. Camus, you're so pale. And you're trembling."

"I'm not afraid to die, believe me, I'm not afraid. All that food in the freezer, what will become of all that food in the freezer?"

"You could arrange to send it to Russia."

"Water, Nellie. A glass of water."

After sipping some water, color returned to Theresa's cheeks. She loosened the belt around her waist and felt even better. "I know they expect to divide everything."

"Who?"

"Rose and her husband. Norton and his wife. That rotten Chester I used to dote on. Well," she said after a long, contemplative pause, "I don't expect them to love me ever, but it would be nice to know they thought kindly of me after I'm gone."

"Oh, Mrs. Camus, now I know God is smiling at you."

"Why? I made a joke?"

The following morning, Theresa visited her lawyer and dictated a new will. Her lawyer, a soul of discretion until bribed, was somewhat astonished by her about-face, her lavish generosity to her family. He was astonished further when she awarded them the full contents of her freezer to do with as they wished. She was especially generous to Nellie Baker, whom she described as "my devoted servant and friend." As she dictated, her face took on a rare, beatific expression. It was as though Theresa expected to be rewarded with sainthood some time in the future. But just as suddenly, the visage of the virago returned and Theresa said to the lawyer:

"I think they were responsible for spreading the rumor."

The lawyer looked perplexed. "Which of the many?"

"The one that claimed I murdered my husband, that I poisoned Vernon and made it look like acute indigestion."

"I'm sure you didn't."

"I wouldn't put it past Chester to try to sell that to some supermarket rag. Oh God, I was once such a loving and unsuspicious woman. But now, look at me, in the coda of my life, trying so hard not to be so mean and rotten and hateful and nasty before it's too late." She sighed and very slowly began to put on her gloves. "When will the will be ready for me to sign?"

"Let me see, today's Tuesday. How's about Thursday afternoon?"

"What time?"

"Any time after lunch."

"I'll be here at three o'clock. I'll bring you some of my yak's cheese blintzes. You'll love them."

The lawyer had paled but she hadn't noticed. "I'm sure I will."

"Unpasteurized yak's cheese," said Theresa. "It's got more flavor unpasteurized."

Only her doctor was aware that Theresa had but a short time to live. Nellie Baker suspected it, but Theresa was so friendly and cheerful these days that Nellie was beginning to believe in miracles. Theresa had made overtures of friendliness to the family, sending them hampers of food, and twice she had Rose and Titania to tea, favoring them with a preview of her whale-blubber crepe suzettes.

On the day she signed the will, Theresa took a walk on the main street. Several toddlers in carriages, now wise to her, hid their goodies under their blankets and were startled that Theresa merely favored them with a wink or a friendly flutter of her fingers and kept on about her business. Every afternoon in her kitchen, there was a rush of activity as Theresa cooked dish after dish, each an exquisite culinary creation. These were wrapped and placed on a special shelf in the freezer.

Theresa dictated so many columns to her secretary that the poor girl's fingers almost went paralyzed at the typewriter. She filmed her television program twice daily, and soon had enough on hand to cover the next year of her contract. Theresa went at a feverish pace and her associates marveled that she hadn't spent herself. Her doctor begged her to curtail eating her own cooking and stick to the bland diet he'd prescribed for her, but Theresa dismissed him with a disdainful wave of the hand, thinking of the turn-of-the-century gourmand Diamond Jim Brady, who when warned by his doctor that his eating indulgences would lead to his premature death, indulged himself with a massive banquet for one, thereby eating himself to death.

Rose Folger said to her husband Oliver one evening as they were dressing to go to Chinatown to celebrate the Year of the Skunk with a thirty-five course repast, "Something's wrong with Mother."

"There always has been," said the doctor.

"This is different. Nellie Baker says she's getting her house in order, like maybe Mother doesn't have much longer to live."

"You think so? Well, if what that crooked lawyer of hers told you is true, you're coming into one hell of an inheritance."

"Oh, my," said Rose, and blushed.

"You know what, hon, we've never been to a luau in Hawaii. When you get your money, what say we fly to Hawaii and have them do us one slap-up of a luau. Suckling pig, baked dog, breaded donkey brains ..."

Rose was salivating. "Oh, hurry, hurry, let's get down to Chinatown before I starve to death."

A curtained hearse drove past Norton and Titania's split-level home in Parkchester. A hail of bullets tore through the walls of the house and broke windows while Norton flung Titania to the floor and held her tightly to him. She was screaming hysterically while Norton attempted to comfort her. "When we get my mother's money, we'll bulletproof the house. Won't that be nice?"

Titania stopped screaming and growled, "And in the meantime, what will the neighbors think?"

Chester Camus sat at his typewriter in his filthy studio apartment on the Lower East Side, his fingers moving swiftly across the keys, knowing that one day soon he would be able to afford a superior model word processor. But now, his old Olivetti would make do as he wrote his grandmother's epitaph. Nellie Baker, who still adored him, had tipped him off that the doctor said Theresa's days were numbered, and Chester had struck a deal with *People* magazine to provide them with an exclusive grandson's-eye view of the last days of the celebrated *cuisinière* Theresa Camus. The phone on the desk rang and he said, "Yes?"

"It's me." He recognized Nellie Baker's voice. "She's going. I'm in the bedroom with her. She's babbling away."

Chester's fingers flew as Nellie spoke.

In the bedroom, Theresa lay on the bed, a crucifix entwined with her fingers. A priest sat in a chair administering last rites and wondering if he dare ask Nellie for a ham and cheese on rye with lots of mustard. Theresa's babbling was making him hungry.

"Asparagus vinaigrette au Liechtenstein . . . veal scallopini à la Minelli . . . heart of artichoke in peanut butter sauce with a waft of pesto . . . reindeer tongue braised with Welsh leeks . . ." Her eyes stared ahead lifelessly, but miraculously enough, she looked young. She was a girl again. She was a student at Vassar and last night she had met Vernon Camus, the man she intended to marry, the man she would one day poison to death as punishment for his perfidy. "Vernon . . ." she whispered.

Nellie spoke softly into the phone and Chester typed: " 'Vernon,' she whispered, evoking her late husband's name . . ." Then Chester heard a strange sound. "What was that?"

"She burped," said Nellie. And Theresa Camus was dead.

The Camus mansion was alive and breathing with the odor of haute cuisine. Nellie Baker was preparing for Theresa's family the special meal the old lady had been cooking at a feverish pace in those frantic days before she died. Seated around the dining room table were Rose and Oliver Folger, Norton and Titania Camus, and their son Chester. They were praising Chester's story on his grandmother's last moments effusively.

"You'll win a Pulitzer Prize!" predicted his father. The five babbled away merrily as Nellie brought in savory dish after savory dish, each a triumphant culinary memorial to the magic of Theresa Camus. Nellie heard the phone ring; the nearest one was in the kitchen. She hurried to get it and it was a food columnist calling. He wanted to know the menu of Theresa's last supper and Nellie was delighted to tell him. She spoke for about ten minutes and then felt something was wrong. It was very quiet in the dining room all of a sudden. She excused herself, hung up the phone, and hurried to the dining room.

Theresa Camus' last meal became a legend. She had succeeded in poisoning her son and daughter, their spouses, and her one grandchild. To the very end, she was mean and nasty and awful and rotten, and Nellie Baker built a monument to her in Mayflower's one public park. Nellie endowed a chain of cooking schools and took a lover. True, Andre du Blancmange was a bit of a philanderer, but on the other hand, Nellie had been taught by Theresa to cook some of her more intricate and exotic dishes. To think, thought Andre, that Theresa Camus had left all that money to her housekeeper. The lovely and charming Nellie Baker, who would finally consent to marry the charming and persuasive Andre du Blancmange and then slowly and miserably become mean and rotten and nasty and horrible, and finally, one afternoon, would cook a special dish for her husband, from a very special recipe created by Theresa Camus.

Veal Meat Again

2 pounds veal, thinly sliced
2 medium onions, chopped fine
2 teaspoons butter
2 pounds very small pared potatoes
1 pound button mushrooms
1 cup heavy cream (more if needed)
2 tablespoons vermouth (more if needed)
⅛ teaspoon black pepper
⅛ teaspoon paprika

Saute the onions in butter and add the veal, sauteing 2 minutes on each side. Add the mushrooms. Boil the potatoes, and place all cooked ingredients, seasoned to taste with black pepper and paprika, in Dutch oven. Stir in heavy cream and vermouth and let simmer in a 400° F. oven for 30 minutes. Serve with rice or kasha.

—George Baxt

The Maggody Files:
Spiced Rhubarb
by Joan Hess

"I haven't seen Lucinda Skaggs since a week ago
Tuesday," Lottie Estes mentioned to a friend in the
teachers' lounge. The fourth period bell precluded further analysis. Although it was of no botanical significance, the next morning it was discussed at the garden
club meeting. It took several hours to reach the Empo-
rium Hardware Store, but then the pace picked up and
by midafternoon it was one of the topics at Suds of
Fun Launderette next to the supermarket, in the supermarket proper, and even at the Dairee Dee-Lishus (although the teenagers moved on to more intriguing
topics, such as blankets alongside Boone Creek and
which minors had been caught in possession of what
illegal substances).

Thus the tidbit—not a rumor, mind you—crept up
the road, moving as slowly and clumsily as a three-
legged dog on a frozen pond, until it reached Ruby
Bee's Bar & Grill. This is hardly worthy of mention
(nor was the fact that Lottie had not seen Lucinda
Skaggs since a week ago Tuesday, but for some reason
it was being mentioned a lot), since Ruby Bee's Bar &
Grill was the ultimate depository of all gossip, trivial
or boggling or outright scandalous, within the city lim-
its of Maggody, Arkansas (pop. 755). Despite occasional attempted coups, it was acknowledged by almost
everybody that the proprietress, Ruby Bee Hanks, was
the guardian of the grapevine.

"So?" Estelle Oppers responded when she was presented with the tidbit. She took a pretzel from the bas-

ket on the bar, studied it for excessive salt, and popped it into her mouth.

"So I don't know," said Ruby Bee. "I was just repeating it, for pity's sake."

"Has Lucinda Skaggs disappeared, or has Lottie lost her bifocals?"

"All I know is that Lucinda hasn't been seen in nearly two weeks now." In retaliation for the skeptical reception, Ruby Bee pretended to polish the metal napkin holder while surreptitiously inching the pretzels out of Estelle's reach. "Lottie said you can set your watch by Lucinda's comings and goings. She's real big on 'early to bed, early to rise,' and Lottie says not one morning goes by that Lucinda doesn't snap on the kitchen light at six sharp, put out the garbage at six fifteen, and—"

Estelle recaptured the pretzels. "I'm not interested in Lucinda Skaggs's schedule, and I'm a mite surprised Lottie and certain other people, present company included, find it so fascinating. If you're so dadburned worried about Lucinda—and I don't know why you should be, what with her being so holier-than-thou and more than willing to cast the first stone—why don't you call her and ask her if she's had a touch of the stomach flu?"

"I might just do that," Ruby Bee muttered, wishing she'd thought of it herself but not about to admit it. "When I get around to it, anyway."

She went into the kitchen and stayed there for a good five minutes, rattling pots and pans and banging cabinet doors so Estelle would know she was way too busy to fool with calling folks on the telephone to inquire about their health. When she returned, the stool at the end of the bar was unoccupied, which was what she'd been hoping for, so she hunted up the telephone number and dialed it.

"Buster," she began real nicely, "this is Ruby Bee Hanks over at the bar and grill. I was wondering if I might speak to Lucinda about a recipe?"

Estelle pranced out of the ladies' room and slid onto

the bar stool. She waited with a smirky look on her face until Ruby Bee hung up the receiver. "Glad you found time in your busy schedule to call over at the Skaggses' house. What'd she say?"

"I didn't talk to her. Buster says she's gone to visit her sister up in Hiana." She hesitated, frowning. "I seem to recollect Lucinda telling me that her sister was doing so poorly they had no choice but to put her in a nursing home in Springfield."

"Maybe she's back home now."

Ruby Bee tapped her temple with her forefinger. "It was a case of her being able to hide her own Easter eggs, if you know what I mean. Lucinda was real upset about it, but there wasn't any way her sister could take care of herself. 'God helps those who help themselves,' Lucinda said to me awhile back at the supermarket, over in the produce section, 'but all my sister's helping herself to is costume jewelry at the five and dime when she thinks nobody's watching.' Why would Buster lie about it?"

"He's most likely confused," Estelle said, yawning so hard her beehive hairdo almost wobbled, but not quite. "She could have gone to visit her sister in the nursing home, or she had to see to some family business in Hiana, or—"

"I don't think so," said Ruby Bee. She picked up the damp dishrag and began to wipe the counter, drawing glittery swaths that caught the pastel light from the neon signs on the wall behind her.

I stared at my mother, who, among other things, is the infamous Ruby Bee. The other things include being a dedicated and undeniably adept meddler, an incurable gossip, and a critic of my hair, my clothes, my face, and my life in general. I'll admit my hair was in a no-nonsense bun, my pants were baggy, my use of makeup was minimal, and my life was as exciting as molded gelatin salad, but I didn't need to hear about it on a daily basis.

I took a gulp of iced tea and said, "You want me

to arrest Buster Skaggs because you couldn't get
Lucinda's recipe for spiced rhubarb conserve? Doesn't
that seem a little extreme—even to you?"

"I didn't say to arrest him," Ruby Bee said. "I said
to question him, that's all."

"He probably doesn't know her recipe. Why don't
you wheedle it out of the chef herself?"

Ruby Bee sniffed as if I were a stalk of ragweed pol-
luting the barroom. "I would, Miss Smart Mouth, but
no one's laid eyes on Lucinda for a good two weeks,
and when I called and asked to speak to her, Buster
had the audacity to say she was visiting her sister in
Hiana."

"Oh," I said wisely. "How about a grilled cheese
sandwich and a refill on the tea?"

"I wish you'd stop worrying about your stomach and
listen to me," Ruby Bee said in her unfriendliest voice.
"You are the chief of police, aren't you? It seems to
me you'd be a little bit worried when someone ups and
disappears like this, but all you care about is feeding
your face and hiding out in that filthy little apartment
of yours. That is no kind of life for a passably attractive girl who could, if she'd make the slightest effort,
find herself a nice man and settle down like all her
high school friends have. Did I tell you that Joyce is
expecting in October, by the way?"

I was torn between stomping out in a snit and staying there to feed my face, about which I cared very
dearly. For the record, my apartment was dingy but not
filthy, and I may have been reading a lot lately, but I
was in no way hiding out. Hiding out would imply
someone was looking for me, and as far as I could tell,
no one was.

"Okay," I said, "you win. I'll put a real live bullet in
my gun and march over to the Skaggses' house. If
Buster refuses to divulge the recipe for rhubarb conserve, I'll blow his head off right there on the spot.
About that sandwich . . ."

"I just told you Buster said Lucinda was visiting her

sister in Hiana. I happen to know Lucinda's sister is in
a nursing home in Springfield."

The conversation careened for a while, with me being called various names and being accused several
times of failing to behave in a seemly fashion (a.k.a.
one resulting in wedding vows and procreation). I par-
ticipated only to needle her, and when the dust settled
back on the barroom floor, I was standing on Lucinda
Skaggs's front porch. The paint was bubbling off the
trim like crocodile skin and the screen was rusted, but
behind me the grass was trimmed, the flower beds
were bright with annuals, and the vegetable garden in
the side yard was weedless and neatly mulched.

"Hey, Arly," Buster said as he opened the door.
"What can I do for you?" He was a small but muscular
man with short gray hair and a face that sagged whenever his smile slipped. He was regarding me curiously,
but without hostility.

I could have saved time by asking him if he'd murdered his wife, but it seemed less than neighborly. "Do
you mind if I visit for a minute?"

"Sure, come on in." He pulled the door back and
gestured at me. "You'll have to forgive the mess.
Lucinda's been gone a couple of weeks, and I'm not
much of a housekeeper."

With the exception of a newspaper and a beer can on
the floor, the living room was immaculate. The throw
pillows on the sofa were as smooth and plump as
marshmallows, the arrangement of wildflowers were
centered on the coffee table, the carpet still rippled
from the vacuum cleaner. No magazines or books were
in view, and unlike most living rooms in Maggody, no
television set dominated the decor. On one wall an embroidered sampler declared that this was home, sweet
home. Another hypothesized that a bird in the hand
was worth two in the bush, and a third, ringed with coy
pink storks, proclaimed that Shelley Belinda Skaggs
had weighed seven pounds two ounces on November
third, 1975.

"Lucinda's hobby," Buster said as I leaned forward

to feign admiration for the tiny stitches. "She says that it relaxes her, and that the devil finds work for idle hands."

"They're very nice," I murmured. I sat down on the sofa and declined iced tea, coffee, and a beer. "I understand Lucinda's visiting her sister."

He gave me a wary look, but I chalked it up to the inanity of my remark. "Yeah, she's strong on family ties. There's a sampler in the kitchen that says, 'The family that prays together stays together.' I guess she and her sister have been on their knees going on two weeks now."

"I don't think I've seen Shelley around town in a while. Did she go with her mother?"

"Not hardly," he said with a brittle laugh. "Shelley took off a couple of weeks ago. I keep thinking we'll get a call from her, but we haven't had so much as a postcard."

"Took off?"

He shrugged, but he didn't sound at all casual as he said, "Ran away is more like it, I suppose. She and Lucinda had an argument, and the next morning there was a note on the kitchen table. According to Lucinda, the acorn can't stray far from the oak, but she may be wrong this time."

I glanced at the sampler behind me and did a bit of calculation. "Shelley's a minor. Have you notified the police in the nearby towns and the state police?"

"I wanted to, but Lucinda kept saying good riddance to bad rubbish. She was real upset with Shelley for coming home late one night and called her a slut and a lot of other nasty names. She's always been real stern with Shelley, even when she was nothing but a little girl in pigtails. When Lucinda wasn't whipping her, she was making her sit in a corner in her room and embroider quotations from the Bible. I can't tell you how many times I've heard Lucinda say—" He broke off and covered his face with his hands.

It was not a challenge to complete his sentence: Spare the rod and spoil the child. I barely knew

Lucinda Skaggs, but I was increasingly aware of how much I disliked her. She seemed to live from cliche to cliche, and I suspected she would have some piercing ones for yours truly.

I waited until Buster wiped his eyes and attempted to smile. "I'll call the state police and alert them about Shelley. While you make a list of the names and addresses of your family and friends, I need to look through her things to see if I can find any leads. Also, we'll need a recent photograph."

Buster nodded and took me to Shelley's bedroom. It was as stark as the living room, with dreary beige walls, a matching bedspread, a bare lightbulb in the middle of the ceiling, and only the basic pieces of furniture. A brush and comb were aligned on the dresser. The drawers contained a meager amount of folded underthings, sweaters, and T-shirts. In the closet, skirts and blouses were separated and hung neatly; had it been plausible, I was sure they would have been alphabetized. There were no boxes on the shelf, no notebooks or diaries in the drawers, no letters hidden under the mattress. The only splash of color came from a braided rug on the hardwood floor. The room, I concluded, could have passed inspection in a convent. Handily.

I paused to see which pithy statements Lucinda had chosen for her daughter's walls. "Pride goeth before a fall." "Honor thy father and thy mother." "For dust thou art, and unto dust shalt thou return." Not quite as lighthearted as posters and pinups of movie stars, I thought as I returned to the living room.

Buster gave me a photograph of a teenaged girl, her smile as starched as her white blouse. Her hair was pulled back so tightly that there were faint creases at the corners of her eyes, which regarded the camera with contemptuous appraisal. I was not surprised that she wore no makeup or jewelry.

I put the photograph in my shirt pocket. "I'll return this to you as soon as possible."

"Here are a few addresses of relatives," he said as

he handed me a piece of paper, "but I've already spoken to them and they promised to let me know if Shelley shows up."

I skimmed the list. "What about Shelley's aunt in Hiana?"

"She wouldn't set foot in that place, not with her mother being there." He looked down for a moment. "The telephone was disconnected, but I'll run up there this evening and fetch Lucinda. It's getting too quiet around here with both of them gone."

I promised to let him know what the police had to say, although I doubted it would amount to much. As I drove away, it occurred to me I'd exchanged a pseudo-missing person for a real one. The reverse would have been more palatable. And Ruby Bee's scalloped potatoes would have been more palatable than the can of soup I planned to have for dinner, but I wasn't quite prepared to deal with the thumbscrews served alongside them.

"Guess we got all excited over nothing," Ruby Bee said with a sigh. "Lucinda came home last night, and sent Buster by first thing this morning with the recipe." She squinted at the index card. "This won Lucinda a blue ribbon at the county fair last fall. As soon as I get a chance, I'm going to try it."

Estelle pensively chewed a pretzel. "What did Arly have to say about her little visit yesterday?"

"I haven't laid eyes on her," Ruby Bee admitted, wondering if she could get decent rhubarb at the supermarket across the road. "But now that Lucinda's back, I guess it was nothing but a wild goose chase. Of course, we only have Buster's word that she really is back."

"Lottie said she caught a glimpse of her at six fifteen, putting out the garbage by the back door like she always does. She thought Lucinda looked thin, but I suppose all that bother with her sister must be worrisome."

Ruby Bee put down the recipe, propped her elbows

on the bar, and tugged on her chin. "I still don't know why Buster lied about that. It doesn't make a whisker of sense, him saying Lucinda was in Hiana with her sister."

"He was addled," Estelle said firmly.

This time Ruby Bee did not resort to wiping the counter. Instead, she picked up the card, studied it with a deepening frown, and then, in a peculiar voice, said, "I don't know, Estelle. I just don't know."

I figured I had two options. I could park by the skeletal remains of Purtle's Esso station and nab speeders, or I could sit in the PD and swat flies. Both required physical exertion, and I was taking a nap when Ruby Bee and Estelle stormed through the door.

Ruby Bee banged down a small bowl on my desk. "I told you so."

In that she told me some fool thing every hour, I wasn't sure how to field this one. "Told me what?" I finally said.

"I told you that Lucinda Skaggs didn't visit her sister in Hiana. Just taste this."

"And don't be all day about it," Estelle added. "This is an emergency."

I leaned forward and studied the goopy red contents of the bowl, then shook my head. "Sorry, ladies, I never taste anything that could be a living organism. A primeval one, to be sure, but perhaps in the midst of some sort of evolutionary breakthrough."

Ruby Bee put her hands on her hips. "Taste it."

"Oh, all right, but it better be good." Trying not to wince, I put my fingers in the goop, plucked out a bite-sized lump, and conveyed it to my mouth without dribbling on my shirt. I regretted it immediately. My lips were sucked into my mouth, and the interior of my cheeks converged on my retreating tongue. Only decorum prevented me from spitting it out. "Yuck! This is awful!"

"No, it's not," Ruby Bee said, "or it's not supposed to be, anyway. It's Lucinda Skaggs's spiced rhubarb conserve, and it won a blue ribbon at the county fair last year."

I washed out my mouth with lukewarm coffee. "If it did, there was a good deal of bribery. This is absolutely awful. Maybe you didn't follow the recipe correctly, because this nasty stuff could turn someone's face inside out."

Estelle flapped an index card at me. "Are you saying Ruby Bee doesn't know how to follow a recipe, Miss Cordan Blue? There's not much to it—you slice your orange and your lemon, add your water, your vinegar, and your rhubarb, put in a little bag with gingerroot, cinnamon candies, mace, and cloves, and simmer until it gets nice and thick." She paused so dramatically that I realized I was holding my breath. "Your raisins are optional."

"And I followed the recipe right down to the cup of raisins," Ruby Bee snapped. "Now what do you aim to do about Lucinda Skaggs?"

I was still sipping coffee to get rid of the painfully tart taste in my mouth. "Decapitation? Force feeding?"

"She never came home," Estelle said, enunciating slowly so that the less perceptive of us in the PD could follow along. "This spiced rhubarb conserve proves it."

"Wait a minute," I said. "She came home yesterday evening. Buster told me he was driving to Hiana to fetch her, and she did give you the recipe for this vile concoction, didn't she?"

Ruby Bee glowered at the offending goop, and then at the offending chief of police. "Buster said she copied it down for me, but she didn't. She may not be the most charitable woman in town, but she did win a blue ribbon and there's no way on God's green earth that she sent this recipe to me."

"Why not?" I asked meekly.

Estelle stuck the card under my nose. "Just take a look for yourself, missy. Where's the sugar?"

"That's right," Ruby Bee said, looming over me like a maternal monolith. "Where's the sugar?"

* * *

This time was I was standing on Lottie Estes's front porch knocking on her door. A curtain twitched, and shortly thereafter, Lottie opened the door, gave me a crisp smile, and said, "Afternoon, Arly."

"I wanted to ask you a few questions about your neighbors," I began. Before I could continue, I was pulled inside, placed on the sofa, and cautioned to stay quiet until the shades were lowered and the curtains were drawn.

"We can't be too careful," Lottie whispered as she sat down beside me and patted my knee. "Now what would you like to know?"

"Is Lucinda Skaggs home?" I asked.

"Why, I believe she is. This morning when I happened to be in my guest bedroom hunting for a pattern, I noticed that the light went on at six and she put out the garbage at exactly six fifteen. At seven thirty, Buster came out and got in his truck, then stopped and went back to the door. Lucinda handed him a card, and he returned to the truck and left, giving me a little wave as he drove by."

"And you saw her?"

Lottie's wrinkled cheeks reddened as she took off her bifocals and cleaned them with a tissue that appeared almost magically from her cuff. "I didn't want them to think I was spying on them, so I did stay behind the sheers. But, yes, I saw Lucinda for a second when she put out the garbage, and I heard her speak quite sternly to her husband when she gave him the card. She said something along the lines of 'a friend in need is a friend indeed.' I couldn't hear Buster's response, even though I had opened the window just a bit to enjoy the morning breeze."

I was amazed that she hadn't used binoculars and a wiretap. I thanked her for her information, but as I started for the door, an unpleasant thought occurred to me. "Two weeks ago," I said, "did you happen to be hunting for a pattern in the guest bedroom and see

Buster carrying a duffel bag or a rolled carpet to his truck?"

"Oh, heavens no," she said with a nervous laugh. "However, I was doing a bit of dusting one morning when I saw him carry a braided rug *into* the house."

I could feel bifocaled eyes on my back as I walked across the yard to the Skaggses' house. I knocked on the door, then turned around to gaze at the garden. The bushy bean and pea plants were already thick, and the zucchini leaves were broad green fans. The tomato plants, although not yet a foot high, were encased with cylindrical wire cages.

The door opened behind me. Without turning back, I said, "Your garden's coming along nicely. I suppose Lucinda does a lot of canning in the fall."

"Tomatoes, beans, beets, turnips, greens, all that," Buster murmured. "A penny saved, you know . . ."

"Is a penny earned," I said, now looking at him. "I thought of another one while I was walking over here. Like to hear it?" He nodded unenthusiastically. "Little strokes fell great oaks."

"Is there something you wanted, Arly?"

"I'd like to speak to Lucinda about her recipe for spiced rhubarb conserve. Ruby Bee made a batch of it this afternoon, and it was inedible."

"I can't imagine that. It won a blue ribbon at the fair."

I opened the screen door, but he remained in the doorway, his arms folded. "I brought it with me so Lucinda could check it," I said, showing him the card.

"She's asleep. She's real fond of the one about the early bird catching the worm. I'd rather have ham and eggs myself." He reached out to take the card, but I lowered my hand. "I'll have her take at look at it in the morning. If there's something wrong, she can fix it up and I'll get it back to Ruby Bee."

"I had a call from the state police," I said, ignoring his vague attempt to reach the recipe card. "You'll be delighted to know they've located Shelley at a shelter in Farberville."

"They have?" he said uncertainly. He swallowed several times and licked his lips until they glistened like the surface of the rhubarb goop. "That's great, Arly. I was really worried about her. So was Lucinda, although she won't admit it. That was the reason she left the next day to visit her sister in Hiana. I'll tell her first thing in the morning."

"You said something interesting when we were discussing where Shelley might have gone," I continued. "You said Shelley wouldn't go to Hiana because her mother was there. How would Shelley have known her mother was there?"

He shook his head and gave me a bewildered look, but I wasn't in the mood to play Lieutenant Columbo and drag the ordeal out until the last commercial.

I held up the card once more and said, "The handwriting matches the list you wrote for me yesterday. You copied the recipe, but omitted the sugar. Lucinda wouldn't have, since she's made it often and is a meticulous person. Let's return to Mr. Franklin's 'Little strokes fell great oaks.' Lucinda might not have cared to be characterized as a tree, but I doubt it took little strokes to fell her. What did it take?"

His face and everything else about him sagged. "She was screaming at Shelley, spitting on her and slapping her. I couldn't stand it any more. I told her to shut up. She started screaming at me, and I pushed her away from me. She fell, hit her head on the edge of the kitchen table."

"I don't think so. When we do an investigation, we'll determine the details, but it didn't happen in the kitchen. It happened in Shelley's room, which is why you took Shelley to Hiana and brought back a braided rug to cover the bloodstains."

"It was an accident," a defiant voice said. Shelley joined her father in the doorway, dressed in a dowdy robe. Her head was covered with hair rollers and a scarf; no doubt Lottie was convinced she'd spotted Lucinda for a second at the back door. "I was the one who pushed her, but I didn't mean for her to hit her head. Or maybe way in the back of my mind, I wanted it to happen."Although her expression did not change, her eyes filled with tears that began to slink down her cheeks.

Buster put his arm around his daughter. "I pushed her. God know she's had it coming for twenty years."

Shelley looked up at him. " 'The heart of the fool is in his mouth.' "

" 'But the mouth of the wise man is in his heart,' " he countered sadly.

"We'll sort those out later," I said before we got lost between quotation marks. "Where's the body?"

Neither answered, but both of them glanced furtively over my shoulder. I studied the neat rows of tomato plants, each ringed with mulch and exuding the promise of a rich red crop later in the summer. I cast around in my mind for a suitable quote, and although my Biblical training was sparse, I found one. " 'They that sow in tears shall reap in joy.' "

Buster managed a wry smile. "Lucinda would have appreciated it. As she was so fond of saying, 'Waste not, want not.' "

Blue-Ribbon Spiced Rhubarb Compote

Thinly slice and remove seeds from:

1 medium orange
1 lemon

In a small bag made of cheesecloth, assemble:

2 whole cloves
½ ounce grated gingerroot
¼ pound cinnamon candies ("Redhots")
1 blade mace

Place all of the above in a saucepan, along with:

½ cup of water
¼ cup of cider vinegar

Simmer until the fruit is tender, and then add:

1 ½ cups sliced rhubarb
3 cups sugar
¼ cup raisins (optional)

Continue simmering until the compote is thick (30 minutes or more). Do not omit the sugar unless you're in the mood to be accused of murder.

—Joan Hess

Blown Up
by Robert Barnard

"Would you like another cheese-and-onion twisty?" asked Annie Monkton in the passenger seat, pushing the bag in the direction of the steering wheel.

"No thanks, Ma. I've got the prawn cocktail crisps," said her son Herbie, speeding up the M1, but brandishing the bag with his free hand.

"You like those, don't you? I like them now and *again*."

"Have one, Ma."

"Ta, I don't mind if I do."

Her arm wobbled over toward the bag and her elbow pushed itself companionably into her son's comfortable belly. Herbie was six foot three and seventeen stone, and Annie was five foot six and thirteen stone, so their bodies in the little Fiat were touching constantly. But they'd had many trips over the years in the small car and had learned to cope without friction.

"That was nice for a change," said Annie, munching. "Tasty. Do you remember that seafood cocktail we had at the Monk's Head in Kendall that year?"

"That was brilliant!" said Herbie enthusiastically. "That had everything: prawn, crab, cod, smoked haddock. It was Dad recommended that hotel."

"He was good on hotels, was your dad. It was him having been a traveler, I suppose."

"You'd remember, wouldn't you, where you'd had really good nosh, and where it hadn't come up to standard."

They sped through the county of Nottinghamshire,

their eyes on the highway, except when they dropped to the bags in their hands.

"I've got coconut ice in my handbag," said Annie. "Fancy a bit, son?"

"No, I think I'll stick with the smoked almonds."

They munched contentedly. Herbie was thinking. "Do you remember that coconut ice we got in the market in Leeds last year—with all the glacé bits in, and the peel?"

"I do. I've often thought about that coconut ice."

"Now," said Herbie, when he had got his thoughts in order, "what I'm wondering is, are we going to stop for lunch at the White Hart in Hunstable or at the Fox and Newt in Carditch? Or we could even try the May-flower at Kirkby again."

"Is that the pub your father took us to? Said he'd had a marvelous rump steak there that nearly filled the plate? Then when to took us it was very disappointing. Mingy little portions, and tough at that, and hardly enough chips to feed a baby?"

"It'd changed management."

"It had. They ought to warn people. I remember your dad after that meal. Hardly said a word all afternoon. No thank you, we won't try there again. I won't be done twice over. Let's see, the White Hart's where they do that lovely steak-and-mushroom pie, isn't it?"

"That's right. Massive portions. With jacket potatoes with grated cheese on."

"Oh, yes. I remember that. Melted in the mouth. And the Fox and Newt's where we had that lovely plaice and chips, where the chips was practically un-limited."

"That's right. I don't know when I've had better plaice and chips."

"Still, I think I fancy the steak-and-mushroom today. We'll have time to digest it before we have our din-ner."

So they stopped at the White Hart, and it hadn't changed hands, and they had the steak-and-mushroom,

and the potatoes with the melted cheese, and a very
generous helping of boiled carrots. Annie washed
hers down with a gin-and-tonic, and Herbie washed his
down with a pint of bitter. Just when they thought
they'd finished, Herbie wondered whether he couldn't
manage a piece of that Black Forest gâteau he'd seen
at the food bar and Annie wondered whether she
couldn't, too, and she said she'd buy another round of
drinks to go with it if Herbie would just fetch them
from the bar. So they had the gâteau, too, and another
round of drinks, and they were very pleased they did.

"That was lovely," Annie said. "That was almost as
good as that Black Forest gâteau they make at the
King's Head in Shoreditch. You know, the one your
dad always swore by."

"That's right. He loved his Black Forest gâteau,
didn't he? We must go out to the King's Head again
sometime. We haven't been there since he died."

"Not since he had his attack, in actual fact. I didn't
like it after your dad had his attack. I mean, we
couldn't get around as we'd been used to, could we?—
Still, I must say, that gâteau we've just had was almost
as good and very nice-sized portions, too. That should
keep us going until dinner."

As they went toward the car, Annie said: "Even your
dad would have been satisfied with that meal. Walter
was always less snappy when he'd really got his money's worth, wasn't he?"

They opened the boot, and Annie got out her large
holdall and took from it a supersize bar of fruit and
nut, some licorice comfits, and a bag of bacon mun-
chies. Herbert took a packet of potato sticks and a tin
of cashews—because, as he said, he'd had enough
sweet things for the moment. They drove on, out of
Nottinghamshire and into Yorkshire, perfectly happy.

"I like Yorkshire," said Annie. "They always do you
proud in Yorkshire."

"They know how to appreciate food in the North,"
said Herbie.

"They do. You can see it in the people."

"The question is," said Herbie, lighting up a cigarette between the potato sticks and the smoked almonds, "are we going to drive on up to the Lake District tonight or are we going to stop off in Yorkshire somewhere?"

"Oh, I thought we'd agreed. Stop off. No point in overdoing it. We're not in a race. We've got the whole weekend, and we don't have to be home till Monday night. There's lots of lovely hotels in Yorkshire where they always make you ever so welcome. There's Manor Court, just outside Ilkley, where they do that marvelous table d'hôte for six pounds fifty a head."

They talked over the various alternatives and finally decided to save Manor Court for the Sunday on the way back and to spend the night at the Devonshire Arms in Spenlow. They enjoyed a pre-dinner lager-and-lime in the bar while they went through the menu. Finally, Herbie ordered the smoked salmon, followed by rump steak with French fries, and Annie ordered the seafood platter, followed by filet of pork Wellington. Herbie had a pint of bitter at table and Annie a snowball and they were as near as possible in a state of perfect bliss when Annie, over the pork Wellington, which she happily observed nearly covered the plate, suddenly remembered something.

"Here," she said, "it's just come to me. The Devonshire Arms was the last place we ever stayed with your dad. Last trip we ever had. We stayed here at the Devonshire Arms on the way down from Skye and the Western Isles."

"Did we, Ma? I'd never have remembered that."

"Well, you should. Three days later he had his first attack."

"I remember it was soon after we got back."

"And do you know what he had for his dinner that night? Filet of pork Wellington!"

For a moment the remembrance of things past seemed to cast a shadow over the meal. Annie looked at the great expanse of pork that had been set before her, and she gave the dead Walter the tribute of a passing sigh. Then she took a sup of her snowball, smiled at her son, and set to again with a will.

"Doesn't do to take things like that, does it?" she said.

"Thinking won't bring him back," said Herbie.

Next morning, they had an English breakfast of egg, bacon, sausage, tomatoes, mushrooms, and fried potatoes, with the Yorkshire addition of black pudding, which Herbie pronounced "not bad, but I don't think I'd want it as a regular thing." He considered the porridge excellent, though, especially with the golden syrup over, and Annie gave her blessing to the marmalade.

"It's one of my criterions," she said. "You can tell the real class of a hotel. That's none of your cheap stuff—" and she waved her pudgy hand at the pot "—because there's no question of skimping here."

When they'd paid their bill, Herbie humped their luggage to the car—just the one small case because Herbie hated lugging heavy cases and considered it shortened your life span—and they set off again.

"People are silly, giving up good English breakfasts," said Annie as they drove out of the drive. "They set you up for the day." She slipped into her mouth a piece of chocolate nougat and chewed contentedly. "That meal last night," she said, "the pork Wellington, would have been one of the last good meals your dad ever ate. Apart from the ones I cooked him, of course. The *very* last meal he ate out. He liked eating out, your dad. I never knew a better judge of whether he'd had value for money."

"Wasn't any point in him eating out, not after his attack," said Herbie. "Not with the sort of stuff he was allowed to eat."

"No. Imagine going into an Italian restaurant and saying 'I want a nice piece of boiled fish and some boiled potatoes to go with it.' They'd split their sides laughing."

"I don't think Dad had the *heart* to eat out again," said Herbie.

"That's it. It was funny, really. Do you remember that mini-cruise we took to Norway—oh, back in 'seventy or 'seventy-one it must have been—and how Dad hated all that boiled fish and boiled potatoes we had? It was boiled potatoes with every meal, wasn't it? Just the most uninteresting way of having potatoes, *I* always say. Your dad was really disgusted, considering the price we'd paid. And then when he comes out of hospital, to have to have boiled fish and boiled potatoes and all that horrible invalid food. It was almost as if the doctor who drew up the diet sheet knew about Dad's likes and dislikes and was trying to get his own back. Because your dad was not an easy patient. Short-tempered—"

"Well, you was very good to him, Ma. You cooked it all for him, didn't you?"

"I did. Though it turned my stomach sometimes, quite apart from the extra work. I mean, the only thing we could've eaten that was on his diet was the shepherd's pie, and he wasn't to have that more than once a week. So there was his little messes to do, on top of the things for ourselves. It was pitiful watching him eating it."

"And watching *him* watching *us*, eh, Ma?"

Annie Monkton gurgled a little laugh.

"Well, he *was* a picture, I'll give you that. But I still think it was diabolical, that diet sheet. It can't have been necessary. I'm no doctor, but I do know a grown man's got to eat enough to keep body and soul together. To see him sitting there with his pea soup, and the rusk he was supposed to have with it, while we were tucking into the steak pizzaola with the sauté potatoes and the baked eggplant—well, I said at the time it wasn't right."

"I think it was the sweets that got him most, Ma. That peach Melba you used to make, with the thick whipped cream and the black cherry jam on top. He used to look at that, gaze you might say, like he was transfixed, like he begrudged us every mouthful. We haven't had your peach Melba lately, have we, Ma?"

"Here, don't go so fast," said Annie, as they sped along the shores of Lake Windermere. "We don't want to get to Keswick too early for lunch."

They both had fresh Scottish salmon for lunch, with French fries, peas, and beans. "You pay for Scottish salmon," said Herbie, "but it does have that touch of class." The thought of how much they'd paid for the salmon made them shake their heads reluctantly over the cheese and walnut gâteau. Afterward they both had a little nap in the car park of the Keswick hotel where they'd eaten and then Herbie got out his map and they decided where to stay for the night, nibbling at a little bag of savory sticks. It was a question of whether to go over to Buttermere and then on to the coast and stay at Whitehaven, or whether to take a leisurely trip around Ullswater and overnight at Penrith.

"I'd go for Penrith," said Annie. "The Borderer at Penrith. I've got a fancy to try their venison again. I know it's extravagant, but we *are* on holiday."

She had woken from her nap with her mind greatly refreshed. "Do you know," she said as they started, "I don't think they put as much fruit in fruit-and-nut chocolate as they used to. Or as much nut, come to that."

"That's the way the cookie crumbles," said Herbie, not altogether appositely.

They drove along the north shores of Ullswater, passing as they did so, though without seeing them, several hosts of golden daffodils.

"This is a good road now," said Herbie, increasing the speed. "A sight better than when we first came up, eh, Ma? Then you really had to dawdle 'round, because of the potholes."

But his mother's mind was on other things.

"I didn't *really* enjoy your father gazing at us eating like he used to after his attack," she said, switching from the fruit-and-nut to the peppermint fondant. "I'm not cruel, you know that, Herbie. In fact, though it was a bit of a laugh at first, after a time I found it really put me off my food, being watched like that. I just wasn't enjoying it any more. I remember sitting there eating a slice of one of my homemade pork pies—with all that lovely jelly, just as I like it—and your dad was toying with his omelette and just looking at my plate greedily—because, not to speak ill of the dead, he could be greedy, your dad—and I thought: I can't enjoy this like I should be doing, not with Walter looking on like he wants to grab every forkful from me. It was as much as I could do to finish it."

"Perhaps he should have ate separately, Ma."

"That would have been like putting him in an insulation ward. No, no, we was a family and we ate as a family. I must say I was glad when they said he could start relaxing the diet."

Herbert drove on again, dipping into his bag of salt-and-vinegar-flavored crisps.

"I think they meant gradually, Ma."

"Well, of course! That was how we went, wasn't it? The whole of the first week we hardly changed his old diet at all. I just gave him a bit of stewed apple or a tiny bit of jam roly-poly for afters. I said to him, I said: 'Keep well *under* for the first few days, then you can go *over* on Sunday, have a bit of a blowout.' "

Herbert was quiet for a bit, then he said: "Well, he enjoyed it, I will say that."

"Oh, he did. He'd been looking forward to it all week. You could feel the juices running. We talked it all over, you know. There was the lobster paté, which was his favorite, as starters, with the little fingers of buttered toast. Then there were the pork steaks with the mushroom cream sauce that he loved, and the scalloped potatoes and the glazed carrots and the cauliflower in cheese sauce. Then there was the Madeira chocolate cake with the sherry-cream topping—the one I got the recipe for out of *Women's Own*. We'd planned it all. It was a lovely meal."

"A meal fit for a king," admitted Herbie.

"And I didn't make any trouble over cooking it, though none of it was convenience foods. I had to do it all with my own hands, but it was a pleasure to me to do it. I loved cooking it for him."

"And he loved eating it," said Herbie. "Even the chocolate cake."

"Well, it was the best I'd ever made. I thought so myself when I ate up the rest the next day. It was perfection. Maybe it was *so* good that in a way he—couldn't stand it."

"It wasn't a bad way to go," said Herbie.

"It was a very *good* way to go. I hope I go like that when my time comes. And it was quick, too. We'd hardly got him upstairs into the bed before he was gone. A darned sight better than lingering, that's what I say."

"It's what I'd call a good death."

"So would I. And I'd have been almost happy about it if it hadn't been for that bleeding doctor," said Annie, getting almost agitated and taking out of her handbag a tiny handkerchief, which she dabbed at her eyes.

"Doctor Causley?" said Herbert, surprised. "He never said anything out of turn in the bedroom."

"No. It was when he came downstairs. I never told you this, son, because I thought it would make you wild. I'd gone downstairs, being upset, to have a bit of a weep by the fire in the dining room. And he came downstairs and he came in, and he was just starting to say something when—Well, you see, the plates with the sweets was still on the table, with his bit of the chocolate cake still uneaten, which had gone to my heart when I came in, and he saw that, and he saw the other plates piled up on the sideboard and he looked at them—in*spected* I'd call it, in a thoroughly nasty way—and he said, 'Had he been eating this?' and I said yes, and explained we'd been sort of saving up on the calories so he could have one good blowout, and he said, 'What exactly did he have?' and so I told him. And do you know what he said?"

"No, Ma. What did he say?"

"He said: 'That meal killed him as surely as if you'd laced it with strychnine.' "

Herbie didn't go wild, but he thought for a bit.

"That wasn't very nice of him."

"It was diabolical. You could have knocked me down with a feather! Me just widowed not five minutes since."

"It was a liberty. These professional people take too much on themselves."

"They do. Your dad always said that, too. It was a wicked, cruel thing to say. And you notice he never had any doubt about signing the death certificate. That's why I changed my doctor. I never could fancy going back to Doctor Causley after that. I know I haven't got anything to reproach myself with."

They went quiet after that and Annie Monkton found a sucky sweet in her bag and comforted herself with it. Quite soon they were drawing up in the courtyard of The Borderer. Herbie got out and made sure they'd got rooms. Luckily the tourist season was only just beginning. He came back smiling.

"Couldn't be better. Two nice singles. I took a peek at the dinner menu, Ma. You'll be able to have the venison. I've worked up an appetite, so I think I'm going to fancy the mixed grill."

As he took the case from the boot and they started toward the main door, Annie's good humor returned. She nudged Herbie with her fat arm.

"It's nice being on our own, though, isn't it, son?"

Pork Fillet Chasseur

1 pound pork fillet (cut into 3½-inch strips)
1 tablespoon olive oil
4 ounces button mushrooms (thinly sliced)
2 shallots (chopped very fine)
½ ounce flour
2 tablespoons brandy
1 cup dry white wine
7½ fluid ounce of jellied stock
1 teaspoon fresh chopped basil
2 ounces butter
½ teaspoon tomato purée
1 teaspoon Dijon mustard
⅛ teaspoon salt
⅛ teaspoon pepper

In a frying pan heat the oil, and when hot drop in 1 ounce of the butter. Fry the pork strips. When they are brown on all sides remove from the pan and keep hot in a low oven.

Put the rest of the butter in the pan and cook the mushrooms, and then add the shallots. After they have cooked for 1 or 2 minutes blend in the flour, then add the brandy, the white wine, the Dijon mustard, the tomato purée and the stock. When the mixture is boiling add salt, pepper, and basil and return the pork to the frying pan. Let the pork and the sauce simmer for about 20 minutes, and then serve.

Good with mashed or scalloped potatoes.

This will serve 3 people of normal appetite. It will make an average meal for one of the Monktons.

—Robert Barnard

Alfred Karns, Accessory
by T. M. Adams

Mr. Karns entered his favorite restaurant, hungry, carefree, and whistling. He found his usual booth in the corner, fringed and hidden by potted palms, and took his seat in the dimness he thought of as "atmosphere." The waitress appeared and he ordered the Lobster Surprise, content in the knowledge that it would take at least half an hour to prepare. He didn't mind. This booth was the one he liked best because it was discreetly invisible, and because its acoustics served up the meat of the conversations going on around him.

It wasn't, he would assure you, that he was an eavesdropper. His interest was not in learning intimate secrets. It was just that now that his wife was gone and his children grown up, he missed the conviviality of mealtimes. He hadn't the slightest intention of remarrying or rooming with other people his age—his pension was small enough to preclude the first possibility and large enough to prevent the second.

No, he just wanted to hear voices at mealtime, the bland but solid conversation of people who were out and about in the world. It was enough to know, each day at lunchtime, that the wheels and seasons were still turning, that the bosses and children were still screaming, that the neighbors and governments were still overspending—in short, that Life was still continuing, with or without Mr. Karns's active participation.

To be sure, at dinnertime he always hoped for something a little spicier—the more malicious office gossip, perhaps, or the careful plans of lovers. Words like those were usually whispered, of course, but on nights like this one, when the restaurant was almost empty, it was possible to hear even the whispers from the table he was now facing. It was his preferred table for listening-in for another reason: although he could see whoever sat there, they were not likely to see him.

He was pleased to find the facing table empty tonight; he liked to monitor a conversation from its beginning, although there were times when it was more fun to try to guess the subject of a discussion intercepted in mid-course. Now that he was in position, however, he wanted the other table occupied as soon as possible.

The waitress, a blank-faced young woman with blonde hair, stopped by to inform Mr. Karns that his Lobster Surprise would take a little longer than expected. He nodded affably and noted that a pair of chatting women were approaching the facing table.

The waitress seated the pair—a charming white-haired lady of some frailty and her rather sharp-faced middle-aged companion. The deliberate dowdiness of the younger woman's dress disappointed Mr. Karns; he had been hoping to overhear something light and frivolous.

The waitress gave them menus and left. "And what would you like tonight, Mother?" the younger woman finally asked, going up a notch or two in Mr. Karns's estimation for her solicitousness.

The older woman's fingers fluttered uncertainly at the catch of her purse. She decided at last, and her voice was very sweet, Mr. Karns thought, soft but clear.

"Well, dear, I think I'd like the salad with French dressing, the baked stuffed clams for an appetizer . . . the candied ham and a side order of Brussels sprouts. Iced tea to drink, and later the strawberry shortcake and coffee."

Mr. Karns marveled at her appetite. How few of us stand up to old age so well, he thought.

"I think I'll have the same," the daughter said, which Mr. Karns thought a little odd with so much to choose from. What was more puzzling was the old woman's reaction to her daughter's choice—a hunching of the shoulders and very evident agitation.

The waitress bobbed up to their table again and the younger woman ordered crisply: "Salad with French, please. The clams for appetizer, the candied ham, and an order of Brussels sprouts. And I'll have the iced tea with that, thanks."

Her mother, who had looked throughout as though she were desperately anxious to interrupt, cut in as soon as her daughter had finished and added, in an almost pleading tone, "I'll have the same, please."

"A bowl of chowder and a glass of hot tea for my mother," the younger woman ordered.

"No, that's all right, dear. I'll have the same as you," her mother said hastily.

The younger woman gave the waitress a cold tight smile.

"Please excuse my mother," she said, a little too loudly. "She is completely senile and doesn't know what she is saying. She will have a bowl of chowder and a cup of hot tea."

Her mother was now quite motionless, except for the fingers still playing aimlessly with the catch of her purse. The waitress turned away and Mr. Karns caught a glimpse of her face. It was still blank, but not, he thought, effortlessly so.

What ghastly behavior! Mr. Karns spent the next five minutes hoping the awkward silence that had descended on the pair would continue unbroken. Eventually the salad arrived. And the chowder. The waitress departed hastily.

The older woman picked up her spoon and stirred the chowder, looking into the bowl distastefully. "I hate chowder," she murmured, as though to no one in particular.

Let's face it, Mr. Karns thought. Some of us, as we grow older, cannot follow our doctors' instructions. The daughter may just be looking out for her mother's welfare. Doing that day in and day out, she could easily get a little fed up, especially if her mother insisted on ordering things she was not supposed to eat. Perhaps this one time she had lost her temper—

"I hate salad," the younger woman said succinctly, "but I'm going to enjoy this one. Do you know what this salad is for, Mother?" She gestured with a forkful of greens, then bent forward slightly, dropping her voice as she said, "This is for Harvey Rice, Mother. The boy you threw out of the house for not wearing a necktie, remember? This is for Harvey Rice, who never called on me again." And she delicately but rapidly consumed the salad, making an exaggerated show of pleasure, while her mother looked on, listlessly sipping her chowder.

This was horrible—this brief glimpse through a maiden-lady's keyhole would trouble Mr. Karns's sleep for years. As the waitress swooped by to deposit his appetizer, Mr. Karns wished she would offer him a loud assurance about his Lobster Surprise, calling attention to his presence so that this dreadful woman would realize she was being overheard and stop her embarrassing performance—

"Do you know what *this* is for, Mother?" The younger woman brandished her little shellfish fork above the largest of the clams. "This is for twelve years of piano lessons at Mrs. de Puy's." She pointed to the second largest clam. "And this is for Iris Anderson's birthday party, which you wouldn't let me go to because it rained." Again, pointing to a clam, "And this is for the kitten you wouldn't let me keep."

And her eating of the clams was an extravagant burlesque of delectation, accompanied by such eye-rolling and lip-smacking that by the time the main course arrived, Mr. Karns thought that he himself would never want to eat anything again. The worst of it was the way the old lady's eyes followed each forkful of her daughter's food, as though she hadn't eaten at all that day, as if she hadn't had a real meal in many days.

It's sickening, Mr. Karns thought. He couldn't possibly complain to the waitress about it. No, that would mean confronting the daughter, and there was something too—too intimate about even talking to her. He had to keep her at arm's length, but still manage somehow to stop her. For he felt that no matter how many times she had staged this little scene before, this time she was going too far—

"Do you know what this ham is for, Mother? This is for the college education I never had because you were sick that year. And the Brussels sprouts are for all the years I nursed you."

I could clear my throat, Mr. Karns thought. Just clear my throat, and she would hear it and realize that I can hear her, and then she would stop. That's what I could do.

Then, as the waitress passed between them, he considered the unfairness of it. Couldn't his own children raise a similar host of grievances? Couldn't any children? Where does this hatred of hers come from, this hatred unforgiving enough to abuse the helpless?

He would clear his throat, and that would be that—

"And the shortcake? That's for our forty-three years together, Mother. Forty-three years. Why don't you finish your chowder, Mother? Or your tea? Don't you like tea, Mother?"

He couldn't do it. He couldn't make a sound. She had gone too far and he had listened. He couldn't humiliate them now. Yes, it would be his humiliation, too. His, the old woman's, and—but the worst of it was that the unnatural daughter might be beyond embarrassment. She might even address him directly, draw him into it!

No, he had to sit here, quiet and unmoving, until they left. And would he be able to eat then? And would he be able to look his face in the mirror that night, his old face, his own helpless face—

It was over. The younger woman, after a final verbal blow at her mother, left for the women's lounge. Mr. Karns felt a slight easing of tension. But that feeling did not last long.

As soon as her daughter was out of sight, the old

woman reached into her purse and fumbled among the pharmacopoeia of green- and brown-tinted bottles until she located the one she wanted. Quickly, without even glancing around, she pried off the cap and emptied the contents of the bottle into her daughter's coffee; then she picked up the spoon next to the cup, stirred the coffee, wiped the spoon clean on her napkin, and replaced both spoon and bottle.

Oh, my, thought Mr. Karns—

The old lady was finishing her chowder when her daughter returned. The younger woman seated herself and raised her coffee cup carelessly, just holding it, the way people hold cigarettes. She wore a self-satisfied smile.

He was trying desperately to think whether anything ever prescribed to him could be fatal in a large dose. Undoubtedly, undoubtedly. But surely she'd taste it. And if not—well, he didn't *know* it was poison; it could just be something harmless. Besides, how could he intervene at this stage? What could he possibly say? And if he were wrong—

The younger woman put the cup to her lips.

"What's *that* for?" her mother asked abruptly. "The coffee?"

The younger woman's reaction was at first as astonished as Mr. Karns'. But then, slowly, the saccharine smile came back to the daughter's face. Her reply had the corrosive sweetness of cheap candy; it made the teeth hurt.

"Mother, this is for bringing me into the world."

And as she emptied the cup, her mother said, "Fair enough, dear. Fair enough."

He had to stop it. He would have to admit he'd been spying on them, have to tell her she'd been poisoned. No. How about, "Couldn't help but notice—happened to overhear your remark about your mother's mental state—she seems to have accidentally—"

They had paid their bill by now. His view of them was blocked by the waitress bearing his Lobster Surprise on a tray. When she turned away from him to clear the newly vacated table, he caught sight of them at the door.

He couldn't sit still and be accessory to a murder. Wasn't it bad enough that he had allowed that shameful scene to go on for so long? It wasn't as though the two acts of omission canceled each other out—

He cleared his throat to attract the waitress's attention, found himself staring at their table, which was as clear as if they had never been there, and glanced back at the door.

They were gone.

"Yes, sir, is your lobster all right?" the waitress was asking, her face as blank as ever. Uncomprehending. Unsympathetic. Young.

He stammered, and then, as though it were a reasonable comment to make after calling her over, he heard himself saying, "Fair enough."

She looked back at him, puzzled. Probably thinks I'm completely senile, he thought. Probably thinks I don't know what I'm saying. He suddenly realized that he was very hungry.

The Case of the Amateur Detective and the Chicken

by James A. Noble

Police Captain John Evert liked his young new detective sergeant, not only because he had already solved an extremely difficult case that had been lying around in the files for five years, but also because of his logical mind and enthusiasm. Of course, the captain would never admit that to anyone, so when Detective Sergeant Mark Murphy entered his office carrying a cardboard box, he feigned irritation.

"Murphy, if you haven't solved another case, I don't want to see you."

"I guess you'll want to see me then," said Mark, putting the box on a chair along the side wall and closing the door. He pulled a small cassette player and a cassette tape from the box and set them down on the captain's desk.

"How'd you get so dirty?" asked the captain. There were dark smears and spots all over the detective's shirt and suit.

Mark looked down at his shirt front. "I've been collecting some evidence."

"And is that a shiner I detect developing?"

"Huh?" replied Mark. He winced as he reached up and touched the left corner of his eye. "Oh. I had a difference of opinion with a guy who works on one of those city sanitation trucks."

Captain Evert's curiosity got the better of him. "This story I've got to hear. Which case is it?"

"The Mannerly murder and accidental death."

"That happened Monday night and today is Thursday. You mean it took you three whole days to figure this one out?"

"Actually, I would have figured it out in one day, but I had to wait for some reports. Wait till you hear this."

Mark loaded the cassette tape into the machine and held down the rewind button. The captain leaned back in his wooden desk chair and prepared himself for what he knew would be an entertaining trip into the world of "detectivery" as only Mark could do it.

Mark Murphy was the son of Jim Murphy, one of the best street cops the city had ever seen. When Jim had been killed in the line of duty five years ago, Mark had applied all his energy toward becoming a policeman. In that five-year period, he made detective sergeant, and the first major case he solved was one leading to the arrest of his father's killers.

Mark had not acquired many of the traits of his tough Irish father. Jim had been a big strapping fellow with light wavy hair and steel grey eyes—slow talking and easygoing when he wanted to be, lightning quick and rough when he had to be. His son Mark, on the other hand, was tall and gangly with dark hair and eyes. He was constantly in motion and possessed of all the nervous habits likely to drive his wife crazy, or anyone else he was around. He wore his suits loose and his ties thin. Both seemed to take a few moments to catch up with him whenever he took off running. The only time Mark acted like his father was when he was deep in thought or partaking of his much loved after work beer. If you closed your eyes and listened to Mark talk during those times, you would swear you were hearing Jim Murphy.

"This is the Alvin Mannerly murder confession," began Mark, when the tape had rewound. "We found it in the living room along with the body and the smashed cassette recorder. Relatives have identified the voice as that of Mr. Mannerly. Listen." Mark pushed the play button, and the sound of someone clearing his throat could be heard. The voice was that of an obviously upset, distraught man.

"My name is Alvin Mannerly. I am making this tape so that anyone listening to it will understand the reasons for my actions.

"I have always believed that when a man and woman are married, they should remain faithful to each other no matter what happens. While I have been faithful, my wife, Audrey, has not. I have suspected for some time that she was having an affair with another man, but it isn't until today that I was able to obtain proof. I'm not neurotic or anything, it's just that when I started paying attention to certain little facts—undeniable facts—I knew she was telling me lies about where she was and what she had been doing today.

"First, there was the matter of her car. It started raining early this afternoon, and when I pulled my car into the garage next to hers at around four fifteen P.M., I noticed it was wet. I compared its odometer reading with the one I had written down before I left this morning. Like I said, I'm not nuts or anything. I just wanted to collect some information on her activities because I felt something was going on. Anyhow, the reading on the odometer indicated she had driven the car exactly eight miles. When I asked her where she'd been, she said she'd never left the house. I also discovered that her coat in the hall closet was damp. I didn't say anything, but she wasn't fooling me.

"Then there were her clothes. She always gets dressed when I do. Then she goes downstairs and makes breakfast for us before I go to work. This morning she put on slacks and a pullover, but when I came home, she had on a blue skirt and a blouse. I asked her if she wanted to go out tonight, figuring she was dressed good enough to do so, but she said she didn't feel like it. Little wonder—she had already been out. I could think of a good reason for her changing clothes, but I kept quiet.

"She told me another lie at dinner. Like I said, I was keeping my eyes open and my mind sharp. I really like fried chicken. You know, the way they make it at some of those fast-food chicken places. Audrey experimented a little bit and came up with a thin, seasoned batter. She puts lots of oil in a big cast iron frying pan, dips the chicken in this special batter of hers, and it makes fried chicken just about like you would get from one of those fast-food joints, only a lot cheaper. Anyway, she told me she had spent much of the afternoon cutting up and frying this chicken I had brought home from the supermarket a couple of days ago. I know there was only one chicken in the freezer when I left this morning. When I got back this afternoon and sat down at the table, there was a platter full of cut-up fried chicken all right, only there was an additional wing and two too many legs. I haven't seen a chicken yet that could sprout three wings and four legs. Not only that, it didn't taste exactly like the stuff she normally cooks. I figure it was bought from one of those chicken joints. And she never left the house? I checked the freezer and the icebox, but the chicken that had been there was gone. She probably hid it somewhere. I've got to give her credit for having some brains.

"What really makes me mad is she must have brought her lover into our house this time. I have proof. While I was making mental notes to myself this morning, I saw that the matchbook by the big ashtray in the living room had all its matches in it. Now, I'm the only one who smokes in this house, but when I got home from work, five or six of the matches were missing from the book and the burnt remains of those matches were not in the ashtray. In other words, the ashtray had been cleaned so I wouldn't find her boyfriend's cigarette butts, but I'm too smart for her. I saw the matches.

"Finally, there were the wine glasses. We always keep them in the kitchen cabinet over the sink. We don't have much use for them, so we keep them behind the water tumblers. This afternoon, I found two of the wine glasses in front of the water tumblers. We don't even have any wine in the house. A little thing, but if you pay attention like I do, you notice things like that.

"I put all the clues together and figure it happened this way. After I leave this morning, Audrey drives to her lover's place and picks him up. He brings along a bottle of wine. They use her car because they don't want the neighbors noticing a strange vehicle hanging around my house or driving into my garage. After they get here, she and him go to the bedroom, drink a little wine, and ... well ... she's cheating on me, that's all! Then she changes clothes and they come back downstairs and the guy smokes a couple of cigarettes using those matches I planted ... I mean, I noticed this morning."

"Humph!" interjected Captain Evert.

"It starts getting late," the voice on the tape continued, "and they know I'm going to be home soon, so they hop into her car and pull out of the garage and into the rain which has since started, thus providing me with another clue: the wet car. You understand?

"After dropping the bum off, she stops by one of those fried chicken outfits and gets a bucket of the stuff. Another mistake. Three wings and four legs in the bucket. Who's she kidding?

"When she gets home, she leaves the car in the garage, puts her wet coat in the closet, and starts trying to cover up what she has done before I arrive. She puts the already-cooked chicken into the frying pan full of oil and turns on the burner, then she gets a bag or something and puts the whole chicken from the freezer, the empty wine bottle, the empty cardboard chicken bucket, and the ashes from the big ashtray into it and hides it somewhere. Next, she washes the wine glasses and mistakenly puts them in front of the water tumblers in the kitchen cabinet. Finally, while she is straightening the upstairs, she hears me drive in and rushes downstairs to make it look like she was in the kitchen cooking, only she doesn't realize she forgot to change out of her skirt and blouse.

"There you have the whole story. Undeniable evidence which I have compiled and analyzed. Proof of my wife's infidelity. If it had happened to you, I am sure you would have done the same thing I did. I have shot and killed my wife Audrey, and as soon as I have finished this recording, I will turn the gun on myself and take my own li . . ."

At this point, there was a loud, sharp noise on the tape followed by silence.

"Is that all?" asked Captain Evert.

"Yep," replied Mark, switching off the cassette player.

"You mean to tell me because of a few things he couldn't explain around his house," said the captain, "Alvin Mannerly set himself up as judge, jury, and executioner?"

"Looks like it," acknowledged Mark. "But worse, he also played amateur detective. Based on five clues— the wet car and coat, the extra and different tasting poultry pieces, the missing matches, his wife's clothing changes, and the two wine glasses—he created a scenario that was logical but not very probable."

"Sounds like he was not a well man," observed Captain Evert. "Perhaps if he hadn't committed suicide, he might have gotten help."

"He didn't kill himself. Remember I said the case was a murder and an accidental death."

"Wasn't that sharp noise at the end of the tape Mannerly's gun going off?"

"Nope," said Mark, shaking his head. "That was the sound of the Mannerly house exploding just before the tape recorder was demolished by the blast. Fortunately, the tape popped free of the machine and survived."

"Blew up? How?"

Mark reached back into the cardboard box he had brought and pulled out some official-looking forms. "It's all here in this fire investigation report, which also provides a logical explanation of each of Alvin Mannerly's five clues."

Captain Evert picked up his glasses from his desk

and slipped them on. He took the forms from Mark and started reading.

FIRE INVESTIGATION REPORT
November 8, 1982
Explosion and fire—Mannerly residence—
116 Westminster Drive
REPORTING OFFICER: John Lofter, First Company
Fire Marshal/Investigator

BRIEF SUMMARY OF INCIDENT:

7:01 P.M. Explosion and fire reported at Mannerly residence by Mr. Joseph Wright, 118 Westminster Drive, a next door neighbor of the Mannerlys.

7:18 P.M. No. 4 hose truck and No. 1 tanker truck from Company 1 arrive at the Mannerly house.

7:23 P.M. Fire extinguished. Two bodies found. One male: apparent victim of the explosion. One female: probable shooting victim. Police notified.

7:35 P.M. Police investigative unit arrives.

7:40 P.M. Departure of Company 1 firefighting equipment.

INVESTIGATIVE REPORT:

Major damage to the two story frame structure occurred during the explosion. The center of the blast was in the area of the kitchen. The subsequent fire was small and confined to a part of the kitchen area. The fire was quickly extinguished by the fire department.

Cause of the blast was an accumulation of gas from a faulty kitchen stove. Helpful information concerning the cause of the explosion was provided by a next door neighbor, Mrs. Emily Wright, who had been in the house a few hours prior to the blast. A transcript of her testimony is included in this report followed by an analysis of her statements as they relate to this investigation.

TRANSCRIPT OF TESTIMONY OF
MRS. EMILY WRIGHT
November 8, 1982; 9:10 P.M.
INTERVIEWING OFFICER: John Lofter
Fire Marshal/Investigator First Company

"I went over to the Mannerly house to return some wine glasses I had borrowed and to offer Audrey some extra chicken pieces I had. When I walked into the house, I found her on her hands and knees trying to re-light the pilot lights and burners on her stove with some matches. I helped her for a few hours until we finally got the pilots lit; however, the burner on which she was cooking her own chicken plus the extra I gave her kept going out every so often. She certainly does use a lot of oil to fry chicken.

"It started to rain, so I helped her close some of the windows in the house.

"Before Audrey went upstairs to change her clothes—she had gotten quite dirty working on the stove; I always clean my stove every week—anyway, before she went upstairs to change, I asked to borrow her car. You see, our car has been in the shop this week being fixed and Audrey, rest her soul, had lent me her car once before when we were having trouble with ours. I also borrowed one of her coats from the hall closet because of the rain, you understand. I hadn't brought one with me when I came.

"When I got back from the store about a half hour later, I went in to return the coat. Audrey told me the stove had quit working altogether. The chicken she was cooking for dinner that night was only half done so I took it to my house and finished it as best I could. I wasn't about to use that much oil, however. When I took the chicken back to her house, I noticed a faint odor of gas, but I didn't say anything to her because I figured she was trying to relight the stove again. After I left, I saw her husband Alvin come home at around 4:15 P.M.

"At approximately 7:00 P.M., I heard this terrible explosion and looked out my window and saw their house (Mannerly residence) had blown up. I went over to try and help while my husband Joe called the fire department. When I got there, I smelled the gas and saw the fire. I was frightened so I ran back home. That's all I know."

ANALYSIS OF INVESTIGATION:

Failure of the burners on the stove to remain lit indicates probable leakage in the feed lines leading to the burners.

The closing of the windows in the Mannerly home, particularly in the area of the kitchen, significantly increased the rate at which gas accumulated.

Analysis of the faulty stove parts indicates that Mrs. Mannerly had failed to turn off one of the burners. If the burner had gone out, it is likely an additional amount of gas was collecting in the kitchen.

While it is likely Mr. Alvin Mannerly was the victim of the explosion due to his close proximity to the kitchen, it is the considered opinion of this fire investigator that Mrs. Audrey Mannerly was not the victim of the explosion or the fire. Because of the location of her body away from the blast area and from the nature of her wounds, police investigation is recommended.

"Do you think the explosion was accidental?" asked the captain, handing the papers back to Mark.

"Probably. Alvin had already indicated on the tape that he was going to use a gun to commit suicide—not gas. Anyone trying to blow up the house intentionally or to kill someone with gas from the stove would have turned on all the burners and the oven."

"One thing the fire investigation report does show," said Captain Evert. "Mr. Mannerly had incorrectly interpreted his clues."

"The report offers answers to all of Mr. Mannerly's so-called evidence of his wife's infidelity," the young detective sergeant agreed. "The extra chicken and the wine glasses came from a borrowing neighbor. The matches were used to try to relight the stove; the burnt matches were discarded in the kitchen. She changed her clothing because of its being soiled. The car and coat were wet because she lent them to the borrowing neighbor that rainy afternoon. The neighbor had partially cooked the chicken in a manner somewhat different from the way Mrs. Mannerly would have, thus contributing to its different taste. Yeah, it would appear that everything adds up."

"Apparently Mrs. Mannerly was telling her husband

the truth all along," observed Captain Evert. "But in his sick mind, he exaggerated the facts he had learned and killed his wife and nearly succeeded in killing himself, except that the gas explosion did the second job for him."

"So we seem to have a logical conclusion to the Mannerly case. Only one problem," said Mark.

"What's that?"

"Why are there so many pages left in this story?"

"Beg your pardon?"

Mark laughed. "If you were an avid mystery reader like myself, you would understand. You'd be reading right along and, all of a sudden, you reach a logical conclusion. All the questions have been answered, all the good guys and bad guys have been determined, and the mystery appears to be solved. Yet when you look ahead to see how many pages are left, you find several. 'Why are there so many pages left in this story?' is another way of telling you that the mystery isn't finished and there's more to tell."

"What more can there be?" asked Captain Evert.

The detective picked up the box from the chair and set it on the captain's desk. Inside the box was a bulging brown paper shopping bag.

"What's in it?" asked the captain.

"One whole chicken, one empty wine bottle, discarded material from a cigarette ashtray, and one cardboard bucket from Annie's Insta-Chicken."

"Huh?"

Mark reached into his pocket and pulled out a smaller bag. He handed it to the somewhat confused captain. "And this is what put me on to it."

The captain opened the small bag and looked inside. "Bones," he announced, flatly.

"Right!" said Mark. "Chicken bones, to be more specific."

"You mean to tell me Alvin Mannerly was right in his little novice investigation after all? What about the testimony of Mrs. Wright?"

"It's past quitting time," said Mark, looking at his

watch. "If you'll buy me a beer at Kelly's, I'll explain the whole thing."

"I'll buy you a six pack, but what . . ."

"Come on." Mark collected all his items and returned them to the box. "Let's stop by the refrigerator and drop this bird off so it doesn't go bad, then we'll go to Kelly's and hoist a few."

Captain Evert looked at the young detective with the soiled clothing and the shiner. He wasn't sure he wanted to be seen in public with this walking disaster, but it was either that or not find out what really happened in the Mannerly case. He chose the former.

They walked the half block down to Kelly's Bar. The place was crowded with other people who had just gotten off work, but Mark managed to find an empty table in the back while Captain Evert ordered.

"Okay," said the captain, arriving at the table with the beers. "Give."

"Wait a minute," said Mark, lifting the mug and downing half its contents. Captain Evert sighed a deep, impatient sigh.

"Doesn't it bother you that Mrs. Wright's testimony to the fire marshal offered all the answers necessary to refute Alvin Mannerly's allegations against his wife?" began Mark after he set the mug down.

"Maybe . . . I see what you mean."

"Like any good detective, I had to check out all possible leads, even if those leads were refuted by someone's impartial testimony. I decided to start with Mr. Mannerly's suspicion that his wife had bought a bucket of chicken instead of cutting up and cooking the whole one he had brought home earlier. That's where those bones you saw come in."

"The chicken bones," said Captain Evert.

"Right. You see, my wife is always buying that precooked chicken from those little fast-food places because she knows there are some pieces of chicken I just won't eat. You know, the back, the neck, those sorts of things; the pieces you get when you buy a supermarket chicken and cook it yourself. Nearly all those precooked-chicken places, including Annie's, don't put parts like that in their mixed buckets. If Mrs. Mannerly did cut up and cook the whole chicken from the refrigerator, those parts had to be somewhere in the Mannerly kitchen."

"What about the fire and explosion?"

"Like the fire investigator indicated, the fire was small and not very intense. It was hot enough to burn paper and blister paint, but not hot enough to destroy chicken bones. Mrs. Mannerly might have put the neck and the back in the refrigerator or she might have thrown them away like my wife would have done. Alvin Mannerly never acknowledged the presence or absence of those parts from his platter of fried chicken, so, like me, he probably doesn't eat them.

"The contents of the refrigerator were intact, but unfortunately I didn't find the neck or back there, which meant the only other place they could be was in the kitchen garbage. Problem was, the explosion blew the contents of the garbage pail all over the kitchen, so I had to search for the bones."

Captain Evert tried to picture this tall, lanky detective crawling among the rubble and trash on his hands and knees, collecting chicken bones. "What did you find?"

"It's what I didn't find," corrected Mark. "No backbones or neckbones. The chicken had to come from a fast-food chicken restaurant. I checked the phone book and the closest restaurant of that type is Annie's Insta-Chicken, exactly four miles away. Remember what Alvin Mannerly had said on the tape. His wife's car had been driven eight miles that day—or four miles each way."

"What about Mannerly's contention that his wife picked up her lover?"

"The mileage wouldn't have added up unless her lover lived along the route to Annie's place," replied Mark. "A more likely possibility was that her lover lived within walking distance of the Mannerly home. It would have to be someone who, if observed walking into the Mannerly house, would not arouse undue suspicion among the neighbors. We're getting away from the main point, however."

"Which is?"

"Since Audrey Mannerly lied to her husband about cutting up and frying the chicken from the refrigerator," said Mark, shaking his finger, "Emily Wright had to have lied to the fire investigator about finishing the chicken in her own kitchen."

"Why would she do that?"

"For the same reason she had to disprove all the evidence Mr. Mannerly had compiled. She didn't want anyone investigating the possibility that Mrs. Mannerly had a lover."

"How could she possibly know what evidence she had to disprove?"

"Elementary, my dear captain," said Mark. "She listened to the tape. While her husband phoned the fire department, Mrs. Wright ran over to the Mannerly house after the explosion to try to help. Instead, she found Audrey Mannerly shot to death and the body of Mr. Mannerly lying on the floor of the living room along with the gun, the smashed tape recorder, and the cassette tape. Figuring there might be information on the tape that would help in the investigation of the shooting death of Mrs. Mannerly, she rescued it for the police. The only problem was, when she returned to her own house, she played the tape back on her own cassette player. She already had her suspicions, but when she heard the tape, she put two and two together and realized who Audrey Mannerly's secret lover was."

"But the tape was found in the living room with Mannerly's body," observed the captain.

"Of course," replied Mark. "Mrs. Wright knew the police would expect to find a tape near the smashed recorder along with the gun and the body. She also knew that if the police launched a thorough investigation because of a missing suicide or confession tape, they might discover who Audrey Mannerly's lover was.

Suddenly she realized how she could use the tape to her advantage. The tape made Alvin Mannerly sound like a nut case already. All she had to do was come up with a story that would disprove his evidence. The police, then, couldn't help but believe that his clues were the products of a deranged mind. The result would be no investigation into the secret lover theory. She knew she had to get the tape back into the living room with the smashed recorder, but that presented no problem. From the time she listened to the tape, probably about seven ten P.M. or seven fifteen or so, she had twenty, maybe twenty-five minutes to get the tape into the room. All she had to do was toss it through the blown-out window before the investigation team arrived."

"Okay, but why did she do it?" asked the captain.

"Because she didn't want anyone to find out that the lover was her husband, Joseph Wright. She was trying to protect him in spite of his actions, but it was the discovery of the bag containing all the stuff supporting Alvin Mannerly's theories that helped me piece together what she was up to."

"And where, may I ask, did you find the bag?"

"I found it in the Wrights' outside trash can, just where Joseph Wright stuck it when he sneaked back to his own house after his interlude with Mrs. Mannerly. The same place Emily Wright saw him put it. Later she went out to compare its contents with what the Mannerly tape had said would probably be in it. The same place I just barely managed to get to before the sanitation truck emptied the can."

"So that's how you got the black eye," snickered Captain Evert.

"I had no idea those guys were so possessive of their trash," said Mark, touching the corner of the eye again.

"I suppose Mrs. Wright knew about the problems with the stove from some earlier conversation with Mrs. Mannerly," observed the captain.

"No doubt."

Mark paused a moment to down the remainder of his beer. "I've already learned from the fellows in the lab that the fingerprints of Audrey Mannerly, Joseph Wright, and Emily Wright are all over the empty wine bottle. . . . Say, do you think that dust they use for fingerprints will ruin that chicken? It just doesn't make good sense to waste a perfectly good . . ."

Captain Evert cracked up. "Come on, you know you can't get fingerprints off a chicken," he roared.

"That's right. They have claws,'" said Mark, starting his own laugh.

And Captain Evert realized he had been the victim of one of the most insidious creations of western civilization: the chicken joke.

Just Desserts
by *Stanley Ellin*

To those like myself who, though American born and bred, are addicted to *haute cuisine* in the grand tradition of Escoffier—calories beyond counting and each one the devil's delight—the Restaurant Sacoche on the narrow rue Sacoche near the Bourse is the greatest restaurant in Paris, meaning, of course, the world. Small, unpretentious, and democratic of spirit, it does not feature its clientele but its food. Anyone who can scan a truly staggering bill at the conclusion of his repast without the blood perceptibly draining from his face is welcome here. Of course, reservations must be made well in advance or else there is nothing left to do but glumly settle for such as Lapérouse or La Tour d'Argent.

The reason for the divine place of La Sacoche in the culinary order is simply stated: the presiding genius of its kitchen is Georges Bordeloup himself, that emperor among mere kings as even his peers grudgingly acknowledge. He looks the part, too. Short and stout, with a formidable mustache and an air of calm command, he wears his starched white chef's *toque* like the crown of an emperor.

An awesome figure, yet he can unbend on occasion. That evening in question he did unbend. It was close to midnight, my dinner companions had left for their homes while I, a hotel dweller, remained alone at our table savoring a cognac and cigar. The restaurant almost deserted now, the day's work done, Monsieur Georges, as was his custom, seated himself at a table near the kitchen door to enjoy his own repast.

When in the mood he had marvelous tales to tell of culinary triumphs, so as he happened to glance my way I raised my glass to him in a toast trusting this would earn me an invitation to join him, and it did. His repast was simple—indeed, gemlike in its simplicity—a *gras-double*, which is a Bordeloup specialty of tripe simmered in minced onions and herbs and a vast improvement over the drearily familiar *tripes à la mode de Caen*—and it was accompanied by nothing more than a loaf of bread and a bottle of champagne. He tucked away a mouthful and washed it down with a glass of champagne before remarking to me with rough good humor, "So it's back here to Paris once again, eh? The airlines must be growing rich on that employer of yours in New York, my friend."

"Possibly. But," I said teasingly, "if you were to open a discreet little restaurant of your own in my country—"

"Ah, no!" He held up both hands in protest. "Don't even say it. Your country? Never." His face was bleak. "The nature of the crimes that can take place there—"

"Oh, come. What you read in the papers—"

"I was once there, my friend. And with these two eyes I witnessed a crime so depraved, so horrid, that I still shudder at the memory of it." He fortified himself with another glass of champagne. "Perhaps I should tell you about it. Of course, if you feel it may wound your patriotic feelings—"

"No, no," I said. "Go right ahead."

"Very well," said he, "I will. Just remember afterwards that it is with your consent."

It all commenced (said Monsieur Georges) on a July afternoon during that tranquil period between lunch and dinner when the restaurant is empty. I was seated at this very table having a small collation—a slice or two of Bayonne ham garnished with fresh figs—when a stranger approached me. A young man, plainly an American, very tall, thin, and with sunburned features, especially the nose. An amiable type with an engaging awkwardness about him. "Mr. Bordeloup," said he, "may I have a word with you, sir?"

I was moved by curiosity. "You may," I said.

"Mighty kind of you, sir," he said. He seated himself and handed me a small card on which was inscribed *Herbert Dobson, Sunshine Spread, Texas.* "That's me," he said. "And the reason I'm here is that some people whose judgment I trust told me you were the finest chef to be found anywhere."

"Their judgment is correct," I assured him.

"Right. I found that out sure enough when I was eating here this week. I also found out that this restaurant closes up for the whole month of August. Now I want to offer you a business proposition. I want to hire your services for that month. All you have to do, sir, is name your price and pack your bags."

I could not believe my ears. "You wish to engage me as your personal chef for that period?"

"Well now," said the fellow apologetically, "it's a little more than just chef. What I really want you to do is give me some cooking lessons. I know my way around French cooking already—done quite a bit of it—but now I need some real blue-ribbon expert help at it."

I should have been outraged by his astounding presumption, but, in truth, he was so ingenuous in manner that I found myself a trifle amused by it. I said, "In a nutshell, I, Georges Bordeloup, who have spent a lifetime mastering the sacred art of *la cuisine classique,* am now to repair to your distant home in the wilderness and there make you master of it in precisely one month? No, no, Monsieur Dobson. This joke has gone far enough, and since I wish to lunch in privacy—"

"Believe me, sir, it's no joke. And I'm not looking to learn the whole art. All I want to do is turn out some choice samples of it. Especially your kind of soufflé." His sunburned features took on an ecstatic expression, the kind of muttonheaded expression a very youthful poet might wear while inscribing a poem to his beloved. "A really great soufflé. And all you have to do, Mr. Bordeloup, is name your price. Any price at all."

I regarded him with scorn. "Oh, indeed? And what if I were to demand a hundred thousand francs? Or better yet, why not a million?"

"Why not?" said he eagerly, whipping out a checkbook. Then as I sat there struck dumb by astonishment he filled out a check and thrust it at me. "Good for a million at the Banque de Paris," he said. "Just phone them now, and they'll confirm that."

And that was how only three days later, my brain still in a whirl, I found myself descending in his private airplane—a monstrous jet plane with full accoutrement of sitting room, bedrooms, and baths—to the airport in the city of Houston of the state of Texas.

At this point I must note that like any sensible Frenchman I have no enthusiasm for travel to foreign cities. What is such travel after all but a series of inconveniences inevitably landing one in an unattractive metropolis crowded with strangers? It was a relief therefore to find that the residence of Herbert Dobson where I was to undergo my month's penance was outside the boundaries of the singularly unattractive city of Houston. Sunshine Spread, it appeared, was a suburban community of enormously wealthy Texans, scions of those oil tycoons who had originally filled the family coffers with gold. Magic coffers indeed, because no matter how deep the following generations dipped into them they remained overflowing. Unbelievable, yes, but true.

If evidence of this was needed, it was provided by those vast estates which comprised Sunshine Spread. Despite their grotesque architecture, the Sun King himself, our Louis Fourteenth, would have been impressed by them. The dimensions of them, their furnishings, the landscaping, the equipage, the host of servants, all indicated what even a tribe of primitives could do about their living accommodations given unlimited wealth to do it with.

Most interesting—even touching—was the discovery

that the primitives occupying this community had
come to feel a dim yearning for civilization, the first
evidence of which is always to be found in *la cuisine*.
World travelers on a fantastic scale—they took flight
in their airplanes to foreign places as one would take a
stroll to the nearest bistro—they had discovered with
enthusiasm the raptures of fine cookery such as I for
one could provide.

Here it is necessary to explain two curious qualities
in these male Texans. One is a compulsion to display
a prowess at cookery, most often demonstrated by what
is known in that region as the barbecue. A sort of sav-
age rite, in fact, which consists of placing bloody portions of cattle on an open fire until they are charred
beyond recognition and then smearing them with
sauces that are not merely an abomination but a punishment.

Their other notable quality is an instinct for com-
petition that borders on madness. Not to beat your
neighbor into the dust with your fists—that had been
the crude practice of their ancestors, as I was given to
understand—but to beat his pride into the dust and joy-
ously leap up and down on its tattered vestiges, ah,
there was the true richness of life as these inhabitants
of Sunshine Spread saw it.

The result? Inevitably a contest among them in *la
cuisine*. It had even become a contest surrounded
by formalities. Precisely twelve of them—a round
dozen—had banded into a fanatical fraternity which
gathered on the last Friday evening of each month at a
different estate to share dinner. Each dinner, so the
rules went, must be prepared in its entirety by its host,
and each must demonstrate a mastery of *la grande cuisine* down to the selection of the sorbet used for clearing the palate between courses. At the conclusion of
the repast would be a solemn discussion of its merits
and deficiencies, and either an accolade bestowed on
its chef, or a shrug of the shoulders, or, tragically, a
contemptuous shake of the head.

And, as Herbert Dobson assured me, his eyes alight

with the challenge, accolades were notoriously hard to
come by. Now he was determined to win one when, on
the last Friday of this month of August, he would be
host of the occasion.

I must admit that during those first few days when I
was being introduced with almost embarrassing rever-
ence to the other members of this fraternity I took the
matter a bit lightly. After all, how far must a Georges
Bordeloup extend himself to overwhelm these childlike
barbarians, even through such an unlikely instrument
as Herbert Dobson? I soon learned better. These men,
with the same demonic intensity with which their
grandpapas had undertaken to sharpen their knives for
the taming of the American wilderness, had undertaken
to sharpen their palates to an exquisite edge. All, including my young friend Herbert, knew their way
around a kitchen. All could pass the most severe tests
in the judgment of a serious wine. No need to ask
where so many of the finest vintages of France had
disappeared to in recent years. Apparently, most of
them were stored in the cellars of Sunshine Spread.

A formidable challenge, but after all I am Georges
Bordeloup. So to work, first in the selection of a menu.
Here I determined to play a little trick on the fraternity.
Lately, I was informed, it had been engaged in a duel
of extravaganzas, pitting the most elaborate dishes
against each other. How effective then, to take the opposite direction. To present only some basic dishes of
la cuisine borgeoise which is, after all, the heart and
soul, the very foundation on which *la grande cuisine*
has been constructed.

Thus, as in a symphony, an opening of hot sausage
in crust and artichokes on foie gras simply to sound the
theme. Then *truite en bleu* followed by quail potted
with fresh grapes to develop it *accelerando*. Then a
masterstroke, responding as it would to the local taste
for beef, an *entrecôte Florentine*. And for the wine list,
the most clever device of all: a single wine, champagne. A Dom Perignon of excellent year which, as a
sensitive piano accompanist rounds out the perfection

of the violinist's efforts, would support to perfection every dish of the prescribed menu.

One problem then presented itself.

In the selection of a dessert my otherwise pliant protégé insisted that nothing would do but a soufflé. And no mere soufflé but my exquisite *soufflé Bordeloup* which he had sampled at the Restaurant Sacoche. He was obsessed by this concept, his sunburned nose glowing even redder as he vehemently defended it against all argument.

Need I tell anyone of intelligence, as I tried to tell him, that this was a highly dangerous move on which to risk his accolade? A proper soufflé is an ethereal and timorous creation, and everything in cruel nature conspires against it. It must be served instantly on removal from the oven, and in that perilous instant the least disturbance can mean its ignominious collapse into wrinkled failure. In view of this, as I pleaded with my protégé, how much better a charming mousse or perhaps the dramatic and non-collapsible crêpes Suzette.

But he was adamant. In fact, he pointed out, it was the very risk which made the *soufflé Bordeloup* an essential element of the dinner. Others of the fraternity had lately taken to experimenting with various exotic soufflés, only to fail disastrously. It was not always a case of the concoction's collapsing at the moment of truth. Some hopefuls had come up with recipes guaranteeing to avoid that, but, as was bound to happen, such products always emerged with the consistency of a pudding, more deplorable even than the process of deflation. No, no, said young Herbert stubbornly, the dessert must be a *soufflé Bordeloup,* light as thistledown, succulent as ambrosia, delivered to the table in all its glory. It would be the burning envy of the fraternity. It would stir the same emotions, he assured me earnestly, as if the university of the state of Texas were to beat the university of the state of Oklahoma in a game of football.

His very words. A game of football. I ask anyone to make sense of that.

But considering his emotionalism I yielded the issue. A *soufflé Bordeloup* it would be, and under my instruction why should he not succeed in this coup? And as the time passed I gained increasing confidence in him. We spent endless hours in that luxurious kitchen which, as was true of all the kitchens of the Sunshine Spread, was completely exposed to the dining room. My demonstrations appeared to be working well too, because he was a passionately dedicated student who allowed nothing to distract him from the pursuit of his goal.

Nothing.

Not even a distraction which insisted on presenting itself to him. And what else would that be but a female of the species?

I must make known at once that this was not a *femme fatale,* a veritable Delilah. Far from it. Her name was Bobby Jo Butterworth, daughter of a Monsieur J.F. Butterworth, one of the most rich and powerful of this community, and she was very young—of that age when the child has just discovered her womanhood—and was golden-haired, blue-eyed, and dimpled, with a shape most pleasantly rounded.

She also shared with the females of that region an attribute one does not find in any other American women, an awesome respect for the male and a willingness to acknowledge that he is, as God intended, her superior. Thus where other women may be bold in the demonstration of their desires, the smitten Bobby Jo Butterworth demonstrated hers by a trembling, wide-eyed yearning when in Herbert Dobson's presence. As the sunflower inclines toward the sun, so she inclined toward the man she had obviously marked as her future lord and master.

The informal manners of the community worked in her favor too. There, one did not knock at the door to be admitted to a neighboring home; when in the mood one merely entered it, that was all. Bobby Jo Butter-

worth, I soon observed, took full advantage of this
privilege. Seek out Herbert Dobson, and there she was,
a silent, adoring presence nearby.

Most of the time, of necessity, this meant she was
planted on a high stool in a corner of the kitchen ob-
serving my education of her Prince Charming. Plainly,
a little of this went a long way with her. After a while
she would be hard put to conceal those small signs in-
dicating that she was being bored to distraction: the
drooping eyelids, the stifled yawns, the furtive glances
at the watch.

Then she would screw up her courage and in hon-
eyed tones attempt to make him aware of her existence
and to lure him from his lessons with reminders of the
delights awaiting them elsewhere: a horseback ride, a
swimming party, a game of baseball in the arena of the
city of Houston, even a rendezvous with picnic basket
in the nearby woodland.

To all these sweet supplications he remained deaf
and blind, such was his fierce devotion to his chosen
task. In the end, there was a deplorable scene played
out in my presence. Caught up the evening before by
experimentation on the batter for a proper soufflé, he
had forgotten that this was an evening when he was to
dine *en famille* at the Butterworth estate. The next day,
Bobby Jo made known to him the humiliation this had
caused her. More than that, she expressed the opinion
that in his order of priorities she now appeared to rank
far below his cooking pots. Was that the truth? And if
so, was it not time for a reordering of priorities?

Herbert appeared stricken by this, bewildered, of an
apologetic disposition. However, at that perilous instant he discovered he was stirring a fine batter in the
wrong direction, and, the true chef, hastily devoted
himself to the correction of this error while angrily
railing at himself for his carelessness. I could not have
been prouder of him than I was at that moment.

On the other hand, his fair supplicant gave him a
long mournful look as he bent to his labors and then
turned on her heel and departed. Nor did she make any

further appearance on the scene as the time moved close for the grand dinner. I saw with relief that Herbert seemed entirely unaware of her absence, devoting himself now only to the intricacies of the *soufflé Bordeloup*.

One does not lightly divulge the recipe for such a creation, but there can be no harm in explaining that where your ordinary soufflé in the oven rises in rounded loveliness above the level of its baking dish and, with only minute diminution, holds to that level as it is removed from the oven, the *soufflé Bordeloup* poses a special challenge. A collar of oiled paper as wide as one's little finger is long has been fixed around the neck of the baking dish and so the soufflé is required to rise and maintain itself that additional height. Imagine the blowing of a dazzling soap bubble larger than you had ever dreamed it could be blown and then the maintaining of it until you yourself invite its dissolution, that will give some idea of the delicacy of this project.

Then consider the mastery of the project that Herbert Dobson finally obtained when, after endless nerve-racking failures, he could draw from the oven one perfect *soufflé Bordeloup* after another. I knew then that no one, with the exception of myself, could have been better equipped to meet the challenge of that impending dinner.

The company for the dinner arrived long before its designated hour to make sure I had no part in its preparation. I was to be an honored guest, that was all. The others gathered in the kitchen ascertaining that everything done was the handiwork of Herbert alone and engaging in some heavy-handed jesting about that handiwork which in no way disconcerted him. He was, in fact, as cool as a cucumber.

At the table itself when the time came we were waited upon by half a dozen skilled servitors, and here the initial reaction to the early courses appeared to be puzzlement at their very simplicity. Then, as the theme of the menu dawned on all, puzzlement became admiration. More than admiration. Awe. Nothing remained now but the presentation of the *soufflé Bordeloup* to assure Herbert's devastating triumph.

He was plainly visible at the oven as he drew the soufflé from it, the kitchen attendants standing aside breathlessly. All eyes were fixed on him as he bore the precious burden toward the table. Suddenly his rapt expression became an open-mouthed surprise. Everyone looked around toward the foot of the table to see what had occasioned this. And the sight that met us—

Monsieur Georges closed his eyes as if to blot out the memory of that sight.

"Yes?" I prompted.

"It takes all my courage to describe it. Bobby Jo Butterworth had entered silently. She stood there with a gigantic pistol clutched in her hands. She raised the pistol—"

"Good God! She shot him right there in front of you?"

Monsieur Georges looked reproachful. "My friend, I am trying to describe to you the most heinous of crimes, so please consider that for a woman to shoot the adored one who neglects her may be excessive, but it is hardly a crime. No, she did not shoot him. She raised her weapon high, and with a terrible smile on her lips and her eyes closed tight she fired a shot into the ceiling."

Enlightenment dawned. "But of course! At the reverberation of that shot, the soufflé—"

"Collapsed like a punctured balloon. A triumph one moment, a shriveled disaster the next." Monsieur Georges leaned forward and aimed a pudgy forefinger at me. "So don't try to make light of the nature of crime in America, my friend. Not when I myself witnessed there a scene that could take place nowhere else in the civilized world—the premeditated murder of an utterly flawless soufflé!"

I reflected on this. Then I said sympathetically, "And a *soufflé Bordeloup* at that."

After all, what else could I say if I didn't want to be restricted forever after to Lapérouse or La Tour d'Argent?

Twenty-Four Petits Fours
by M. F. K. Fisher

Professor Lucien Revenant felt almost light-headed to be up and about again after his tedious illness. For two days now, he decided with a prim little smile, it was as if he had taken a new lease on life. Suddenly, exactly 46 hours ago, he had begun to feel better instead of worse, well instead of ill.

He looked carefully at the weather outside before putting on his winter topcoat and his brown plaid scarf; that was one of the boring things about being very old—the necessary preoccupation with wind and cold ... and of course he must be especially careful ...

He could not afford to lose any more time on his thesis, which he had been polishing and rewriting for enough years to become almost legendary in the small American college where he had taught since he was a comparatively young man. His habit was to get everything ready to send off once more to the printers, and then, to the delight and exasperated amusement of his colleagues on the faculty, to withdraw it again—to change, they swore, a comma here and a semicolon there.

Work on the great thesis had come to a painful standstill with his illness, and he had spent most of the time since the sudden cessation of his weakness, exhaustion, and pain in putting his big study-table into good order again, ready for hard concentration tomorrow. Meanwhile, he was going to give a little party, here in his familiar shabby lodgings.

It would be a kind of reunion—of five dear people whom he had neglected as they all grew older and more preoccupied in their own dwindling powers. It was the damnable weather, surely, that most hindered the senescent: the constant fear of drafts and of slipping on wet pavements or on bathroom floors, the hazardous burden of breathing into cold winds. We sit by our fires, he admitted regretfully.

But today Professor Revenant defied this creaking cosiness that seemed to envelop them all. He had arranged everything by telephone, after a busy morning. Everyone could come, and the new strength in his own voice seemed to imbue them with quick liveliness—so that Rachel Johnson had sounded almost like a girl again, and Mrs. Mac too.

There would be four men, then, and two ladies—a reunion of classical proportions, almost Greek, he told himself as he closed his door on the new tidiness of his bed-sitting room and walked carefully down the carpeted stairs of the old boarding house.

Outside, it was colder than he had guessed from his warm inside view, but he pulled his hat well down over his shiny head, and walked more briskly than he had for many years toward the shopping district of the little town. There were few people on the streets. He recognized a couple of his graduate students, but they hurried past him, their faces buried between their shoulders against the chill wind.

He would go first to the Buon Gusto. He remembered that faculty wives had told him, before he grew too tired to accept their invitations to dinner, that the best little cakes in town came from this small bakery. It was too bad, he thought in a remote way, that he had never taken time enough from his classes and from his thesis to learn such details personally: he might have had a few tea parties himself, with some of his prettiest students nibbling and tittering in his chaste room. He smiled again primly.

The bakery shop was delightfully warm. He stood looking seriously at the glass cases piled with cakes and cookies, and felt the welcome air against his dry cold skin, and even in behind his ears, until a solid black-browed woman by the cash register asked how she could help him. He cleared his throat. It had been some time since he last spoke with anyone.

"Oh, yes," he said hastily. "Yes. I need some little cakes. For a tea party this afternoon—that is, not tea exactly, but there will be ladies present. In fact, it is a rather special occasion, and I wish the best you have, which I can see is excellent."

He was astonished to hear himself so wordy. It must be the sudden convalescence, the quick recovery, perhaps the warm shop after that cold wind. To cover his vague embarrassment, he rattled on while the woman looked patiently and kindly at him. It was lucky the shop was otherwise empty, she thought: he was one of those talky old fellows who liked to take his time.

"I had in mind something decorated," he said, frowning. "It is a kind of reunion we are having, after a long absence. All of us so busy, you know. In fact, we may even start a little club this afternoon and plan regular meetings."

"That would be real nice," she said. "Ladies like these little petits fours."

"Petits fours!" he exclaimed. "Precisely! I used to buy them in Paris for my dear mother's 'afternoons.' Thursdays, always. Very old ladies came, it seemed to me then." He laughed a little creakily, being out of practice. "But of course we are rather elderly too. Not you, Madame, but my friends this afternoon. Yes, petits fours are just what we need."

"They're easy to chew, too," she said. "No nuts."

Professor Revenant chuckled in an elaborately conspiratorial way which amazed him, but which was very enjoyable. "Ah, yes," he almost whispered. "I understand what you mean, exactly! Geriatrical gastronomy, eh?"

She smiled (a real nice old gentleman, and such a cute accent!), and opened the case which held the tiny squares of cake covered with fancy icings: rosebuds on pistachio green, white scrolls on chocolate, yellow buttercups on orange and pink.

"These are our specialty—made with pure butter," she said. "How many?"

The professor discussed with her the fact that there would be only six at his party, but that they appreciated good food when they saw it and would no doubt be a little hungry.

"Figure on four apiece then," she decided for him, and in a few minutes he went out with the box of twenty-four petits fours dangling carefully from a solid string over his thick woolen glove. He felt buoyant (a very pleasant young woman, and so helpful and understanding!), and his feet hardly seemed to touch the ground.

He turned toward the liquor store nearest his house, so that he would not have to carry the bottle too far: the air hurt his chest a little, and he wished to be at his best, later on.

Somewhat regretfully he asked for a bottle of good sherry. With Rachel and Mrs. Mac to be there, sherry was indicated. What was it his dear mother always offered to the occasional gentlemen who came to her afternoons? Marsala? Madeira? It was brown and sweet, he remembered from what he used to steal from the bottoms of the glasses . . . Then recklessly he asked for a bottle of good scotch as well: it would please old Dr. Mac. In fact, it would taste very good to anyone who wanted it, as the Professor did, suddenly.

"Sure we can't deliver this, Mr.—uh? It's kind of heavy." The clerk looked worriedly at the old man.

"Thank you, no," Professor Revenant said with firmness; he must keep all these supplies under his personal control.

He walked more slowly than before with the two bottles carefully pressed under one arm, and the box of little cakes dangling from his hand, and by the time he reached the boarding house and walked up the familiar wooden front steps, he felt a little hint of his late fatigue creep into him. He shook himself in the dim hall, rather like a bony old dog, and went one at a time up the stairs to his room. An inner excitement reassured him: this would be a good party, worth all the effort and expense, all the weariness.

As he hung his coat neatly in the closet, with his scarf in the right-hand pocket where it had been every winter all these years, and his gloves in the left-hand pocket, he looked approvingly at the big round study-table, cleared now of most of the papers and book catalogues that had piled up during his wretched illness. He had brushed all but the inkstains off the dark red cover, and had brought up six wine glasses from the back of his landlady's cupboard where she kept them for christenings and wakes, and a big hand-painted china plate.

He would put Rachel facing the door, in a faint subtle effort to make her know that if he had only had enough money and had managed to finish the thesis, he might well have asked her to share her life with him and be his hostess. But even before it could be, it had seemed too late. He sighed: too late, yet only some forty-eight hours ago he had realized that nothing need be too late. Rachel had sounded so young and warm and sweet on the telephone.

On one side of her he would put Dr. Mac, the old reprobate. Anyone who had sailed on as many ships and lived in as many foreign ports as he had would break even the ice of their many years of separation— just so long as he did not drink too deeply of the ceremonial scotch. But Mrs. Mac had a way with her, deft from long practice, of keeping an eye on the bottle.

Then on Rachel's other side would be Harry Longman. Rachel liked eccentrics, and Harry surely was that: a well adjusted garage mechanic with a degree in engineering and a Ph.D. and a history of countless liaisons behind him, even in his ripe old years, all with young girls who worked in candy stores. It was the sweets he loved, he always boasted, and he was as round and sane as a butterscotch kiss himself.

Then Mrs. Mac would sit between Harry Longman and Judge Greene, and he himself would sit next to Dr. Mac. It suddenly seemed important to him to let Rachel be the hostess and not to be the host himself, facing her boldly across the red tablecover and the glasses and the little petits fours. And that way Mrs. Mac could keep an eye on Dr. Mac and still flirt a little with the Judge, who was the kind of austere man who said very witty things in a low detached voice.

Professor Revenant put the petits fours in diminished circles on the dreadful hand-painted plate, as soon as his own hands had unstiffened in the warm room. The colors looked pretty: the little pastries in their stiff white fluted cups were like flowers, and he made a centerpiece of them. He uncorked the bottles, and debated whether to put two glasses with the sherry for the ladies, and four glasses with the scotch, and then decided against it: Harry might like sherry because it was so sweet.

For a minute he was sobered to realize that he had only five chairs, counting his bathroom stool and his own work chair. Then he slid the table toward his couch-bed, so that he could sit on that. It looked, he concluded, quite Bohemian.

It was almost time. He was beginning to feel the excitement like wine. What a fine idea of his, to call them together again after such a long dull dropping away!

He thought of how years ago they had used to meet often at the jolly hospitable Macs, all of them perhaps hiding from outside strictures as he was hiding from the faculty dinners—Rachel's ancient mother, the Judge's drear and empty house, even Harry's sweet-sick diet of lollipops.

It might be a good idea to pour himself a little nip, a wee drop, to warm him before the fire of life took over again. He looked with another smile, not prim this time, at the pretty table waiting for the reunion, the beginning of a better and warmer time with his long-absent but still dear friends, and he considered first the bottle of sherry and then the bottle of scotch.

He decided to eat one of the petits fours on the little

waiting centerpiece and then pretend not to be hungry when they came.

He had not seen the Macs and Harry and the Judge, and the sweet Rachel, since their funerals. His own, that morning, had been boring: only the priest and an altar boy and the head of the French Department had been there.

He would clear off the empty plate and glasses tomorrow, and get to work on his thesis, this time definitively . . .

North Country Tart

8 ounces short pastry
1 cup gooseberries, or
   any fruit in season

3 teaspoons sugar
1 cup thick cream
   chilled

Preheat oven to 350 F.

Line a deep baking dish with the pastry and cover with fruit and ample sugar. Put in a layer of the pastry that is a little smaller than the dish, then more fruit and sugar. Repeat this. Then cover the dish with a top layer of pastry, pinch it well around the top, cut a little hole in the center, and bake in a hot oven for about 45 minutes. The fruit and sugar will make a fine rich syrup for the two floating layers of pastry. Serve hot in the winter, cold in the summer, and always with a jug of chilled cream.

This is a really heavenly sweet, as even I will swear to. It should obviously come at the end of a simple and not too heavy family supper rather than a proper party dinner, but I have occasionally used it as a kind of titillation, a gastronomical gambit, in an otherwise more sophisticated menu.

—M.F.K. Fisher

One Can of Peaches
by Edward D. Hoch

It takes more than hatred to make a murderer.

William Willis had hated his wife almost from the day of their marriage 17 years ago, but the thought of murder had never once crossed his mind. He was quite content to live out the days of his life without complaint, driving to the office each morning, returning each evening, and simply shutting his ears to the constant drone of her voice.

In her late thirties, Constance Willis had lost almost all the youthful beauty that had first attracted Willis to her in college. She was flabby of body and mind, hardly ever bothering to read a newspaper or pick up a book. Her days were spent in random shopping excursions with girl friends, at a weekly bridge club and in countless hours on the telephone. But for all his hatred, William Willis had never thought of murder. In fact, he did not even think of divorce until he met Rita Morgan in the apartment downstairs.

Willis and his wife had no children, so they'd remained for many years in the pleasant garden apartment close to the downtown expressway. It was convenient to his office, and the surroundings had taken on the comfortable feeling of home. The apartment was one of the few things in their marriage that William and Constance agreed on.

When Rita Morgan moved into the apartment below them, Willis' evenings and weekends immediately perked up. Rita was a 25-year-old schoolteacher with long blonde hair and the sort of quiet beauty that couldn't have passed unnoticed even among her fifth-

grade pupils. Willis helped her move in, carrying a few
cartons of books up from her car, and they became
friends immediately. She was everything he'd seen in
Constance 17 years before. But more important, she
was intelligent and witty.

"Were you down in Rita's apartment again?" Constance asked on Saturday afternoon.

"One of her faucets was leaking," he explained. "It
only needed a new washer."

"There's a janitor to take care of those things."

He sighed and opened a beer for himself. "You
know she'd have to wait a month before he'd get
around to it."

Constance grunted, but he knew she was unhappy
about his attentions to Rita Morgan. She need not have
worried quite so much, for Rita was a virginal young
lady—at least as far as Willis was concerned—who
treated him only with neighborly good will.

Nevertheless, it was Rita's presence on the scene
that came first to Willis' mind when he read in the afternoon paper about the food contamination. A twelve-
year-old boy had died of botulism in Chicago after
eating canned peaches that had been improperly ster-
ilized. As a rule, peaches were rarely affected by botulism, but these had been processed in a special
manner, making them more susceptible to the deadly
spores.

Reflecting on the blind fate that had killed the boy,
he could not help speculating on a similar fate befall-
ing Constance. Driving home that night, his recent
daydreams of divorce and marriage to Rita shifted fo-
cus. Now he imagined Constance dead, killed by some
trick of fate like an auto accident or contaminated
food.

Constance did not mention the news of the botulism
scare and it passed from his mind for the night. She
kept up so little on current events that he'd often had
to explain at length some happening on the foreign
scene or some new face on the political horizon. Her
interest in events, and in people other than her own cir-

cle of friends, had virtually ceased the day she left college to marry Willis.

But he was reminded again of the canned peaches when one of the secretaries at the office mentioned it. The afternoon paper had further details, including word that all of one lot was being recalled by the canner. Can o' Gold Fancy Prepared Peaches, lot 721/XY258.

Then the daydreams returned. He knew Constance ate canned peaches during the summer, often having them as part of her dessert. And he knew that she sometimes bought the Can o' Gold brand.

He pored over the newspapers that afternoon, even walking three blocks to a store where he knew he could buy a Chicago paper. He read more about the boy's death, and about the deadly effects of botulism poisoning, and the fantasy continued to grow in his mind. By the evening paper all Can o' Gold fruit products were being recalled, and consumers were being warned to avoid lot 721/XY258.

That evening at home, while Constance chatted on the telephone with some friend, William Willis glanced over the cupboard shelves, inspecting the canned goods. There were two cans of peaches, and one of them was Can o' Gold. His heart skipped a beat as he peered in at the lot number embossed on the lid. It was lot 721/XY258. Studying it more closely, he noticed that the can was bulging a trifle—an almost certain sign of gases produced by the bacterial activity inside.

There, standing on a shelf in the cupboard, was one of the deadly cans of peaches.

He said nothing to Constance, but that night in bed the possibilities paraded through his mind. All he had to do was say nothing, and sooner or later Constance would eat the contaminated peaches and die of botulism. Everyone would be most sympathetic. No one would suspect a thing.

And William Willis would be a free man.

He rolled over on his side and gazed into the darkness, thinking of Rita Morgan downstairs.

On his way out in the morning he saw Rita washing her car with a hose. "Hello, there," he called out. "I didn't think teachers ever got up this early in the summertime."

"I'm going on a picnic," she answered, beaming a smile his way. "Trying to get some of the dirt off this thing first."

"If I didn't have to go to work I'd help you out." He stood chatting with her for another few moments, until he noticed Constance watching them from an upstairs window. "Gotta be going," he said finally. "Be seeing you."

That day in the office he tried not to think about it. But after lunch, while reading the latest newspaper account of the can recall, he let the idea of murder cross his mind.

If Constance died from eating those peaches, was he guilty of murder?

No, no—he refused to accept that. He had not even touched the can. Constance had purchased it, Constance would open it, Constance would eat it—possibly during the day when he wasn't even at home. How could it be his fault?

Accident. Or death by misadventure, as the British liked to say. But certainly not murder.

William Willis went back to work and tried not to think of the can of peaches waiting on the shelf for Constance.

When he got home that evening the first sight that greeted him was Constance sitting at the kitchen table eating peaches and ice cream.

"Won't that spoil your dinner, dear?" he asked a bit stiffly.

"It's too hot to cook dinner in the apartment. I thought we might just go out for a sandwich later. All right?"

On any other night he might have grumbled, but this evening he simply said, "Sure," and walked behind her back to the cupboard. The Can o' Gold Peaches were still on the shelf. She was eating the other brand.

They talked very little that night and for the first time in many years he found himself getting through the hours with Constance without feeling the old hatred. When they returned from dinner, Rita came upstairs to borrow some milk, and Constance greeted her in a friendly fashion and even invited her in for coffee. Willis went to bed that night feeling good.

The feeling persisted the next day at the office and he wondered if he might be mellowing toward Constance. He made a point of buying the New York and Chicago newspapers, where the story of the botulism scare was still very much alive on the inner pages. One paper carried a detailed account of the boy's death agonies, of the gradual impairment of various parts of his brain until finally he simply stopped breathing. Willis read it grim-lipped, imagining Constance as she might be during those long hours of dying.

He grabbed the telephone and dialed his home number, but the line was busy. She was chatting with a girl friend again.

His hands were trembling when he put down the phone and he knew he must get a grip on himself. He'd been only an instant from warning her, from telling her of the contaminated can and thereby revealing the dark presumptions that had run through his mind. He must control himself. He was not a murderer. He was not even an instrument of chance.

And yet—if Constance died would he ever be able to look at himself in a mirror again? Would he ever be able to love Rita Morgan without the memory of Constance's death to haunt them?

He picked up the phone and dialed his number again. The line was still busy.

"I have to go home," he told his secretary. "Emergency."

He got the car out of the lot and headed for the expressway. It was nearly midafternoon and he knew she sometimes had her peaches about this time of the day.

The drive home seemed longer than it had ever been at rush hours. Driving fast, almost recklessly, he imagined finding her stretched out dead on the kitchen floor—even though he knew from the newspaper articles that botulism took several hours to show its first symptoms.

He turned into the drive next to the apartment house and parked in his usual spot. The second-floor window of his apartment seemed the same, the place itself seemed unchanged. Perhaps he'd made the drive for nothing, and he'd have to explain it to Constance. And somehow get that can out of the house.

"Dear! I'm home early!"

There was no answer and he went into the kitchen seeking her. The first thing he saw was the open, empty, discarded can of Can o' Gold Fancy Prepared Peaches by the sink. That, and an empty dish, with its dirty spoon and telltale juices.

"Constance!"

She appeared then, coming from the bathroom. Her face was pale and somehow a little strange. "What are you doing home?" she asked.

"I wasn't feeling well."

"Oh."

"Constance, did you eat those peaches?"

She glanced at the empty dish and the discarded can by the sink. Then her eyes met his and there was something in them he'd never seen before.

"Oh, no, dear. That nice Miss Morgan came up to borrow something, and she stayed and chatted, and I persuaded her to have a little snack."

The Herb of Death
by Agatha Christie

Now then, Mrs. B.," said Sir Henry Clithering encouragingly.

Mrs. Bantry, his hostess, looked at him in cold reproof.

"I've told you before that I will *not* be called Mrs. B. It's not dignified."

"Scheherazade, then."

"And even less am I Sche-what's her name! I never can tell a story properly—ask Arthur if you don't believe me."

"You're quite good at the facts, Dolly," said Colonel Bantry, "but poor at the embroidery."

"That's just it," said Mrs. Bantry. She flapped the bulb catalogue she was holding on the table in front of her. "I've been listening to you all and I don't know how you do it. 'He said, she said, you wondered, they thought, everyone implied'—well, I just couldn't, and besides I don't know anything to tell a story about."

"We can't believe that, Mrs. Bantry," said Dr. Lloyd. He shook his gray head in mocking disbelief.

Miss Marple said in her gentle voice, "Surely, dear—"

Mrs. Bantry continued obstinately to shake her head.

"You don't know how banal my life is. What with the servants and the difficulties of getting scullery maids, and just going to town for clothes, and dentists, and then the garden—"

"Ah!" said Dr. Lloyd. "The garden. We all know where your heart lies, Mrs. Bantry."

"It must be nice to have a garden," said Jane Helier, the beautiful young actress. "That is, if you don't have to dig, or get your hands messed up. I'm ever so fond of flowers."

"The garden," said Sir Henry. "Can't we take that as a starting point? Come, Mrs. B. The poisoned bulb, the deadly daffodils, the herb of death!"

"Now it's odd your saying that," said Mrs. Bantry. "You've just reminded me. Arthur, do you remember that business at Clodderham Court? You know. Old Sir Ambrose Bercy. Do you remember what a courtly charming old man we thought him?"

"Why, of course. Yes, that *was* a strange business. Go ahead, Dolly."

"You'd better tell it, dear."

"Nonsense. Go ahead. Must paddle your own canoe, you know."

Mrs. Bantry drew a deep breath. She clasped her hands and her face registered complete mental anguish. She spoke rapidly and fluently.

"Well, there's really not much to tell. The Herb of Death—that's what put it into my head, though in my own mind I call it *sage and onions*."

"Sage and onions?" asked Dr. Lloyd.

Mrs. Bantry nodded. "That was how it happened, you see," she explained. "We were staying, Arthur and I, with Sir Ambrose Bercy at Clodderham Court, and one day, by mistake—though very stupidly, I've always thought—a lot of foxglove leaves were picked with the sage. The ducks for dinner that night were stuffed with it and everyone was very ill, and one poor girl—Sir Ambrose's ward—died of it."

"Dear, dear," said Miss Marple, "how very tragic."

"Wasn't it?"

"Well," said Sir Henry, "what next?"

"There isn't any next," said Mrs. Bantry, "that's all."

Everyone gasped. Though warned beforehand, they had not expected quite such brevity as this.

"But, my dear lady," remonstrated Sir Henry, "it

can't be all. What you have related is a tragic occurrence, but not in any sense of the word a problem for us to solve."

"Well, of course there's *some* more," said Mrs. Bantry. "But if I were to tell you it, you'd know the answer."

She looked defiantly round the assembly and said plaintively, "I told you I couldn't dress things up and make it sound properly like a story."

"Ah ha!" said Sir Henry. He sat up in his chair and adjusted an eyeglass. "Really, you know, Scheherazade, this is most refreshing. Our ingenuity is challenged. I'm not so sure you haven't done it on purpose—to stimulate our curiosity. A few brisk rounds of 'Twenty-Questions' is indicated, I think. Miss Marple, will you begin?"

"I'd like to know something about the cook," said Miss Marple. "She must have been a very stupid woman, or else very inexperienced."

"She was just very stupid," said Mrs. Bantry. "She cried a great deal afterwards and said the leaves had been picked and brought into her as sage, and how was she to know?"

"Not one who thought for herself," said Miss Marple.

"Probably an elderly woman and, I daresay, a very good cook?"

"Oh, excellent," said Mrs. Bantry.

"Your turn, Miss Helier," said Sir Henry.

"You mean to ask a question?"

There was a pause while Jane pondered. Finally she said helplessly, "Really, I don't know what to ask."

Her beautiful eyes looked appealingly at Sir Henry.

"Why not the *dramatis personae,* Miss Helier?" he suggested smiling.

Jane still looked puzzled.

"Characters in order of their appearance," said Sir Henry gently.

"Oh, yes," said Jane. "That's a very good idea."

Mrs. Bantry began briskly to tick people off on her fingers.

"Sir Ambrose—Sylvia Keene, the girl who died—a friend of hers who was staying there, Maud Wye, one of those dark ugly girls who manage to make an effect somehow—I never know how they do it. Then there was a Mr. Curle who had come down to discuss books with Sir Ambrose—you know, rare books— queer old things in Latin, all musty parchment. There was Jerry Lorimer—he was a kind of next door neighbor. His place, Fairlies, joined Sir Ambrose's estate. And there was Mrs. Carpenter, one of those middle-aged pussies who always seem to manage to dig themselves in comfortably somewhere. She was by way of being *dame de compagnie* to Sylvia, I suppose."

"If it is my turn," said Sir Henry, "I want a good deal. I want short verbal portraits, please, of all the foregoing. Sir Ambrose now—start with him. What was he like?"

"Oh, he was a very distinguished-looking old man— and not so very old really—not more than sixty, I suppose. But he was very delicate—he had a weak heart, could never go upstairs—had had to have a lift put in, and so that made him seem older than he was. Very charming manners—courtly—that's the word that describes him best. You never saw him ruffled or upset. He had beautiful white hair and a particularly charming voice."

"Good," said Sir Henry. "I can see Sir Ambrose. Now the girl Sylvia—what did you say her last name was?"

"Keene. She was pretty—really *very* pretty. Fair-haired, you know, and a lovely skin. Not, perhaps, very clever. In fact, rather stupid."

"Oh, come, Dolly," protested her husband.

"Arthur, of course, wouldn't think so," said Mrs. Bantry drily. "But she *was* stupid—she really never said anything worth listening to."

"One of the most graceful creatures I ever saw," said

Colonel Bantry warmly. "See her playing tennis—charming, simply charming. And she was full of fun—most amusing little thing. And such a pretty way with her. I bet the young fellows all thought so."

"That's just where you're wrong," said Mrs. Bantry. "Youth, as such, has no charms for young men nowadays. It's only old duffers like you, Arthur, who sit maundering on about young girls."

"Being young's no good," said Jane. "You've got to have S.A."

"What," said Miss Marple, "is S.A.?"

"Sex appeal," said Jane.

"Ah, yes," said Miss Marple. "What in my day they used to call 'having the come-hither in your eye.' "

"Not a bad description," said Sir Henry. "*The dame de compagnie,* you described, I think, as a pussy, Mrs. Bantry?"

"I didn't mean a *cat,* you know," said Mrs. Bantry. "It's quite different. Just a big soft white purry person. Always very sweet. That's what Adelaide Carpenter was like."

"How old a woman?"

"Oh, I should say fortyish. She'd been there some time—ever since Sylvia was eleven. I believe. A very tactful person. One of those widows left in unfortunate circumstances, with plenty of aristocratic relations, but no ready cash. I didn't like her myself—but then I never do like people with very long white hands. And I don't like pussies."

"Mr. Curle?"

"Oh, one of those elderly stooping men. There are so many of them about, you'd hardly know one from the other. He showed enthusiasm when talking about his musty books, but not at any other time. I don't think Sir Ambrose knew him very well."

"And Jerry next door?"

"A charming boy. He was engaged to Sylvia. That's what made it so sad."

"Now I wonder—" began Miss Marple, and then stopped.

"What?"

"Nothing, dear."

Sir Henry looked at Miss Marple curiously. Then he said thoughtfully, "So this young couple were engaged. Had they been engaged long?"

"About a year. Sir Ambrose had opposed the engagement because, he said, Sylvia was too young. But after a year's engagement he had given in and the marriage was to have taken place quite soon."

"Had the young lad any property?"

"Next to nothing—a bare hundred or two a year."

"No rat in that hole, Clithering," said Colonel Bantry, and laughed.

"It's the doctor's turn to ask a question," said Sir Henry.

"My curiosity is mainly professional," said Dr. Lloyd. "I should like to know what medical evidence was given at the inquest—that is, if our hostess knows."

"I know roughly," said Mrs. Bantry. "It was poisoning by digitalin—is that right?"

Dr. Lloyd nodded. "The active principle of the foxglove—digitalis—acts on the heart. Indeed, it is a very valuable drug in some forms of heart trouble. A very curious case altogether. I would never have believed that eating a preparation of foxglove leaves could possibly result fatally. These ideas of eating poisonous leaves and berries are very much exaggerated. Very few people realize that the vital principle, or alkaloid, has to be extracted with much care and preparation."

"Mrs. MacArthur sent some special bulbs round to Mrs. Toomie the other day," said Miss Marple. "And Mrs. Toomie's cook mistook them for onions, and all the Toomies were very ill indeed."

"But they didn't die of it," said Dr. Lloyd.

"No," admitted Miss Marple.

"A girl I knew died of ptomaine poisoning," said Jane Helier.

"We must get on with investigating the crime," said Sir Henry.

"Crime?" said Jane, startled. "I thought it was an accident."

"If it were an accident," said Sir Henry gently, "I do not think Mrs. Bantry would have told us this story. No, as I read it, this was an accident only in appearance—behind it is something more sinister. I remember a case—various guests in a house party were chatting after dinner. The walls were adorned with all kinds of old-fashioned weapons. Entirely as a joke one of the party seized an ancient pistol and pointed it at another man, pretending to fire it. The pistol was loaded and went off, killing the man. We had to ascertain, in that case, first, who had secretly prepared and loaded that pistol, and secondly who had so led and directed the conversation that that final bit of horseplay resulted—for the man who had fired the pistol was entirely innocent!

"It seems to me we have much the same problem here. Those digitalin leaves were deliberately mixed with the sage, knowing what the result would be. Since we exonerate the cook—we do exonerate the cook, don't we?—the question arises: Who picked the leaves and delivered them to the kitchen?"

"That's easily answered," said Mrs. Bantry. "At least the last part of it is. It was Sylvia herself who took the leaves to the kitchen. It was part of her daily job to gather things like salad or herbs, bunches of young carrots—all the sort of things that gardeners never pick right. They hate giving you anything young and tender—they wait for them to be fine specimens. Sylvia and Mrs. Carpenter used to see to a lot of these things themselves. And there was foxglove actually growing with the sage in one corner, so the mistake was quite natural."

"But did Sylvia actually pick them herself?"

"That, nobody ever knew. It was assumed so."

"Assumptions," said Sir Henry, "are dangerous things."

"But I do know that Mrs. Carpenter didn't pick them," said Mrs. Bantry. "Because, as it happened, she was walking with me on the terrace that morning. We went out there after breakfast. It was unusually nice and warm for early spring. Sylvia went alone into the garden, but later I saw her walking arm in arm with Maud Wye."

"So they were great friends, were they?" asked Miss Marple.

"Yes," said Mrs. Bantry.

"Had she been staying there long?" asked Miss Marple.

"About a fortnight," said Mrs. Bantry.

There was a note of trouble in her voice.

"You didn't like Miss Wye?" suggested Sir Henry.

"I did. That's just it, I did."

The trouble in her voice had grown to distress.

"You're keeping something back, Mrs. Bantry," said Sir Henry accusingly.

"I wondered just now," said Miss Marple, "but I didn't like to go on."

"When did you wonder?"

"When you said that the young people were engaged. You said that was what made it so sad. But, if you know what I mean, your voice didn't sound right when you said it—not convincing, you know."

"What a dreadful person you are," said Mrs. Bantry. "You always seem to *know*. Yes, I was thinking of something. But I don't really know whether I ought to say it or not."

"You must say it," said Sir Henry. "Whatever your scruples, it mustn't be kept back."

"Well, it was just this," said Mrs. Bantry. "One evening—in fact, the very evening before the tragedy—I happened to go out on the terrace before dinner. The window in the drawing room was open. And as it chanced I saw Jerry Lorimer and Maud Wye. He was—well—kissing her. Of course I didn't know whether it was just a sort of chance affair, or whether—well, I mean, one can't *tell*. I knew Sir Ambrose never had really liked Jerry Lorimer—so perhaps he knew he was that kind of young man. But one thing I *am* sure of: that girl Maud Wye, was *really* fond of him. You'd only to see her looking at him when she was off guard. And I think, too, they were really better suited than he and Sylvia were."

"I am going to ask a question quickly, before Miss Marple can," said Sir Henry. "'I want to know whether, after the tragedy, Jerry Lorimer married Maud Wye?"

"Yes," said Mrs. Bantry. "He did. Six months afterwards."

"Oh, Scheherazade, Scheherazade," said Sir Henry. "To think of the way you told us this story at first! Bare bones indeed—and to think of the amount of flesh we're finding on them now."

"Don't speak so ghoulishly," said Mrs. Bantry. "And don't use the word flesh. Vegetarians always do. They say, 'I never eat flesh' in a way that puts you right off your nice little beefsteak. Mr. Curle was a vegetarian. He used to eat some peculiar stuff that looked like bran for breakfast. Those elderly stooping men with beards are often faddish. They have patent kinds of underwear, too."

"What on earth, Dolly," said her husband, "do you know about Mr. Curle's underwear?"

"Nothing," said Mrs. Bantry with dignity. "I was making a guess."

"I'll amend my former statement," said Sir Henry. "I'll say instead that the *dramatis personae* in your problem are very interesting. I'm beginning to see them all—eh, Miss Marple?"

"Human nature is always interesting, Sir Henry. And it's curious to see how certain types always tend to act in exactly the same way."

"Two women and a man," said Sir Henry. "The old eternal human triangle. Is that the base of our problem here? I rather fancy it is."

Dr. Lloyd cleared his throat. "I've been thinking,"

he said rather diffidently. "Did you say, Mrs. Bantry, that you yourself were ill?"

"Was I! And so was Arthur! So was everyone!"

"That's just it—everyone," said the doctor. "You see what I mean? In Sir Henry's story which he told us just now, one man shot another—he didn't have to shoot the whole roomful."

"I don't understand," said Jane. "Who shot who?"

"I'm saying that whoever planned this thing went about it very curiously, either with a blind belief in chance, or else with an absolutely reckless disregard for human life. I can hardly believe there is a man capable of deliberately poisoning *eight* people with the object of removing only *one* of them."

"I see your point," said Sir Henry, thoughtfully.

"And mightn't he have poisoned himself too?" asked Jane.

"Was anyone absent from dinner that night?" asked Miss Marple.

Mrs. Bantry shook her head.

"Everyone was there."

"Except Mr. Lorimer, I suppose, my dear. He wasn't staying in the house, was he?"

"No, but he was dining there that evening," said Mrs. Bantry.

"Oh!" said Miss Marple in a changed voice. "That makes all the difference in the world." She frowned vexedly to herself. "I've been very stupid," she murmured. "Very stupid indeed."

"I confess your point worries me, Lloyd," said Sir Henry.

"How insure that the girl, and the girl only, should get a fatal dose?"

"You can't," said the doctor. "That brings me to the point: *supposing the girl was not the intended victim after all?*"

"What?"

"In all cases of food poisoning the result if very uncertain. Several people share a dish. What happens? One or two are slightly ill, two more, say, are seriously indisposed, one dies. That's the way of it—there's no certainty anywhere. But there are cases where another factor might enter in. Digitalin is a drug that acts directly on the heart—as I've told you it's prescribed in certain cases. *Now, there was one person in that house who suffered from a heart complaint.* Suppose he was the intended victim? What would not be fatal to the rest *would* be fatal to him—or so the murderer might reasonably suppose. That the thing turned out differently is only proof of what I was saying just now—the uncertainty and unreliability of the effect of drugs on different human beings."

"Sir Ambrose," said Sir Henry, "you think *he* was the person aimed at? Yes, yes—and the girl's death was a mistake."

"Who got his money after he was dead?" asked Jane.

"A very sound question, Miss Helier. One of the first we always ask in my late profession," said Sir Henry.

"Sir Ambrose had a son," said Mrs. Bantry slowly. "He had quarreled with him many years previously. The boy was wild, I believe. Still, it was not in Sir Ambrose's power to disinherit him—Clodderham Court was entailed. Martin Bercy succeeded to the title and estate. There was, however, a good deal of other property that Sir Ambrose could leave as he chose, and that he left to his ward Sylvia. I know this because Sir Ambrose died less than a year after the events I am telling you of, and he had not troubled to make a new will after Sylvia's death. I think the money went to the Crown—or perhaps it was to his son as next of kin—I don't really remember."

"So it was only to the interest of a son who wasn't there and of the girl who died herself," said Sir Henry thoughtfully. "That doesn't seem very promising."

"Didn't the other woman get anything?" asked Jane. "The one Mrs. Bantry calls the pussy woman."

"She wasn't mentioned in the will," said Mrs. Bantry.

"Miss Marple, you're not listening," said Sir Henry. "You're somewhere far away."

"I was thinking of old Mr. Badger, the chemist," said Miss Marple. "He had a very young house-keeper—young enough to be not only his daughter but his grand-daughter. Not a word to anyone, and his family, a lot of nephews and nieces, full of expecta-tions. And when he died, would you believe it, he'd been secretly married to her for two years? Of course, Mr. Badger was a chemist, and a very rude, common old man as well, and Sir Ambrose Bercy was a very courtly gentleman, so Mrs. Bantry says; but for all that, human nature is much the same everywhere."

There was a pause. Sir Henry looked very hard at Miss Marple who looked back at him with gently quizzical blue eyes. Jane Helier broke the silence.

"Was this Mrs. Carpenter good-looking?" she asked.

"Yes, in a very quiet way. Nothing startling."

"She had a very sympathetic voice," said Colonel Bantry.

"Purring—that's what I call it," said Mrs. Bantry.

"You'll be called a cat yourself one of these days, Dolly."

"I like being a cat in my home circle," said Mrs. Bantry. "I don't much like women anyway, and you know it. I like men and flowers."

"Excellent taste," said Sir Henry. "Especially in put-ting men first."

"That was tact," said Mrs. Bantry. "Well, now, what about my little problem? I've been quite fair, I think. Arthur, don't you think I've been fair?"

"Yes, my dear."

"First boy," said Mrs. Bantry, pointing a finger at Sir Henry."

"I'm going to be long-winded. Because, you see, I haven't really got any feeling of certainty about the matter. First, Sir Ambrose: well, he wouldn't take such an original method of committing suicide—and on the other hand he certainly had nothing to gain by the death of his ward. Exit Sir Ambrose. Mr. Curle:

no motive for death of girl. If Sir Ambrose was intended victim, he might possibly have purloined a
rare manuscript or two that no one else would miss.
Very thin, and most unlikely. So I think Mr. Curle
is cleared. Miss Wye: motive for death of Sir
Ambrose—none. Motive for death of Sylvia—pretty
strong. She wanted Sylvia's young man, and wanted
him rather badly—from Mrs. Bantry's account. She
was with Sylvia that morning in the garden, so had
opportunity to pick leaves. No, we can't dismiss Miss
Wye so easily. Young Lorimer: he's got a motive in
either case. If he gets rid of his sweetheart, he can
marry the other girl. Still it seems a bit drastic to kill
her—what's a broken engagement these days? If Sir
Ambrose dies, he will marry a rich girl instead of a
poor one. That might be important or not—depends
on his financial position. If I find that his estate was
heavily mortgaged and that Mrs. Bantry has deliberately withheld that fact from us, I shall claim a foul.
Now Mrs. Carpenter: you know, I have suspicions of
Mrs. Carpenter. Those white hands, for one thing, and
her excellent alibi at the time the herbs were
picked—I always distrust alibis. And I've got another
reason for suspecting her which I shall keep to myself. Still, on the whole, if I've got to plump, I shall
plump for Miss Maud Wye, because there's more evidence against her than anyone else."

"Next boy," said Mrs. Bantry, and pointed at Dr.
Lloyd.

"I think you're wrong, Clithering, in sticking to the
theory that the girl's death was meant. I am convinced
that the murderer intended to do away with Sir Ambrose. I don't think that young Lorimer had the necessary knowledge. I am inclined to believe that Mrs.
Carpenter was the guilty party. She had been a long
time with the family, knew all about the state of Sir
Ambrose's health, and could easily arrange for this girl
Sylvia to pick the right leaves. Motive, I confess, I
don't see; but I hazard the guess that Sir Ambrose had

at one time made a will in which she was mentioned. That's the best I can do."

Mrs. Bantry's pointing finger went on to Jane Helier.

"I don't know what to say," said Jane, "except this: why shouldn't the girl herself have done it? She took the leaves into the kitchen after all. And you say Sir Ambrose had been against her marriage. If he died, she'd get the money and be able to marry at once. She'd know just as much about Sir Ambrose's health as Mrs. Carpenter."

Mrs. Bantry's finger came slowly round to Miss Marple.

"Sir Henry has put it all very clearly—very clearly indeed," said Miss Marple. "And Dr. Lloyd was so right in what he said. Between them they seem to have made things so very clear. Only I don't think Dr. Lloyd quite realized one aspect of what he said. You see, not being Sir Ambrose's medical adviser, he couldn't know just what kind of heart trouble Sir Ambrose had, could he?"

"I don't quite see what you mean, Miss Marple," said Dr. Lloyd.

"You're assuming—aren't you?—that Sir Ambrose had the kind of heart that digitalin would affect adversely? But there's nothing to prove that's so. It might be just the other way about."

"The other way about?"

"Yes, you did say that it was often prescribed for heart trouble?"

"Even then, Miss Marple, I don't see what that leads to."

"Well, it would mean that he would have digitalin in his possession quite naturally—without having to account for it. What I am trying to say—I always express myself so badly—is this: supposing you wanted to poison anyone with a fatal dose of digitalin. Wouldn't the simplest and the easiest way be to arrange for *everyone* to be poisoned—actually by digitalin leaves? It wouldn't be fatal in anyone else's case, of course, but no one would be surprised at one victim because, as Dr. Lloyd said, these things are so uncertain. No one would be likely to ask whether the girl had actually had a fatal infusion of digitalis. He might have put it in a cocktail, or in her coffee or even made her drink it simply as a tonic."

"You mean Sir Ambrose poisoned his ward, the charming girl whom he loved?"

"That's just it," said Miss Marple. "Like Mr. Badger and his young housekeeper. Don't tell me it's absurd for a man of sixty to fall in love with a girl of twenty. It happens every day—and I daresay with an old autocrat like Sir Ambrose it might take him queerly. These things become a madness sometimes. He couldn't bear the thought of her getting married— did his best to oppose it—and failed. His jealousy became so great that he preferred killing her to letting her go to young Lorimer. He must have thought of it some time beforehand, because that foxglove seed would have to be sown among the sage. He'd pick it himself when the time came, and send her into the kitchen with it. It's horrible to think of, but I suppose we must take as merciful a view of it as we can. Gentlemen of that age are sometimes very peculiar indeed where young girls are concerned. Our last organist— but there, I mustn't talk scandal."

"Mrs. Bantry," said Sir Henry. "Is this so?"

Mrs. Bantry nodded. "Yes. I'd no idea of it—never dreamed of the thing being anything but an accident. Then, after Sir Ambrose's death, I got a letter. He had left directions to send it to me. He told me the truth in it. I don't know why—but he and I always got on very well together."

In the momentary silence, she seemed to feel an unspoken criticism and went on hastily. "You think I'm betraying a confidence—but that isn't so. I've changed all the names. He wasn't really called Sir Ambrose Bercy. Didn't you see how Arthur stared stupidly when I said that name at him? He didn't understand at first.

I've changed everything. It's like they say in magazines and in the beginnings of books: 'All the characters in this story are purely fictitious.' You'll never know who they really are."

Seven Art Soups
by Stringfellow Forbes

"In a year of change, when I learned many things, when I refined every aspect of my way of living, I came to the art of soup, an art so apt to life, so satisfying to every sense, so worthy of following as daily discipline and definition of the state of the soul, that I have begun this little book of teaching. There may be art in any seriously considered process of choosing, but I think there are few who can express themselves through soup, who know that every situation and emotion can be defined through this simple elemental food.

"To begin: However we may live, each of us is alone, a condition to be cherished—and to be overcome. There will be a time, if you live creatively, when your singleness is unbearable to you, when your fullness of self overflows and becomes treasure you are compelled to share, to give with joy, unfolding petal by petal your richness, your capacity for valuing all things. Fortunately, it is at just this time of ripeness that such singleness will be unendurable also to the perceptive Other, who will be attracted by your perfection and claim it as his—or hers—by right of recognition. At this time of coming together you will make the Soup of Perfect Unity . . ."

It will begin this way, my slim book. I have it all in my head. Papa would be surprised—he would never have thought I could write anything but a business letter.

But it will have depth, Papa, and weight, as you always said the best things do. Because I've learned such a lot since I was freed to—

I miss him so, my poor papa.

—to live in an outward way, no longer penned by your notions of what a large daughter can do, no longer countering your rich owning with my bareness, your charm with my dry getting to the point, your masculine, almost European elegance—

Once I got into a taxi, Papa, that was full of your after-shave scent, and I fell back years and years to my desperate childhood, when I loved you so.

—no longer countering your elegance with my business suits and clipped hair, my blocky overweight disdain.

I have come into a lot lately. Papa died, a thing I had never thought of, and everything is now mine—every secret of business and old letters, of closets and attic, every lustrous chair and table, every warm, heavy piece of silver. Why had I not imagined it? He was not young. But he was eternal, the unending corrective force.

It made me sick that he was gone. I wasted, couldn't eat, couldn't move. I was in the hospital for weeks, a puzzle to dozens of doctors. They did without me at Dobson and Aimes, though the new girl still calls me several times a week. I may never go back. When my downtown apartment building was converted to condominiums, I bought this small house and it was here I came when the doctors finally said they could do nothing for me, to regain my strength, strength that has come back as power. I can choose now, I have money, I have all Papa's beautiful things. I decide what I will take and what I will not.

You were always severe to me, Papa, about choices. But the choices started too soon, before I was trained in them. Mother died when I was only ten and you wanted me to be to you what she had been. It makes me laugh that anyone could have expected the scrawny child I was to come near the image of my elegant mother, who wore beads and flowered dresses, whose loose wavy hair just managed to stay in its bun, who rested in the mornings because of her bad heart and

came downstairs at three o'clock in the afternoon
bathed and dressed, smelling of powder and perfume,
and who could inspire Hilda to go exactly by the recipe and produce palatable food.

I can see now how it was: I was not your beautiful
wife, you were not my comforting mother.

I tried, Papa, I really tried. My room stayed as
Mother had arranged it. Even after I was a teenager, I
kept the dolls and teddy bears, the ruffled bedspread. I
brought my friends home to play—and later to play
records, very low. I shopped with love and care for
your presents. I wore the clothes chosen for me by
your widow friends—dressed with lace collars, with
piping and ribbons, white tights, black patent-leather
shoes—until I realized how different this made me
from the others, and then I did my own shopping, buying jeans, sweatshirts, and running shoes at the dis-
count stores Hilda took me to, finding approval at last
for the cheapness of my selections.

And it was always, "Great God, where did you find
that shirt—or those hideous shoelaces, or that idiot
friend, or this awful tie? We can't have it, send it to
perdition, my dear." And you would laugh, and make
your women friends laugh, too.

The shame, the hot twisting shame that sent me fly-
ing to destroy or to rid myself of whatever or whom-
ever it was. Once, in my frenzy, I cut up a shirt and
tried to flush it down the toilet, which overflowed and
ruined the dining-room ceiling. I screamed at my only
boy friend until he fled and told everyone in junior
high that I was schizophrenic. And how many of your
birthday and Christmas presents came to adorn trees,
iron fences, dogs, drunks on the street as I cast them
from me, Hilda shouting shame at me for the waste of
it all?

Finally, unbearably sensitized, I wore only brown
and beige and white. I saw my friends at school, but
increasingly fewer of them outside as I gained weight,
stopped studying, withdrew into solitude. I didn't dare

to make choices, Papa. I owned nothing but essentials. I was heavy and dull, living a dull life.

But now lightness has entered everywhere—sun from outside, strength from digging, zest from accomplishment, health from the garden harvest. Soup as the essential refinement, art from making soup. Eating no meat or other gross food, I have become slim. I have let my hair grow and found it wavy, the red only lightly dimmed by the grey, and I put it up in back like Mother did. My poles have shifted, the negative charge has become positive.

Papa is lost from this lovely world. How sad that he can't see his fourposter bed, his Biedermeier desk, his leather chair, his Adam table in my little white house where the curtains blow in the breeze . . .

Healing for me began in the yard, when I turned from boredom with languishing and idleness to clearing and digging. And through the spring the garden developed, as new plants were delivered several times a week—poppies, cyclamens, freesias, dahlias, cannas, rose geraniums. I bought strong-colored flowers and they looked beautiful together. It is not possible now to make a mistake.

That was how I met Richard, that was how, having gone so far beyond myself, I went further and took him for my own.

Would you be happy for me, Papa? You would see that I have changed, but would it make you happy?

Richard. Broad, clear, and honest as his name. He was the driver of the package delivery truck that brought me fresh plants all spring. He came with a box of herbs the day I painted the front door.

"Now would you look at that," he said. "Dark blue on the door and red on the frame. How did you think of that?"

"I like color now. It's rich, don't you think, blue and red?"

"This whole place is. You can tell someone cares for it. You must stay here and work on this yard all the time. Or does your husband help you?"

"No. No husband."

"My wife's gone, too. Not that she ever did anything much around the house. She was always out, even after the children came. Half the time I was the one had to feed them when I got home at night, open a can of soup or something."

"Soup is a wonderful food, but it's best homemade."

"I never had much soup made at home."

"Soup and gardening go together. I have fresh vegetables and herbs right here. I cook a bit, come out and hoe a bit, go back and add to the pot. I find it a very agreeable way to live, making soup and working the garden."

I looked at him—at his wide forehead, his eyes steady on mine, his mouth so clearly modeled, his shoulders and chest broad and deep. He was asking, waiting. I felt a great quiet in myself, a reaching and growing toward this most daring of choices.

A delivery man, Papa.

I asked him for soup on Sunday. And I made
                    The Soup of Perfect Unity

"This soup is a blend of potatoes and leeks, chicken broth with not a trace of fat, and cream. It is chilled, and garnished just before serving with delicately fried parsley leaves which glisten with olive oil. With it you need only the shyest of white cheeses, French bread, and a simple mountain wine. I am not wise about wines and do not believe in great expense for them. Soup should not be dominated by any other part of the meal."

Richard arrived at noon, his hair black and falling onto his forehead, the sleeves of a white-cotton shirt loose on his big arms. We walked around the garden and sat a while on chairs in the shade, then we ate the perfect soup in the shadowed dining room. Afterward, standing in the back doorway looking out at all the green and coolness, his chest behind my shoulders, I felt him sigh. His hand came to loosen my combs but he held it back. He would come again, he said.

The Soup of Conviviality

"Here everything comes together, to float up into the spoon one surprise after another, as you tell your lives to each other, as you turn the facets of wit, sympathy, experience, good humor, and fantasy and let them sparkle. You will mingle chicken, beef, and sausage, noodle twists, and beans, parsnips, carrots, squash, beets, tomatoes, onions, and cabbage for their common ancestry in soups. There will be bread to break off from the loaf and a raw red wine."

The day was warm and still. We sat in the chairs under the tree as we ate and talked. He was divorced last year, he said, and lived now across town from his family in an apartment that seemed very empty.

We made love on Papa's high curtained bed. It was my first time and Richard was astonished. Richard, my own, I said. He said, Ah.

Your bed had not been a lonely couch, Papa. Lawyer to widows, you often had company at home and I was in the way, playing my radio just a little too loudly, hiding behind the noise. Many are the law offices that lost clients to you as word got around among widows as to how serious and courteous you were, how handsome in your rich dark clothes.

Though you never actually wore velvet, Papa, there was always some touch of it about you, some ancestral heritage of portrait elegance. You told the widows what they should do and they always profited from your competence and knowledge. You were their escort at concerts and parties, their adviser at auctions and antique shops, their agent with difficult family members. You never said there is no one so generous as a grateful widow, though you knew it well. You loved them all, Papa, that was your secret.

The Soup of Dark Delight

"It is frightening to know that he is yours, for how will you then sufficiently guard your ownership? And owning is not allowed for persons, anyway—women these days know that. But your hidden joy is there, to be expressed in this soup. Black beans and garlic, pureed to perfect smoothness, will be animated at the last minute by a spoonful of Spanish sherry and decorated with curves of avocado and a shaved slice of lemon."

They loved you, too, Papa. I found letters. My partridge, you called them. My pigeon. My dove. Ah, Papa, how sad that you are gone.

Richard was happy—his joy was there to match mine. I never explained to him the significance of the soups, trusting him to know everything with the intuitions of love.

We both thought he should come here more often, but he said he was too tired on working days. So the next weekend we planned supper for Saturday. I spent two days making

The Soup of Ease and Loving

"It is not hot, nor is it cold, but serve it warm as the air—mixed sorrel broth, sour cream, and minced shrimp, melded a day in the refrigerator, then gently warmed. It is the simplest of soups but needs care to mature properly. It is ordinary and rare, tart and rich, and nourishing without obvious potential."

At six-thirty, half an hour before I expected him, he walked in the front door, calling to me in the kitchen.

"I've brought a surprise," he said, holding up a bulky package wrapped in white paper.

I thought candy, I thought books.

"Steak!" he cried.

"But," I said, "I can't possibly—"

He put the heavy package in my hands and I dropped it on the counter. Already he had turned and was going back out to his car. I followed and watched him take a square box and a long bag from the trunk. "See," he said, starting around the side of the house to the back. "I've thought of everything. Portable grill—" he slapped the box "—and charcoal." He rattled the bag. I could only watch as he blithely set up the grill near the chairs under the tree.

It was August, very hot. Next door on the left, the

Albert family had already lit their grill. I had been
smelling the fumes from it even in the house all summer. Their children were noisy on the swing set and
the baby was crying. On the other side, Cindy Appol-
linaris was lying in her lounge chair. I knew that because it grates on the concrete of her patio when she
sits down. She and her husband sometimes party until
late, but tonight she was alone—he pilots a plane for a
local corporation and she had told me he was asked to
fly to Brazil with only one day's notice and it was
lucky he kept his passport up to date.

Richard sang to himself as he flamed his charcoal,
waving to the Albert children when they swung into
sight over the fence. I saw him wave to Cindy, too.

In the kitchen, finishing the soup that was supposed
to celebrate our intimacy, I put the cheese out to warm
and the raspberries in to chill, set the table, opened the
wine, and checked the temperature of the big pot on
the stove. When I looked out again, Cindy was standing on her side of the fence, talking her southern talk
and laughing with my Richard. I heard him ask her to
share our supper, but she glanced at the kitchen window and declined. Her golden head with its ridiculous
just-out-of-the-shower hairdo disappeared.

"All ready in here!" I called.

"But we have a good twenty minutes to wait before
the fire's hot enough. When steak is grilling, steak is
king!" He was merry, in charge.

While I was thinking how to tell him he would have
to eat his steak alone because I could never have such
a thing on a plate in front of me, he came in and embraced me. "There's time," he said into my ear. "If we
go up now, the coals will be just right when we come
down."

I tore myself away, too outraged to speak, grabbed
the soup pot off the stove and tipped the Soup of Ease
and Loving into the sink. I could barely breathe, my
hands were shaking, my feet felt numb. He didn't say
anything, but I could see his dismay. Rushing past him,
I flew upstairs to the bedroom, slamming the door be-

hind me so that he couldn't misinterpret my choice of destination.

From the window I saw him wander back to the grill and sit on a chair with his hands hanging. I saw Cindy approach the fence and speak to him again. To his credit, he barely answered her. He got up, picked up the bundle of meat, and left. The charcoal glowed on long after dark.

Did they betray you, Papa, your partridges and doves? Did they disappoint you with coarseness and lack of romance? Was it ever like this for you, did you ever sit desolate among your beautiful objects? And how did you entice them back?

The Soup of the Cloud of Thorns

"Chicken Velvet Cream is soothing, but it bears floating an airy cake of crisp prickles. This accords with your suspicions, alternately denied and stabbingly felt. Cut peeled salsify into tiny tiny sticks, mix them with flour, and fry into cakes, one for each serving, to be laid on the hot cream soup just before eating."

He came again, after phoning and phoning to apologize in a baffled way.

I could tell he didn't know what he had done wrong, and that only made it worse. It was settled that we would have lunch on Saturday. He ate the soup impatiently, splashing it onto the tablecloth when he tried to break up the floating cake of salsify. What was salsify, anyway? he said. And hadn't I got any beer? Couldn't we have just an ordinary meal sometimes? The less I answered him, the more he heaved himself around in his chair.

Miserable, I had lost all my lightness and freedom—I was back in my defensive cage of silence and fear. When he had gone, I thought of Papa.

They never left you, Papa. You smiled and courted until they returned, until you could be the one to do the casting aside, such a specialty of yours. You were merciless. I've seen the letters and how they pleaded.

I willed myself to calmness and called him on Sunday night. A woman's voice answered, a woman who made three syllables of the word hello, a woman whose bottle-blonde hair always looks wet. I cut the connection without speaking.

You gave up on me, Papa, putting me aside as cruelly as you dismissed your erring widows. You sent me out to work at eighteen, moving me into my own apartment, a freedom I didn't crave as my contemporaries did.

I lived in that echoing, brown place, not daring to make it my own, as if it were a bus station. But haven't I, after all, learned your lessons?

I could no longer doubt it. Richard had betrayed me, departing from the honest character I had seen in him. What of perception, what of shared sympathies, what of romance? I had been so sure in this choice.

"Send him to perdition, my dear."

First I must smile and court. This I did on the telephone, until he agreed to come once more.

The Soup of Parting

"Mussels there must be, not for flavor but to mask by their chance of sand any grittiness from the weed poison you will add. And put in tomatoes, chopped celery, canned white beans, wine vinegar—every wryness you can think of. He will eat it because he will be contrite. You may merely taste, too overcome by the reunion to be your normal self. Then get him out of the house, because he will soon be very sick."

I washed all the dishes and pots and buried the mussel shells.

Richard was indeed very sick. In fact, he died.

After all, Papa, one must have pride in one's discrimination.

The Soup of Consolation

"As simple and clear as life going on, this soup contains the balm of fish, white and innocent, and the bitterness of raw endive shredded into it, the black pepper of knowledge, and the lemon of slight regret. And it is red with tomato juice, for grief, for courage. It looks very nice in the bowl, vivid and interesting—a soup with character."

Could that be the doorbell? I've been musing so, stirring the pot, setting the table. Now who, at this time of evening—

Yes, officer. Oh, two of you. But I was just about to sit down to a bowl of soup. Soup is a specialty of mine. Oh, that is what you want to talk to me about? About soup?

If Cooks Could Kill
by Robert Gray

"Okay," said Henri Cavanaugh, pacing across the carpet, "read me your list of all likely suspects."

Laura, sitting at the large oak desk in their study, picked up her notepad and examined it for a moment. Of the two dozen names originally listed there, all but four had been crossed out during this discussion.

"Well, here's what we've narrowed it down to. Alice, the woman from Rochester who's done this kind of thing off and on for nearly twenty years; Mary, a local girl, the one who was her mother's nurse until the poor lady died recently; Stella, the Italian woman, new to Saratoga, but with a reputation in New York we can't easily overlook; and Monique, inexperienced, lacking apparently all motivation ..."

"Ah yes, Monique."

"A finalist only because you insist and, need I add, extremely attractive, if you like your women petite, with sweetly accented, servile voices."

"Of course, how else?" Henri asked, grinning. "Why do you think I married you?"

"Uh-huh. So these are our prime suspects, Mr. Cavanaugh. Now all we have to do is choose one."

Henri sighed and walked over to one of the four stained glass windows in the booklined room, which was grudgingly letting in the faintest hint of soft blue light. The afternoon outside had turned cloudy. A storm was imminent.

He studied the nineteenth century hunt scene depicted on the window, particularly the horses, whose spreadeagled gait had been created when artists had no

idea how a horse ran. The haughty gentlemen atop
them looked as if they were riding hobbyhorses in
somebody's lush playroom.

"I'm still not convinced we've got a motive here,
Laura. You already have someone in three days a week
to clean the place. And since I do the cooking when we
don't go out . . ."

"Ah, Watson. I believe you've stumbled upon a key
clue there."

"Okay, okay. So my cooking presently leaves something to be desired."

"Like taste."

"But did I criticize your sleuthing abilities when we
first began working as a team?"

"Henri, dear. There is absolutely no detective equiv-
alent for last night's dinner."

"You mean my roast capon?"

"I mean your charred pigeon."

Henri surrendered with a shrug. "Okay, you win. We
get a live-in cook/housekeeper."

"Poor baby. I promise I'll arrange kitchen visitation
rights for you during negotiations. Now, assuming that
we can eliminate your friend Monique on the grounds
that she's just another pretty face, I nominate Stella."

"God, wasn't she the fascist? Came on a little strong
for my taste."

"Nonsense. She's just a take-charge kind of gal. Precisely what this operation needs. Somebody to whip us
into domestic shape, as it were. Agreed?"

"Does it matter?"

Laura smiled. "You know how much I value your
opinion on crucial domestic matters."

Before Henri could think of an appropriate come-
back, the telephone rang and Laura answered it.

"Oh, hello, Mother. How are you?"

Henri breathed a sigh of relief. He and Laura's
mother were not on the best of terms, never had been.
She considered him a hopelessly lowbrow golddigger,
unworthy of her daughter. On the rare occasions when
she called their home, if Laura didn't answer, the witch

hung up without speaking. Henri would dutifully relay the message to his wife and she'd call her mother back.

Laura, who loved them both, had miraculously remained neutral.

Henri watched his wife stretch out her lanky frame in the swivel chair and run a hand through her long red hair as she listened. Occasionally she tossed in a "Yes, Mother" or "Of course you are," just to prove she was listening. Henri loved the sound of her seductively raspy voice.

As the phone conversation continued, Henri noticed a change in Laura's tone, from politely noncommittal to concerned, emphasized further by her particularly intriguing question, "Then you're saying he's dead?"

Henri moved away from the window and sat down in one of the two leather armchairs in front of the desk. He read shock and worry in his wife's face.

"Mother! Mother, control yourself. I know it's terrible, but we must be calm about this. . . . Of course I'll try to help you, if I can. No, I know you don't approve of my doing this sort of thing. Yes, this is a special case. . . . No, he won't, not if you don't want him to. . . . Mother, that isn't fair. You know it isn't. He's no such thing."

Henri had a pretty good idea who was being discussed here.

"All right, Mother. Now start from the beginning. . . . The *beginning,* Mother."

This seemed like an opportune time for drinks. Henri went over to the antique rolltop desk in a secluded corner of the study and poured two scotch and sodas from the small bar they kept there. When he returned to his chair, he placed one of the drinks within Laura's reach on the desk. She glanced up from her notepad and smiled faintly.

Five minutes later, Laura hung up the phone. She swallowed what remained of her drink, sat back in her chair, and stared at Henri.

"What is it?" he asked.

"Would you believe we have a client?"

Not the Wicked Witch of the West, thought Henri. "Not your mother," he said.

Laura nodded. "A man who was staying with her this week is apparently now dying."

Henri suppressed a wisecrack. "Tell me about it."

Laura picked up her notepad. "Well, to begin with, each autumn at this time Mother organizes her Champignons Harvest Festival."

"Translation?"

"She and a select group of friends belong to a gourmet club of sorts. At various times during the year one of them is responsible for an appropriate banquet, depending upon the particular fruits of that season. Mother has always focused on various dishes prepared with freshly picked wild mushrooms. At all of these banquets, the ladies of the club choose three local chefs to prepare their feasts."

"Back up just a sec. By wild mushrooms, I take it you mean the kind that, if you don't know what you're doing . . ."

"Are poisonous, deadly. But the club has been holding this dinner for decades without incident. Mother and her friends are experts at identifying edible fungi."

Again Henri nobly resisted a punchline.

"I gather somebody blew it this year?"

"So it would seem. One of Mother's guests began showing symptoms last night, about twenty-four hours after the dinner. He isn't dead yet, but there doesn't seem to be much hope. The police have been at Mother's house all day. And, you'll no doubt be pleased to hear, one detective in particular has been a constant irritant to her."

"Mac?"

Laura nodded. Detective Sergeant David McKerney had worked, involuntarily for the most part, with the Cavanaughs on several previous cases. He was usually the beneficiary of their hard work, since they shunned notoriety for many reasons, not the least of which was the fact they were unlicensed.

"She said Mac refuses to cooperate with her in keeping this scandal out of the newspapers. Her friends in the club are all mortified, naturally, and are blaming one another for selecting the bad mushrooms."

"What about the chefs?"

"I don't know. I'm sure the police will be in touch with them."

"Does she have a copy of the menu?"

Laura shook her head. "She threw it away the day after the banquet. She's not one for keeping things, you know. She's rather obsessed with neatness and order. She said she remembers many of the dishes that were served, but I don't think it would hurt to go directly to the chefs for the details."

"I just thought of something. If some of those mushrooms were poisonous, and everyone ate together, how is it that only one person suffered the consequences?"

"That, dear Henri, is why people employ detectives."

Laura had Henri drop her off at her mother's house. She even managed to coerce him into trespassing all the way up the oaklined drive to the stone portico of the front entrance.

There were nine cars in the parking area near the carriage barn, which was located on the left side of the house. Laura recognized only Mac's brown Chevrolet sedan, looking odd and ungainly in the distinguished company of all those Mercedes and Cadillacs.

Saunders, who had been the Woodwards' butler for all of Laura's forty years and most of his eighty, escorted her to the parlor, where a somber crowd had gathered. Sixteen of them were proper Saratoga society matrons, all suitably attired as such. They were seated primly on the stiff Victorian furniture scattered throughout the cavernous room, and sipped almost in unison from delicate china teacups as Laura made her entrance.

Mac was standing near the marble fireplace, his elbow resting on the mantel and his undivided attention focused on her mother, who was obviously giving him a stern dressing-down on the proper respect he should be showing to his superiors.

"Ah, here she is now," said Laura's mother.

Mac did a nice job of disguising his surprise upon seeing who this nasty woman's daughter was. He guessed from Laura's formal attitude that their past dealings were not family knowledge, and made no sign of recognition.

Laura walked over to the fireplace. A gauntlet of elderly ladies greeted her as she walked past them, their polite smiles doing little to mask the strain evident on their powdered faces.

"Sergeant McKerney, this is my daughter, the one I've been telling you . . ."

"Mother, please. What have you been saying?"

Mac smiled grimly. "Your mother says you've had some kind of experience with this stuff. She insists that I direct all my inquiries through you so that she and her friends here can be spared the embarrassment of a public spectacle. I keep telling her it just ain't that easy. There are laws, ma'am."

"I'm afraid this gentleman is right, Mother. I know this is all terrible and upsetting for you, but the poor man has a job to do and he does need your assistance. Now . . ."

Laura could see that her mother was on the verge of tears again, and not hearing any of this. She asked Mac if he could temporarily direct his questions to some of the other ladies. He agreed. She led her mother out of the parlor and upstairs to her bedroom. The canopied bed was flawlessly made and covered with a pale blue spread that matched perfectly everything in the room, from the drapes to the rug to the furniture, even down to the jars on her dressing table.

Sometimes it was hard for Laura to believe that anyone had ever lived in this house. It always had the undisturbed atmosphere of a museum, as if the rooms should be roped off from the public. Yet she had spent nearly thirty years here. Living with Henri had quickly altered most of previous assumptions about neatness and order.

They sat together on the edge of the bed and Laura handed her mother some tissues to dry her eyes. "I want, when you feel strong enough, for you to tell me everything you can about this poor man and how the tragedy came about."

"Oh Laura, it's all so horrid. I still want to believe it was only a dream. His name ... his name is Philip Booker. Have you heard of him?"

"No."

"Well, he has, or had, a cooking show on public television. He's quite famous in culinary circles."

"Henri might know him, but then he doesn't watch much on television besides movies and sports programs."

"Hmmph. As I was saying, Philip is an extremely charming and amusing young man. He came from this area originally, of common stock you understand, but he studied in European culinary schools after leaving here. The television show came about from his reputation as a chef at a fine restaurant in New York, along with his cookbook and, of course, his singular wit and intelligence."

"How did you snare him for your dinner?" asked Laura.

"Quite devious of me, actually, though now I wish I'd never thought of it. Knowing his roots in this region, and not coincidentally being a stockholder in the company that underwrites his show, I simply made a few calls, and naturally he accepted my invitation."

"Naturally."

On Sunday afternoon our club had its annual mushroom outing. Philip accompanied us. He is quite famous for his mushroom dishes, which is another reason I thought it would be fun to have him here for my dinner. In fact, he introduced us to one particular variety that even we didn't know was edible. And he regaled us with many stories of his adventures in Europe and New York. Since the members of the club are all well-traveled themselves, they could appreciate his anecdotes more than most people he knows. He said as much himself. All in all, it was a splendid afternoon. We discovered a bounty of mushrooms and returned to the house positively giddy with anticipation."

"What time?"

"Oh, relatively early. Before tea anyway. The chefs were already here and we delivered our harvest to the kitchen immediately so they could begin their preparations."

"Did the cooks check your mushrooms to be certain none were poisonous?"

"Well, only one of them was really at all versed in the field. Chef William Finley. He owns a restaurant out on the lake called William's. I did see him inspecting the mushrooms individually. In fact . . . oh my God! You know, I remember Philip made a joke as we were leaving the kitchen, cautioning Chef William not to make any mistakes. Chef William just grumbled. He's not the most pleasant of men sometimes, though of course an adequate cook.

"After we changed for dinner, we met again in the parlor for cocktails. This was about five o'clock. There were seventeen of us, the ladies in the club, plus Philip. Once again he occupied center stage and entertained us with his stories. He was particularly amusing in his recounting of the early days in his career, working for some of the seedier Saratoga establishments, though of course he wouldn't tell us which ones no matter how we teased. His wit is very sharp and bold, and he has an impressive talent for making everyone in a group feel as if he were speaking to her alone, which is precisely why he comes across so well on the television."

"Were appetizers served?"

Her mother looked at Laura as if she had just questioned the existence of God. "Of course they were, Laura. Let me see. Chef William served Deviled Mushrooms and Stuffed Mushrooms with Cheese and Walnuts; Chef Anton tiny Mushroom and Port Wine

Creampuffs; and Chef Jon, um, oh yes, Marinated Raw Mushrooms. All delicious, though I felt the marinated ones were a touch on the vinegary side for my taste. I think he ..."

"Mother," said Laura, though she was glad to see her mother's mind distracted for the moment.

"Sorry, dear. Did you want to know what they served for dinner? As I said, I disposed of the menu, but perhaps I could recall ..."

"No, I can get that later, in detail, from the chefs themselves. Tell me a bit more about the incident."

"The incident? It's odd, really, but there was no incident to speak of. As I told you over the phone, Philip was perfectly healthy. We dined at seven. The conversation remained spirited and intelligent. Afterward, we had coffee and brandy in the parlor and watched the sunset. A local string quartet played Handel and Mozart pieces. We broke up into smaller groups. A few of us played some bridge. Nothing extraordinary."

"However ..."

"Late yesterday afternoon Philip began complaining of stomach pains and we canceled a dinner date. Because we've never had such a thing occur before, I foolishly made no immediate connection between his discomfort and the mushrooms. However, as the evening progressed, the attacks grew worse and were accompanied by various ... intestinal difficulties. I called an ambulance. Today I learned ..."

She could not hold back the tears. Laura embraced her as she collapsed, and decided there had been enough questioning for one day.

After leaving his wife at her mother's place, Henri drove to Albany through a dense, pounding rainstorm. He arrived at two thirty and headed directly for a suburban restaurant called Chateau D'Orville.

Anton Lapierre may have been French by ancestry, but he was more than a few generations removed from the old country, as far as Henri could tell. His accent showed more Brooklyn than Bordeaux. He seemed

about tens years younger than Henri, in his early for-
ties maybe, but half as tall and three times as wide, an
apparent tribute to his own cooking.

When Henri arrived, the kitchen was quiet except
for Anton, who was chewing out a young prep cook
for throwing away some chicken bones instead of add-
ing them to a huge stock pot that was bubbling on the
nearby stove. While the chef screamed, the intimidated
kid pawed through a trash can, retrieving the carcasses
and leg bones of a half dozen chickens. Fortunately, it
looked as if a new bag had been recently put in the
can. The prep cook juggled the piles of chicken bones
against his soiled white apron as he hurried over to the
stove and dumped them into the steaming cauldron.

When Anton caught sight of Henri approaching, he
spun around as if he were going to continue his act on
a new victim. But his face softened and a smile played
across his lips. The youngster took advantage of the
distraction and made his retreat.

"Kids!"said Anton by way of explanation.

Henri nodded sympathetically and introduced himself, mumbling something indistinct about his connection with the police investigation of the poisoning. He
hoped Anton would know what was going on. Laura
had neglected to get the name of the victim during her
phone conversation with her distraught mother.

Henri said he would like to get a copy of the menu
Anton had served at Mrs. Woodward's house. He knew
better than to ask for ingredients. None of these guys
would part with a recipe except under court order, but
the menu would at least give him a place to start.

The chef escorted Henri into his small, cluttered office just off the kitchen. "It's a damn shame. I heard
about it a couple of minutes ago on the radio. Mrs.
Woodward's a nice lady in her way. Hate to see her
have to go through this kind of thing, y'know? Leave
it to Phil Booker to make trouble."

"I don't think he's too thrilled about what's happened, either. Do you?"

"Him? Yeah, well . . . I got extra copies of that menu

here someplace. Figured there'd be people after 'em soon's I heard. Guess the newspaper types'll have a field day with us tomorrow, huh?"

Anton began pawing through the mess on his desk.

"Tell me if it's none of my business," said Henri, "but why do I get the feeling you're worried more about Mrs. Woodward and your own rep than you are about the poor guy who's dying?"

Anton shrugged, then shook his head. "I'll tell you somethin', buddy. You hold your breath lookin' for somebody who's broke up over Booker's accident, and you're gonna run out of breaths. He was a jerk when I met him twenty years ago and he's an even bigger jerk now."

"Did you work with him back then?"

"In a manner of speakin'. I came up to this area from New York when I was eighteen. Used to work as a stablehand at Aqueduct and Belmont racetracks, so like everybody I followed the circus up to Saratoga in August. One year I got in this fight with the trainer I was workin' for and I quit. When they all go back to the city, I stay around, starve for a week or so, then land this job washin' dishes at a restaurant called William's, owned by this guy named Bill Finley."

"Finley. Wasn't he at the dinner the other night?"

"Yeah. That was all Mrs. Woodward's doin'. If I'd known there's no way I would've worked that gig. But she's not a lady I can afford to cross, know what I mean? And when I hear Booker's the goddam guest of honor, I'm thinkin' somebody's tryin' to drive me totally nuts."

"What about the third chef?"

"Name's Jon Wilson. He's new up here. Just opened a place in Saratoga called Charades. You musta heard of it."

Henri nodded. "Haven't checked it out yet, though."

"He's already got a rep. Did some nice things the other night. Anyways, like I was sayin', I worked for this Finley as a dishwasher, then bussed tables and eventually wound up in the kitchen full time as a prep cook. That lasted about five years. I picked up a lot, y'know? Covered ground for the cooks that I didn't have to, improved my position, understand? So, when one of the cooks quits, I think this is my big chance to move up in the ranks. But Finley goes and hires this college kid right outta nowhere, meaning Phil Booker, right? He comes in and right off starts throwin' his weight around. I mean, nobody liked him. We mixed it up more than a few times, and I even had it out with Finley himself before I jumped ship. I knew Booker'd go down hard someday."

Henri had a simple question running through his head like an electric current, but there was no way to ask it without blowing his already flimsy cover. He could only hope that it would answer itself as the afternoon wore on.

Who the hell was this Philip Booker?

"I can see you're all broken up," he said.

"Hey! It won't keep me awake nights, right? But believe me, I'm just one of many in this area that feels like that. Booker didn't make no friends here, buddy. Everybody he ever came near's got a story, I bet. Look at me. If I get that job he beat me out of, maybe by now I own my own place instead of still climbin' the goddam ladder, understand? Took me a long, long time to get out from under Finley's badmouthin', let me tell you."

"But you wouldn't have slipped him a mushroom Mickey."

"Christ, if Finley and those nearsighted old bags couldn't tell good mushrooms from bad, it ain't my fault. I only know how to cook the things. I took their word that it was all safe."

Anton finally located the list and handed it to Henri. "And listen, buddy. Don't get your hopes up. Like I said, if I made a list of everybody who hated Booker, I'd run out of paper before I ran out of names. He made friends like I make money."

It was after three thirty by the time Henri got to William's Restaurant, an ivy-covered old stone house near the shores of Saratoga Lake. He and Laura had been there a few times, though they had never met the owner and Henri couldn't recall anything special about the food. With more than fifty restaurants of various quality in Saratoga itself, and hundreds more within easy driving distance, they had neither the time nor the appetites to become friendly with every owner. Besides, despite his culinary forays, Henri had to admit that he usually preferred Saratoga's smaller diners and cafes to these fancy places. Something in his working class background rebelled against the idea of paying twice as much to have his drink weakened by mineral water instead of tap.

Henri discovered William Finley in his office, listing checks on a bank deposit slip. He had passed through the kitchen while searching for the owner, and noticed that the atmosphere was just a bit more harried than it had been at Chateau D'Orville. The staff was beginning to acquire that panicky edge that would be needed to crank out meal after meal at the height of the dinner rush.

When Henri introduced himself, William Finley, a dignified looking man of sixty-five or seventy, politely expressed his deep distress over the tragedy. But Henri saw in his eyes a cool detachment, like that of a sympathetic undertaker. Finley said he had no extra copies of his menu, but could write one out if Henri could wait a minute.

Henri sat in a rickety chair near the desk and watched Finley search through one of the drawers, then extract a sheet of paper.

"Mr. Finley, I hear Phil Booker worked for you many years ago."

William sighed and nodded. "That was before his current fame and fortune, long before. You've been talking to Anton, I gather. He's never forgiven me. I'm not proud of my behavior in that episode. I haven't made many mistakes in this business, but I made a couple of doozies with those two boys, especially Mr. Booker."

"How did you come to hire him? Booker, I mean. Anton talked like the guy appeared out of thin air," said Henri, still wondering about that "fame and fortune" business.

"Almost. Oh, there's no denying Phil Booker had a certain amount of natural ability. But he was also an egomaniacal clod. He walked on people, used them to his own ends and then discarded them. Twenty years ago, as Anton no doubt already told you, I gave Mr. Booker his first real break in this business. Right out of college. He was a theater major, for God's sake. His only experience was a part-time job in a New York deli. He had, however, a letter of recommendation from a well-known chef who will remain nameless. Mr. Booker told me the chef was a friend of the family and had taught him a great deal. The letter extolled the young man's potential, his natural talent, and his drive. It said nothing about his inability to get along with people or to take orders. As it turned out, he had forged the letter anyway. I should have checked it before hiring him, but I was more naive in those days. When I called afterward, just out of curiosity, that chef had, of course, never heard of any Phil Booker."

"And in the meantime Anton had quit."

"Yes. The great irony is that Mr. Booker now works for that same restaurant in New York. He replaced the chef whose recommendation he had forged years before. And have you ever watched his television show?"

"Television?"

"I never miss it, like a penance, you might say. Mr. Booker enjoys telling amusing stories about the stupid things people taught him when he was first learning to cook. I regret to say that ninety percent of those stories were culled from his years with me. I'm something of a laughing-stock in this area now, in the profession anyway. Of course he doesn't use my name on the air, but everyone knows. And then there's the matter of the recipes. Did Anton mention the recipes?"

"No."

"From everyone he ever worked with, Mr. Booker

stole. His mind was a sponge. That book of his that came out this year, the one tied in with his show? What was the title?"

Henri shrugged. He always used old cookbooks himself. Food fads didn't interest him. Finley turned to a bookshelf on his left and ran a finger along the spines, many of which were flour-coated. Finally he stopped and extracted a garish red, yellow, and blue cookbook.

"Oh yes, how could I forget? *Eats of Eden.* Ludicrous title, don't you think? I've gone through this book many times, as I'm sure have others with whom he worked over the years. Any of us can probably pick a half-dozen recipes of our own that he stole, then altered ever so slightly and published as his creations. The man never had an original idea in his entire life. He was like ... like a musician, I suppose. He could read the notes of recipe and play it fluently with his utensils, but he was no composer. Ask Anton. Ask Jon."

"What about Jon?"

"He's a more recent victim. He worked with Mr. Booker in that New York restaurant where they film the TV show. He was fired last spring for insubordination. Seems Jon told Mr. Booker exactly what he thought of him in front of the entire staff. And you just can't treat a star like that."

Henri checked his watch and knew he'd better be going if he intended to get to Jon's place before the dinner rush. He thanked Finley for his help and left.

Driving back to Saratoga from the lake, Henri entered the city on Union Avenue and drove past the thoroughbred track and stables. Less than a month ago, this area had been practically impassable with its crowds and traffic jams every race day. Now it was more like a ghost town, the stable area on the right side of the street silent and devoid of any activity, the grandstand building on the left as empty as an abandoned old warehouse. The city was still recovering from the August invasion, licking its wounds, counting up its profits.

Charades was one of those establishments that had not yet decided what it really wanted to be. Located in a small building on Broadway, its lunch crowd was primarily from the downtown business community, but at dinner the menu and prices climbed into the more rarefied air of an upper class clientele, only to be supplanted one more time after eleven o'clock. Then Charades underwent its finally metamorphosis of the day, and was rapidly becoming the most popular nightspot in town for Skidmore College students.

The kitchen was already in a state of organized chaos. He had timed his arrival badly. Cooks and waitresses rushed about as if the room were on fire. When Henri asked for the owner, one of the passing furies gestured toward the right-hand wall, where two gas stoves stood under a large hood fan. All the burners were fired and most of them were in use. Jon Wilson was at that moment shaking a sauté pan over the heat, vegetables sizzling in oil and occasionally erupting in flames. Simultaneously, he was keeping an eye on several other pots and pans and shouting orders to his workers, sending them away on a variety of missions, all of which sounded of the utmost importance and urgency.

Henri approached tentatively. "Excuse me, Mr. . . ."

"Yeah? What's up?" he asked, somehow managing to look at Henri and the stove at the same time. "You bring me those chickens, man? They said you'd be here at noon."

Henri shook his head. He mumbled something about the police and the poisoning, speaking clearly only when he came to the part concerned with getting Jon's menu.

"I got no time right now, man. I'm buried. You have a paper and pencil?"

Jon turned quickly away from the stove, nearly grazing Henri's arm with the hot pan as he swung past. One of Jon's assistants was right there waiting with two dinners plates, on each of which half a roast duckling lay next to a generous scoop of brown rice. This allowed room only for the vegetables. Deftly Jon poured the pan's contents onto the plates, somehow making the piles evenly divided down to the last onion.

The assistant added an orange slice and a parsley sprig to each plate as a garnish, then hurried away. Jon was already back at the stove, shaking a couple of the other pans, checking under the lid of a saucepan. Another order was called out to him by the salad girl in the corner, who was reading off order slips delivered to her by the waitresses. Without acknowledging the call, he reached into a cooler nearby and took out two pieces of sirloin.

In the middle of all this Jon still managed to dictate the list of dishes he had prepared for the Woodward party. Henri decided not to press for more than that under the circumstances.

Laura sat with her mother for almost three hours, trying to persuade her to take a nap. When she finally relinquished and closed her eyes, Laura covered her with a blanket and returned to the parlor, where only Mac remained. He was sitting on a loveseat near the fireplace, drinking from a teacup, his feet up on the red velvet cushion.

"Mother would have you shot if she saw those shoes on her furniture, Mac."

"Oops." He dropped his feet clumsily to the carpet. "You can dress some people up . . . How's she doing?"

"Sleeping now. I don't think she's had much of that since this all began."

"Here," said Mac, reaching for a silver pot and another cup. "That Mr. Saunders brought me some coffee. Laura, if I'd known this was your family, I maybe could've worked something out, you know."

Laura accepted the cup and saucer. She shook her head. "Thanks, Mac, but no special treatment is necessary. You just do what you have to."

"Your mother have anything to say?"

"Only what little she knows. That Philip Booker was

a charming young celebrity, and that they had a marvelous time until now."

Mac nodded. "Yeah, same story I got from the ladies. And I believe every word of it, if that's what worries her."

Laura shook her head again. "In her heart, I'm certain she doesn't think you suspect anyone in the club of anything worse than poor judgment in picking the mushrooms. But these ladies guard their reputations like crown jewels, Mac. They're terrified of any stain, and the publicity from all this will have social reverberations, in a manner of speaking. Of course they're distressed for Mr. Booker, too. Have you heard from the hospital recently?"

"I called a few minutes ago. Talked to one of the docs. It's just about hopeless. When Booker was brought in, he was already suffering from, if you'll pardon the grisly details, a burning gut, vomiting, fainting spells, body cramps, the works. Now he's starting to have some breathing troubles. They say the symptoms might ease up for a day or so, but at most he probably won't live out the week. They did what they could, pumped him out and whatever, but the mushrooms were already well digested and the poison had spread throughout his system."

"How ghastly."

"The doctors, knowing about this dinner the other night, have, of course, no doubt that it was mushroom poisoning. They called it probably amanita-toxin poisoning, from what we call toadstools and they call *Amanita phalloides*. They said it's the villain in about ninety percent of all mushroom poisoning cases."

"Have you spoken with the cooks?"

"No, not personally. I just sent a couple of my boys out for a preliminary visit, to let them know what's up. Having all that time pass since the dinner doesn't help much as far as evidence goes."

"I don't know if you'll be too thrilled to hear this, Mac, but Henri also made the rounds this afternoon. He might be home by now. I was going to have Saunders take me home but if you'll do the honors, it might be worthwhile for the three of us to compare notes. In anticipation of murder, you might say."

Henri was sitting at the desk in the study when they arrived. He was nearly hidden behind two stacks of cookbooks. On his lap was a clipboard and a yellow legal pad. He was copying down something from one of the books.

"Welcome home, kids. What's new, Mac?"

"Nothing at all, Henri. Just thought I'd stop by to say hello, that's all. You planning dinner?"

Henri shook his head. "I got the party menus from those chefs this afternoon. I'm just looking up recipes similar to theirs for a comparison of basic characteristics and ingredients. Might turn up something. You never know."

"Good idea," said Mac.

Henri looked at Laura. "How's she doing?" It was the closest he could get to a sympathetic question about her mother.

"She'll be okay, I think. A bit shocked, of course."

Laura and Mac sat down in the two armchairs in front of the desk and began talking about the case, comparing her mother's version of the events to those of the other members of the club. Henri divided his attention among listening to them, reading, and writing. He only glanced up when Laura began describing the victim in glowing terms.

"Whoa! Time out. Are we talking about the same person here? The nearly deceased Phil Booker?"

"Of course. Why?"

Mac nodded his agreement. "The ladies all described him in much the same way: charming, intelligent, kind."

Henri shook his head and grinned. "You've obviously been listening to the wrong crowd. An equally brief list of Philip Booker's dominant personality traits, as provided by the local culinary establishment, would replace the words charming, intelligent, and kind with egomaniacal, parasitic, and cruel. We better get some fingerprints, Mac. I think we're talking about two different guys."

Henri told them what he had learned during the afternoon, which left Mac and Laura shaking their heads in confusion.

"It's probably not that odd, when you come right down to it," said Mac. "Booker wouldn't be the first chiseler to suck up to a bunch of gullible old broads. No offense, Laura."

Her expression hovered somewhere between a polite smile and a glare, then softened as her mind moved on to more important matters. "What about the fact that Booker was the only guest poisoned? Does that make sense in terms of logistics? Everyone ate the same food. If somebody was going to poison Mr. Booker, he would have to be awfully careful not to get more victims than he bargained for, or even the wrong victim altogether. And Mr. Booker knew wild mushrooms himself. After all the inspections they were subjected to, I don't see how a significant number of bad ones could have just slipped through."

Henri glanced up from his book again. "If it was attempted murder, it had to be one of the three chefs, right? All of them seem to have sufficient motive, but only one had enough screws loose to actually pull it off. This party was just too good an opportunity for him to pass up. Booker is, from what I hear, at the height of his popularity right now: the TV show, his bestselling cookbook, a prestigious job in a fine New York restaurant. Would there ever be a better chance for revenge than your mother's party? Booker could be killed not only in the presence of multiple suspects, but also with the possibility that maybe it really was just an unfortunate accident."

Mac lit a cigarette. "One of the ladies told me it was pretty hectic in that kitchen all day. Along with the cooks and their helpers, Booker and most of the guests kept running in and out to check on their progress and to second-guess methods of preparation. So there was more than enough distraction and confusion in there for anything to happen."

"But ..." said Henri, reaching for another cookbook, his old favorite, *Larousse Gastronomique,* "we still have the not-so-minor detail of how the bad mushrooms were planted in one particular dish, and in such a way that only Booker would eat them, without noticing anything suspicious. So the murderer had to find a way to get that specific food into Booker's mouth while serving a buffet-style dinner. I read somewhere that you'd need at least twenty grams of poison mushrooms to do the trick."

Laura handed Mac an ashtray. "As far as serving is concerned, part of the floor show that night was for the chefs to be standing behind the banquet tables, doling out portions and describing each of their creations. All three of them were in a position to influence who received what."

"Hmmm ..." Henri turned a page of the *Larousse,* then glanced at his clipboard. "I think we can probably eliminate any dish that was served to the guests from a communal container like a salad bowl or casserole or chafing dish, as well as the finger foods at cocktail hour, over which the cooks had no service control."

"That must involve a good share of the meal," said Laura.

"It would mean dropping, let's see, the Mushroom Bisque, three kinds of salad, Stewed Mushrooms, Champignons Flambé, Mushrooms au Gratin, French-Styled Baked Mushrooms, Mushrooms in Marsala Wine, Kidneys and Mushrooms with Pasta, the three casseroles made with chicken, zucchini, and broccoli, Mushroom Pie, Paprika Mushrooms ..."

Henri was drawing lines through the names on his list.

"What does that leave?" asked Mac, butting his cigarette in the ashtray.

"Not a hell of a lot. Just Mushroom Patties, Tiny Mushroom Soufflés, Mushroom Tarts, and Mushroom Piroshki."

"That must eliminate somebody from our suspect list," said Laura.

Henri checked his notes. "Guess again. William made the piroshki, Jon the tarts and soufflés, and Anton the patties. Right back where we started."

Mac shook his head. "And we still don't even know how he managed to slip at least twenty grams, and probably a hell of a lot more, of poisonous mushrooms into a single item without attracting Booker's attention when he ate it. Henri?"

Absorbed in his studies, Henri didn't look up for several moments. When he finally did, he was grinning. "How, you ask? I'll lay odds on page 636, Mac."

He dropped the heavy book on the desktop and spun it around so they could read a section he had just marked with his pen.

Mac wasn't sure his superiors would approve, but the plan made enough sense to go along with until something better came up. Laura had convinced her mother to arrange a small dinner for the three chefs, scheduling it on a Monday night when all their restaurants were closed. This involved a delay of six days, but since Philip Booker was still clinging tenaciously to life in the hospital, and the newspapers so far were treating it as an unfortunate accident, there did not seem to be any need to rush things.

Before Laura's mother grudgingly extended her invitations to "those fools," one of whom she was certain had made a stupid and deadly error, Mac called them all and let it be known that he expected them to attend. He said he needed their assistance in recalling the events of the dinner and this would be the most convenient way of getting them all together.

Henri generously offered to do the cooking, but Laura insisted on a catered affair, since it was also Mrs. Woodward's cook's night off. The dinner was held in the secondary dining room. There were only six guests: Laura, her mother, Mac, and the three chefs.

The meal was served with a nervous flourish by the

caterer, who appeared to be both delighted and intimidated by his clients. Every time he left the room, his colleagues grumbled about his work.

Mac served as moderator, explaining to the chefs much of what he had discovered thus far, as well as his suspicion that Philip Booker's poisoning hadn't been as accidental as the media was portraying it. He said that the main reason he had asked them there was to solicit their opinions on a theory he was developing.

"I'd like to toss something out to you guys, see what you think of the possibilities. As cooks I mean. Now it's pretty obvious at this point that the murderer had to get the poison mushrooms into something he could serve to Booker specifically, without any risk of hurting the others. I've narrowed the possibilities down to four items: soufflés, piroshki, tarts, and patties."

Mac stared hard at the creator of each one as he spoke its name. They all flinched in turn. "While I was thumbing through some cookbooks, checking out ingredients, I happened to come across an interesting recipe for a concoction called Mushroom Powder. Seems it's used like any spice, to add flavor to the dish you're cooking. It's pretty simple stuff. You just slice up some mushrooms, bake 'em, and, when they've dried out, pulverize them with a mortar and pestle. So I got to thinking, if the mushrooms being used happened to be phalloides, for instance, and you used enough of them, you'd have kind of a powdered death. What do you guys think?"

Jon laughed. "What should we think? Of course it makes sense, man. We've all ground our own spices on occasion for special dishes. And obviously we all have a mortar and pestle. Any decent kitchen does. But it seems to me you're right back where you started. I mean, all of us were here, making potentially lethal dishes, all of us have some kind of motive, and all of us have the know-how and equipment."

Mac smiled, then shrugged. "I guess you're right, but only one of you has a mortar and pestle that was used to grind up poison mushrooms. Now even if you washed the equipment out thoroughly, I'm betting the lab boys can find traces of the lethal substance on them. That's another reason why I asked you all here tonight. I sent one of my boys around to your homes and restaurants to confiscate all mortars and pestles in sight. Just thought it best to do so when you weren't there to . . . interfere."

"You can't just . . ." Anton sputtered, but Mac waved him silent.

"I can and I have."

The chefs erupted in a single, furious voice of protest, but were silenced again by Henri's appearance in the doorway.

"Sarge, sorry to butt in. You said to let you know when I got back. I left those things you wanted on the front seat of your car, okay? They're all in marked plastic bags."

"Thanks. I'll drop 'em off at the station later. Take the rest of the night off."

Henri vanished. Mac turned back to the chefs. "Sorry for the interruption, gentlemen. And sorry also for the secrecy."

The shouting started once more. Mac rested his face wearily against his hand and waited for the storm to subside. Laura glanced at her mother, who was still staring openmouthed at the doorway where Henri had been moments before, like an apparition. She seemed to be trying to decide if what she had seen was what she thought she had seen. Laura thought it best to let the incident remain a mystery.

Mrs. Woodward composed herself and rapped her knuckles on the table, which surprisingly caused all three chefs to stop yelling at the same time.

"Gentlemen, please. If you can control yourselves, there will be coffee and brandy served in the parlor in ten minutes. If you'll excuse us, I've been asked to show Detective McKerney the room where Mr. Booker was staying upstairs. We shall join you shortly. Please make yourselves at home."

"Let's continue this little chat over coffee, okay, guys?" Mac added, as everyone stood.

Laura, her mother, and Mac exited through the door to the hallway. The chefs headed for the kitchen, still growling among themselves, apparently ready to vent their anger on the helpless caterer.

Once out of the dining room, Mrs. Woodward excused herself and went into seclusion in her upstairs bedroom. Mac and Laura headed for the greenhouse and a seldom-used exit from the house. Mac followed Laura across the moonlit lawn and through a small maze of high hedges. When they emerged near the carriage barn, she spotted Henri lurking in the shadows, and they hurried over to join him.

"You booking bets on this one?" asked Mac.

"Against the law," Henri whispered.

They waited five minutes. The cloudless sky allowed a full moon to illuminate the parking area. Crystals in the marble chips sparkled. A slight breeze rustled the oak leaves and stirred wind chimes over by the greenhouse.

At first they couldn't see him, but heard the sound of hesitant footsteps on crushed stone. Then the silhouette of a head appeared near the hood of the Cavanaughs' Mercedes. Crouching behind the car, the figure seemed to be gauging the distance between his hiding place and Mac's car, an open space of a dozen yards or so.

Another long minute passed. Time was running out. Finally the silhouette, still crouching, scurried across the opening and reached for the police car door.

"Freeze! Police!" shouted Mac, rushing from cover. The Cavanaughs followed.

The shadow figure, poised momentarily to flee, thought better of it and stood his ground. Something fell from his hand and clattered on the stones.

Mac shone a flashlight and the shadow suddenly had a face, Anton's fleshy face, looking thoroughly scared and defeated. Training the light on the driveway, Mac located the item that had fallen from Anton's grasp, a mortar and pestle. He had just stolen them moments before from Mrs. Woodward's kitchen, planning to switch them with the ones in the plastic bag marked with his name.

Mac returned the light to Anton's face, told him to put his hands on the car and spread his legs. When he began reciting the Miranda warnings, Henri draped his arm around Laura's shoulders and they walked back to the house.

"She doesn't even let me in the damn kitchen!" Henri complained as he entered the study with a tray on which mugs, a coffee pot, and some fresh Danish had been neatly laid out. "I almost had to slug her just so I could bring this tray in here myself."

Laura shook her head and smiled. "Poor baby. Give Stella a chance. It's her first day. She has to get acclimated. If you can control yourself for a second, I just had a call from Mac. He wanted to thank us again for last night. Also, Philip Booker is still holding on, so murder isn't the operative word here yet."

"Nothing like solving them before they happen. Shame about Booker, though. Did Mac check to see if the lab guys could actually have picked up traces of *Amanita phalloides* on a mortar and pestle?"

"He didn't say. It would be icing on the cake at this point, anyway. Anton made a full confession last night. What a strange man. I was just thinking. If he'd spread the poison around a bit and killed one of the others, or even made a few of them a little sick, there would have been much more reason to think it might be accidental. Yet he didn't take that chance. He gambled with his own life instead of those of Mother and her friends."

Henri sipped his coffee. "Something else is strange about this case. Anton is guilty, yet every one of those guys had the motive and ability to carry out this scheme. For a while there I wondered if it might be a conspiracy, but if Anton's taking the rap there's not much we can do on that score. He seems to have just been unlucky in beating them to a punch they all could have thrown. Speaking of punches, how's your mother handling this?"

"She'll survive. Now that the media have this new bone to chew on, the story will be reborn for a couple of weeks. Mother's pretty shaken up about that, refusing to go out of the house and such. But her ego will get the better of her eventually and this will become yet another grand story for her to tell on the local tea circuit."

Henri grinned, picked up a Danish, and took a small, tentative bite, followed immediately by a larger one. Laura could tell that he was impressed with Stella's baking prowess, but knew he wasn't ready yet to admit defeat.

Henri returned the pastry to the tray and screwed up his face as if he'd just eaten a lemon. "If we'd hired Monique, we could've had fresh croissants every morning."

"That I sincerely doubt," said Laura. "But you'll be pleased to hear that Stella makes croissants, too, as well as dozens of Italian pastries. She's extremely versatile. And she promised to do some croissants just for you tomorrow."

"Laura, she's just not that great. This isn't by any stretch of the imagination the best Danish I've ever had. And she is definitely a fascist. I bet I'll never get to cook in that kitchen again."

"Oh, no," said Laura, putting the back of her hand to her forehead in mock horror.

"Laugh if you want to, kid. But I say there's gonna be war," Henri said as he reached for the Danish again and took another hearty bite.

In Vino Veritas
by A. A. Milne

I am in a terrible predicament, as you will see directly. I don't know what to do. . . .

"One of the maxims which I have found most helpful in my career," the superintendent was saying, "apart, of course, from employing a good press agent, has been the simple one that appearances are not always deceptive. A crime may be committed exactly as it seems to have been committed, and exactly as it was intended to be committed." He helped himself and passed the bottle.

"I don't think I follow you," I said, hoping thus to lead him on.

I am a writer of detective stories. If you have never heard of me, it can only be because you don't read detective stories. I wrote *Murder on the Back Stairs* and *The Mystery of the Twisted Eglantine,* to mention only two of my successes. It was this fact, I think, which first interested Superintendent Frederick Mortimer in me, and, of course, me in him. He is a big fellow with the face of a Roman emperor; I am rather the small neat type. We gradually became friends, and so got into the habit of dining together once a month, each in turn being host in his own flat. He liked talking about his cases and naturally I liked listening. I may say now that *Blood on the Eiderdown* was suggested to me by an experience of his at Crouch End. He also liked putting me right when I made mistakes, as so many of us do, over such technical matters as fingerprints and Scotland Yard procedure. I had always supposed, for instance, that you could get good fingerprints from butter. This, apparently, is not the case. From buttery fingers on other objects, yes, but not from the pat of butter itself, or, anyhow, not in hot weather. This, of course, was a foolish mistake of mine, as in any case Lady Sybil would not have handled the butter directly in this way, as my detective should have seen. My detective, by the way, is called Sherman Flagg, and is pretty well known by now. Not that this is germane to my present story.

"I don't think I follow you," I said.

"I mean that the simple way of committing a murder is often the best way. This doesn't mean that the murderer is a man of simple mind. On the contrary. He is subtle enough to know that the simple solution is too simple to be credible."

This sounded anything but simple, so I said, "Give me an example."

"Well, take the case of the magnum of Tokay which was sent to the Marquis of Hedingham on his lordship's birthday. Have I never told you about it?"

"Never," I said, and I too helped myself and passed the bottle.

He filled his glass and considered. "Give me a moment to get it clear," he said. "It was a long time ago." While he closed his eyes, and let the past drift before him, I fetched another bottle of the same; a Château Latour '78, of which I understand there is very little left in the country.

"Yes," said Mortimer, opening his eyes, "I've got it now."

I leant forward, listening eagerly. This is the story he told me.

The first we heard of it at the Yard (said Mortimer) was a brief announcement over the telephone that the Marquis of Hedingham's butler had died suddenly at his lordship's town house in Brook Street, and that poison was suspected. This was at seven o'clock. We went round at once. Inspector Totman had been put in charge of the case; I was a young detective sergeant at

the time, and I generally worked under Totman. He
was a brisk, military sort of fellow, with a little prickly
ginger mustache, good at his job in a showy, orthodox
way, but he had no imagination, and he was thinking
all the time of what Inspector Totman would get out of
it. Quite frankly I didn't like him. Outwardly we kept
friendly, for it doesn't do to quarrel with one's superiors; indeed, he was vain enough to think that I had a
great admiration for him; but I knew that he was just
using me for his own advantage, and I had a shrewd
suspicion that I should have been promoted before this,
if he hadn't wanted to keep me under him so that he
could profit by my brains.

We found the butler in his pantry, stretched out on
the floor. An open bottle of Tokay, a broken wineglass
with the dregs of the liquid still in it, the medical evidence of poisoning, all helped to build the story for
us. The wine had arrived about an hour before, with
the card of Sir William Kelso attached to it. On the
card was a typewritten message, saying, "Bless you,
Tommy, and here's something to celebrate it with."
Apparently it was his lordship's birthday, and he was
having a small family party for the occasion, of about
six people. Sir William Kelso, I should explain, was
his oldest friend and a relation by marriage, Lord
Hedingham having married his sister; in fact, he was to
have been one of the party present that evening. He
was a bachelor about fifty, and a devoted uncle to his
nephew and nieces.

Well, the butler had brought up the bottle and the
card to his lordship—this was about six o'clock; and
Lord Hedingham, as he told us, had taken the card,
said something like "Good old Bill, we'll have that tonight, Perkins," and Perkins had said, "Very good, my
lord," and gone out again with the bottle, and the card
had been left lying on the table. Afterwards, there
could be little doubt what had happened. Perkins had
opened the bottle with the intention of decanting it, but
had been unable to resist the temptation to sample it
first. I suspect that in his time he had sampled most of

his lordship's wine, but had never before come across
a Tokay of such richness. So he had poured himself out
a full glass, drunk it, and died almost immediately.

"Good Heavens!" I interrupted. "But how extremely
providential—I mean, of course, for Lord Hedingham
and the others."

"Exactly," said the superintendent.

The contents of the bottle were analyzed (he went
on) and found to contain a more than fatal dose of
prussic acid. Prussic acid isn't a difficult thing to get
hold of, so that didn't help much. Of course we did all
the routine things, and I and young Roberts, a nice
young fellow who often worked with us, went round
all the chemists' shops in the neighborhood, and
Totman examined everybody from Sir William and
Lord Hedingham downwards, and Roberts and I took
the bottle round to all the well known wine merchants,
and at the end of a week all we could say was this:

1. The murderer had a motive for murdering Lord
Hedingham; or, possibly, somebody at his party; or,
possibly the whole party. In accordance, we learnt,
with the usual custom, his lordship would be the first
to taste the wine. A sip would not be fatal, and in a
wine of such richness the taste might not be noticeable;
so that the whole party would then presumably drink
his lordship's health. He would raise his glass to them,
and in this way they would all take the poison, and be
affected according to how deeply they drank. On the
other hand, his lordship might take a good deal more
than a sip in the first place, and so be the only one to
suffer. My deduction from this was that the motive was
revenge rather than gain. The criminal would revenge
himself on Lord Hedingham, if his lordship or *any* of
his family were seriously poisoned; he could only
profit if *definite* people were definitely *killed.* It took a
little time to get Totman to see this, but he did eventually agree.

2. The murderer had been able to obtain one of Sir
William Kelso's cards, and knew that John Richard
Mervyn Plantaganet Carlow, 10th Marquis of Heding-

ham, was called "Tommy" by his intimates. Totman
deduced from this that he was therefore one of the
Hedingham-Kelso circle of relations and friends. I dis-
puted this. I pointed out: (a) that it was rather to strangers than to intimate friends that cards were presented;
except in the case of formal calls, when they were left
in a bowl or tray in the hall, and anybody could steal
one; (b) that the fact that Lord Hedingham was called
Tommy must have appeared in society papers and be
known to many people; and, most convincing of all, (c)
that the murderer did *not* know that Sir William Kelso
was to be in the party that night. For obviously some
reference would have been made to the gift, either on
his arrival or when the wine was served; whereupon he
would have disclaimed any knowledge of it, and the
bottle would immediately have been suspected. As it
was, of course, Perkins had drunk from it before Sir
William's arrival. Now both Sir William and Lord
Hedingham assured us that they *always* dined together
on each other's birthday, and they were convinced that
any personal friend of theirs would have been aware of
the fact. I made Totman question them about this, and
he then came round to my opinion.

3. There was noting to prove that the wine in the
bottle corresponded to the label; and wine experts were
naturally reluctant to taste it for us. All they could say
from the smell was that it was a Tokay of sorts. This,
of course, made it more difficult for us. In fact I may
say that neither from the purchase of the wine nor the
nature of the poison did we get any clue.

We had, then, the following picture of the murderer.
He had a cause of grievance, legitimate or fancied,
against Lord Hedingham, and did not scruple to take
the most terrible revenge. He knew that Sir William
Kelso was a friend of his lordship's and called him
Tommy, and that he might reasonably give him a bottle
of wine on his birthday. He did *not* know that Sir William would be dining there that night; that is to say,
*even as late as six o'clock that evening, he did not
know.* He was not likely, therefore, to be anyone at

"Right! The murderer's a man who wanted me to believe all that I have believed. When I've told myself
that the murderer intended to do so-and-so, he intended
me to believe that, and therefore he didn't do so-and-so.
When I've told myself that the murderer wanted to mislead me, he wanted me to think he wanted to mislead
me, which meant that the truth was exactly as it seemed
to be. Now then, Fred, you'll begin all over again, and
you'll take things as they are, and won't be too clever
about them. Because the murderer expects you to be
clever, and wants you to be clever, and from now on
you aren't going to take your orders from *him*."

And of course, the first thing which leaped to my
mind was that the murderer *meant* to murder the butler!

It seemed incredible now that we could ever have
missed it. Didn't every butler sample his master's
wines? Why, it was an absolute certainty that Perkins
would be the first victim of a poisoned bottle of a very
special vintage. What butler could resist pouring himself out a glass as he decanted it?

Wait, though. Mustn't be in a hurry. Two objections.
One: Perkins might be the one butler in a thousand
who wasn't a wine sampler. Two: Even if he were like
any other butler, he might be out of sorts on that particular evening, and have put by a glass to drink later.
Wouldn't it be much too risky for a murderer who only
wanted to destroy Perkins, and had no grudge against
Lord Hedingham's family, to depend so absolutely on
the butler drinking first?

For a little while this held me up, but not for long.
Suddenly I saw the complete solution.

It would *not* be risky if (a) the murderer had certain
knowledge of the butler's habits; and (b) could, if necessary, at the last moment, prevent the family from
drinking. In other words, if he were an intimate of the
family, were himself present at the party, and without
bringing suspicion on himself, could bring the wine
under suspicion.

In other words, and only, and finally, and definitely—if he were Sir William Kelso. For Sir William was the only man in the world who could say, "Don't drink this wine. I'm supposed to have sent it to you, and I didn't, so that proves it's a fake." The *only* man.

Why hadn't we suspected him from the beginning? One reason, of course, was that we had supposed the intended victim to be one of the Hedingham family, and of Sir William's devotion to his sister, brother-in-law, nephew, and nieces, there was never any doubt. But the chief reason was our assumption that the last thing a murderer would do would be to give himself away by sending his own card round with the poisoned bottle. "The *last* thing a murderer would do"—and therefore the *first* thing a really clever murderer would do. For it couldn't be explained as "the one mistake which every murderer makes"; he couldn't send his own card accidentally. "Impossible," we said, that a murderer should do it deliberately! But the correct answer was, impossible that we should not be deceived if it were done deliberately—and therefore brilliantly clever.

To make my case complete to myself, for I had little hope as yet of converting Totman, I had to establish motive. Why should Sir William want to murder Perkins? I gave myself the pleasure of having tea that afternoon with Lord Hedingham's cook-housekeeper. We had caught each other's eye on other occasions when I had been at the house, and—well, I suppose I can say it now—I had a way with the women in those days. When I left, I knew two things. Perkins had been generally unpopular, not only downstairs, but upstairs; "it was a wonder how they put up with him." And her ladyship "had been a different woman lately."

"How different?" I asked.

"So much younger, if you know what I mean, Sergeant Mortimer. Almost like a girl again, bless her heart."

I did know. And that was that. Blackmail.

What was I to do? What did my evidence amount

to? Nothing. It was all corroborative evidence. If Kelso had done one suspicious thing, or left one real clue, then the story I had made up would have convinced any jury. As it was, in the eyes of a jury he had done one completely unsuspicious thing, and left one real clue to his innocence—his visiting card. Totman would just laugh at me.

I disliked the thought of being laughed at by Totman. I wondered how I could get the laugh of him. I took a bus to Baker Street, and walked into Regent's Park, not minding where I was going, but just thinking. And then, as I got opposite Hanover Terrace, who should I see but young Roberts.

"Hallo, young fellow, what have *you* been up to?"

"Hallo, sarge," he grinned. "Been calling on my old schoolchum, Sir Woppity Wotsit—or rather, his valet. Tottie thought he might have known Merton. Speaking as one valet to another, so to speak."

"Is Inspector Totman back?" I asked.

Roberts stood to attention, and said, "No, Sergeant Mortimer, Inspector Totman is not expected to return from Leatherhead, Surrey, until a late hour tonight."

You couldn't be angry with the boy. At least I couldn't. He had no respect for anybody, but he was a good lad. And he had an eye like a hawk. Saw everything and forgot none of it.

"I suppose by Sir Woppity Wotsit you mean Sir William Kelso," I said. "I didn't know he lived up this way."

Roberts pointed across the road. "Observe the august mansion. Five minutes ago you'd have found me in the basement, talking to a cockeyed churchwarden who thought Merton was in Surrey. As it is, of course."

I had a sudden crazy idea.

"Well, now you're going back there," I said. "I'm going to call on Sir William, and I want you handy. Would they let you in at the basement again, or are they sick of you?"

"Sarge, they just love me. When I went, they said, 'Must you go?' "

We say at the Yard, "Once a murderer, always a murderer." Perhaps that was why I had an absurd feeling that I should like young Roberts within call. Because I was going to tell Sir William Kelso what I'd been thinking about by the Leg of Mutton Pond. I'd only seen him once, but he gave me the idea of being the sort of man who wouldn't mind killing, but didn't like lying. I thought he would give himself away . . . and then—well, there might be a roughhouse, and young Roberts would be useful.

As we walked in at the gate together, I looked in my pocketbook for a card. Luckily I had one left, though it wasn't very clean. Roberts, who never missed anything, said, "Personally I always use blotting paper," and went on whistling. If I hadn't known him, I shouldn't have known what he was talking about. I said, "Oh, do you?" and rang the bell. I gave the maid my card, and asked if Sir William could see me, and at the same time Roberts gave her a wink, and indicated the back door. She nodded to him, and asked me to come in. Roberts went down and waited for her at the basement. I felt safer.

Sir William was a big man, as big as I was. But of course a lot older. He said, "Well, sergeant, what can I do for you?" twiddling my card in his fingers. He seemed quite friendly about it. "Sit down, won't you?"

I said, "I think I'll stand, Sir William. I wanted just to ask you one question if I might." Yes, I know I was crazy, but somehow I felt kind of inspired.

"By all means," he said, obviously not much interested.

"When did you first discover that Perkins was blackmailing Lady Hedingham?"

He was standing in front of his big desk, and I was opposite to him. He stopped fiddling with my card, and became absolutely still; and there was a silence so complete that I could feel it in every nerve of my body. I kept my eyes on his, you may be sure. We stood there, I don't know how long.

"Is that the only question?" he asked. The thing that

frightened me was that his voice was just the same as before. Ordinary.

"Well, just one more. Have you a Corona typewriter in your house?" You see, we knew that a Corona had been used, but there was nothing distinctive about it, and it might have been any one in a thousand. Just corroborative evidence again, that's all. But it told him that I knew.

He gave a long sigh, tossed the card into the wastepaper basket, and walked to the window. He stood there with his back to me, looking out but seeing nothing. Thinking. He must have stood there for a couple of minutes. Then he turned round, and to my amazement he had a friendly smile on his face. "I think we'd both better sit down," he said. We did.

"There is a Corona in the house which I sometimes use," he began. "I daresay you use one, too."

"I do."

"And so do thousands of other people—including, it may be, the murderer you are looking for."

"Thousands of people including the murderer," I agreed.

He noticed the difference, and smiled. "People" I had said, not "other people." And I didn't say I was looking for him. Because I had found him.

"So much for that. There is nothing in the actual wording of the typed message to which you would call my attention?"

"No. Except that it was exactly right."

"Oh, my dear fellow, anyone could have got it right. A simple birthday greeting."

"Anyone in your own class, Sir William, who knew you both. But that's all. It's Inspector Totman's birthday tomorrow—"(as he keeps telling us, damn him, I added to myself). "If I sent him a bottle of whisky, young Roberts—that's the constable who's in on this case, you may have seen him about, he's waiting for me now down below"—I thought this was rather a neat way of getting that in—"Roberts could make a guess at what I'd say, and so could anybody at the Yard who knows us both, and they wouldn't be far wrong. But *you* couldn't, Sir William."

He looked at me. He couldn't take his eyes off me. I wondered what he was thinking. At last he said:

"A long life and all the best, with the admiring good wishes of — — how's that?"

It was devilish. First that he had really been thinking it out, when he had so much else to think about, and then that he'd got it so right. That "admiring"; which meant that he'd studied Totman just as he was studying me, and knew how I'd play up to him.

"You see," he smiled, "it isn't really difficult. And the fact that my card was used is in itself convincing evidence of my innocence, don't you think?"

"To a jury perhaps," I said, "but not to me."

"I wish I could convince *you*," he murmured to himself. "Well, what are you doing about it?"

"I shall, of course, put my reconstruction of the case in front of Inspector Totman tomorrow."

"Ah! A nice birthday surprise for him. And, knowing your Totman, what do you think he will do?"

He had me there, and he knew it.

"I think *you* know him too, sir," I said.

"I do," he smiled.

"And me, I daresay, and anybody else you meet. Quick as lightning. But even ordinary men like me have a sort of sudden understanding of people sometimes. As I've got of you, sir. And I've a sort of feeling that, if ever we get you into a witness box, and you've taken the oath, you won't find perjury so much to your liking as murder. Or what the law calls murder."

"But *you* don't?" he said quickly.

"I think," I said, "that there are a lot of people who ought to be killed. But I'm a policeman, and what I think isn't evidence. You killed Perkins, didn't you?"

He nodded; and said, almost with a grin at me, "A nervous affection of the head, if you put it in evidence. I could get a specialist to swear to it." My God, he was a good sort of man. I was really sorry when they found him next day on the Underground. Or what was left of him. And yet what else could he do?

I was furious with Fred Mortimer. That was no way to end a story. Suddenly, like that, as if he were tired of it. I told him so.

"My dear little Cyril," he said, "it isn't the end. We're just coming to the exciting part. This will make your hair curl."

"Oh!" I said sarcastically. "Then I suppose all that you've told me so far is just introduction?"

"That's right. Now listen. On the Friday morning, before we heard of Sir William's death, I went in to report to Inspector Totman. He wasn't there. Nobody knew where he was. They rang up his block of flats. Now hold tight to the leg of the table or something. When the porter got into his flat, he found Totman's body. Poisoned."

"Good Heavens!" I ejaculated.

"You may say so. There he was, and on the table was a newly opened bottle of whisky, and by the side of it was a visiting card. And whose card do you think it was? *Mine!* And what do you think it said? 'A long life and all the best, with the admiring good wishes of—'*me*! Lucky for me I had had young Roberts with me. Lucky for me he had this genius for noticing and remembering. Lucky for me he could swear to the exact shape of the smudge of ink on that card. And I might add, lucky for me that they believed me when I told them word for word what had been said at my interview with Sir William, as I have just told you. I was reprimanded, of course, for exceeding my duty, as I most certainly had, but that was only official. Unofficially they were very pleased with me. We couldn't prove anything, naturally, and Sir William's death had looked as accidental as anything could, so we just had to leave it. But a month later I was promoted to inspector."

He filled his glass and drank, while I revolved his extraordinary story in my mind.

"The theory," I said, polishing my *pince-nez* thoughtfully, "was, I suppose, this. Sir William sent the poisoned whisky, not so much to get rid of Totman, from whom he had little to fear, as to discredit you by bringing you under suspicion, and entirely to discredit your own theory of the other murder."

"Exactly."

"And then, at the last moment he realized that he couldn't go on with it, or the weight of his crimes became suddenly too much for him, or—"

"Something of the sort. Nobody ever knew, of course."

I looked across the table with sudden excitement; almost with awe.

"Do you remember what he said to you?" I asked, giving the words their full meaning as I slowly quoted them. " 'The fact that my card was used is convincing evidence of my innocence.' And you said, 'Not to me.' And he said, 'I wish I could convince you.' *And that was how he did it!* The fact that your card was used *was* convincing evidence of your innocence!"

"With the other things. The proof that he was in possession of the particular card of mine which was used, and the certainty that he had committed the other murder. Once a poisoner, always a poisoner."

"True ... yes. ... Well, thanks very much for the story, Fred. All the same, you know," I said, shaking my head at him, "it doesn't altogether prove what you set out to prove."

"What was that?"

"That the simple explanation is generally the true one. In the case of Perkins, yes. But not in the case of Totman."

"Sorry, I don't follow."

"My dear fellow," I said, putting up a finger to emphasize my point, for he seemed a little hazy with the wine suddenly; "the *simple* explanation of Totman's death—surely?—would have been that *you* had sent him the poisoned whisky."

Superintendent Mortimer looked a little surprised.

"But I did," he said.

So now you see my terrible predicament. I could hardly listen as he went on dreamily: "I never liked Totman, and he stood in my way; but I hadn't seriously thought of getting rid of him, until I got that card into my hands again. As I told you, he dropped it into the basket, and turned to the window, and I thought, Damn it, *you* can afford to chuck about visiting cards, but I can't, and it's the only one I've got left, and if you don't want it, I do. So I bent down very naturally to do up my bootlace, and felt in the basket behind me, because of course it was rather an undignified thing to do, and I didn't want to be seen; and it was just as I was putting it into my pocket that I saw that inksmudge again, and I remembered that Roberts had seen it. And in a flash the whole plan came to me; simple; foolproof. And from that moment everything I said to him was in preparation of it. 'Course we were quite alone, but you never know who might be listening, and besides—" he twiddled the stem of his empty wineglass"—p'raps I'm like Sir William, rather tell the truth than not, and it *was* true, all of it as I told the super, how Sir William came to know about Totman's birthday, and knew that those were the very words I should have used. Made it very convincing, me just repeating to the super what had really been said. Don't think I wanted to put anything on to Sir William that wasn't his. I liked him. But he as good as told me he wasn't going to wait for what was coming to him, and he'd done one murder anyway. That was why I slipped down with the bottle that evening, and left it outside Totman's flat. Didn't dare wait till the morning, in case Sir William closed his account that night." He stood up and stretched himself. "Ah, well, it was a long time ago. Goodbye, old man, I must be off. Thanks for a grand dinner. Don't forget, you're dining with *me* next month. I've got a new cocktail for you. You'll like it."—He swaggered out, leaving me to my thoughts.

"Once a murderer, always a murderer. . . ." And tomorrow he will wake up and remember what he has told me! And I shall be the only person in the world who knows his secret! ...

Perhaps he won't remember. Perhaps he was drunk. . . .

In vino veritas. Wasn't it the younger Pliny who said that? A profound observation. Truth in the bottle. . . .

"Once a poisoner, always a poisoner. . . ."

"I've got a new cocktail for you. You'll like it."

Yes, but—shall I?

A Coffin of Rice
by Martin Limon

The scream from the King's quarters smashed through the inner sanctum of the Secret Garden and brought Chin Ga So, Chief of the Royal Guard, to a rigid sitting position amidst the jumble of his sweat-soaked blankets.

His stomach tightened like a fist preparing for battle. "It didn't work," he thought.

He rose and slipped on a full-length silk robe, richly embroidered with warring dragons and the portentous symbols of long-dead astrologers. He strapped on his sword and in a reflex movement pulled it slightly out of the scabbard and let it drop back into its finely honed position. When he slid back the door of his room, the Royal Food Taster was already there.

Cowering on all fours, he repeatedly bounced his forehead on the carefully raked gravel of the courtyard.

"They should have both eaten," he said. The words almost choked out of his throat. "I can't understand why she is alive."

"Silence!" Chin roared. He slipped on his sandals, stepped down into the courtyard, and stomped his foot down on the Food Taster's head.

Chin bent slightly forward and said it softly. "You vile issue of dog leavings." He rotated his foot and ground the Food Taster's head into the dirt. "If they are not both dead, you will soon wish that your ancestors had fornicated only with the sterile corpses of beasts."

He kicked his foot forward and the Foot Taster rolled over in the dust until he lay on his back with both arms and legs held up in the air like a supplicant canine.

Chin Ga So turned and strode toward the source of the scream.

The fragrant paths of the Secret Garden were interspersed with brightly colored pavilions and resplendent Royal Guards who came to attention and barked out a martial greeting as Chin passed. He came to a small lake that was in the center of the Secret Garden which was in the center of Kyongju, the capital of the Kingdom of Silla.

Only the sound of softly singing birds wafted across the placid, lily pad-filled waters. At the base of a small footbridge two soldiers, armed with pikes and swords, stood guard.

"Has anyone passed this way since I left you early this evening?"

"No one, sir." The young guards trembled.

Chin Ga So got up close to the guard who had spoken until he could see the beads of moisture forming around his wispy mustache. "You will die very slowly," he said, "if you are lying to me."

The guard swallowed hard. "No one has passed tonight, sir."

Chin stepped back and looked at the other guards standing at attention around the small lake. "Has anyone crossed the lake tonight?" he yelled.

They sounded off in unison. "No one, sir!"

He crossed the bridge quickly and unsheathed his sword.

The building was not large but exquisitely made with handcarved and brightly colored rafters and elegant upturned shingles on the roof. Small figurines of monkeys vigilantly straddled the shingles, guarding against evil spirits. Chin chuckled at the failure of the simian protectors to do their work today.

The Chief of the Royal Guard didn't charge into the building right away but instead walked completely around the small island. In the dim light of the dawn he checked carefully for any footprints in the neatly raked sand.

There were none.

He stepped up on the lacquered wooden porch, took off his sandals, and used his key to unlock and then slide back the wood paneled entranceway. He entered and closed the door behind him.

The quarters were just large enough for the King and a few privileged concubines that he chose to favor with his attentions. Chin stepped softly across the heated floor toward the soft whimpering coming from the bed-chamber of the Great King.

Lady Ahn sat on the wrinkled sleeping mats and bedcovers holding her face in her hands and crying softly.

The Great King of Silla, dressed only in his white linen bedclothes, lay face down on the mat. Chin Ga So kneeled and turned him over. A skein of twine rope was fastened around his neck, still biting hard into his constricted flesh. His eyes bulged and his tongue stuck out to one side of his mouth, as if he had made a last, mad face at his tormentor.

"What have you done, woman?" Chin yelled.

Lady Ahn threw her long shimmering black hair back and lifted her face to his. "I have done nothing!" she said. Small bits of solid black coal burned inside her eyes. A large purple welt stood out on her forehead, ob-scenely mocking the unblemished purity of her skin. "I must have been knocked unconscious. And when I awoke . . ." She looked over at the King.

Chin checked for the food. The intricately designed tray and the elegant chinaware remained untouched.

"You didn't eat?"

"No. We weren't hungry."

Chin realized that except for the concubine's whim-pering, the King's chamber had been unusually silent. The cheerful chirping of the King's pet bird, a colorful yet vile creature from some far off uncivilized land, was absent. The small but ornate birdcage was empty, and the little door had been left ajar.

"Did he let the bird out?"

"Yes. He often let him out to play."

"Wasn't he afraid he would escape?"

"No. All the windows and doors were closed."

"Where is the bird now?"

Lady Ahn looked around, puzzled. "I don't know. When we went to sleep he was still flitting about amongst the rafters."

Then someone had entered, Chin thought. "And your forehead?"

"It was the middle of the night." The lady lifted a delicate back hand to her forehead. "Someone grabbed me, and before I could react in any way, he rammed me against the post." She waved her free hand in the direction of the elaborately carved and decorated supporting beam in the center of the room.

Outside, the courtiers, servants, and the curious, who seemed to arise out of the shadows of the Secret Garden, were gathered along the shore in gawking, murmuring clusters.

"Clear them," Chin Ga So ordered and they were cleared.

He allowed no one to cross over to the island. Even the Royal Morticians were forced to wait impatiently on the shore. One by one Chin questioned the two dozen guards who had stood sentry around the lake during the night. Some of them had heard nothing, but a few reported hearing a soft thud in the night sometime after the Hour of the Rat. They had thought nothing of it and had not even bothered to report it, since the King was known to make even more rollicking reverberations during his nightly assignations.

The Royal Alchemist and the Royal Architect were summoned, and they searched the building for the means of surreptitious entry. Chin personally led Lady Ahn across the bridge to her entourage of ladies-in-waiting. She held onto him for balance as she walked and with her free hand held her stomach and looked very pale. A series of gruff and incongruous belches emanated from the lady's slim body, and Chin thought of how upset she must be, but in the fashion of the cultured people of Silla he ignored the impolitic bodily intrusions.

The sliding windows had all been latched and sealed for the night by the Royal Keeper of the Keys, and in any case if someone had approached a window he would have left footprints in the sand and the guards would have seen him easily. The white, lightly oiled paper that filled the window frame was unblemished and unbroken.

The Alchemist came up with a concoction of various powders and started a fire in the central heating system at the outside base of the building that sent red smoke billowing through the underground heating ducts. No smoke came up into the building but as expected ran through the heating ducts, warming the masonry below the highly polished wooden slat floors, and then escaped through the chimney on the opposite side of the building.

The heating system was working fine and allowed no entrance into the building. And from within the building there was no entrance to the heating flues or the chimney that might have provided the bird an escape.

Under Chin's close supervision the Architect checked the walls and the rafters. Each beam and wooden slat was handcarved and fitted perfectly into the grooves of another, making a strong and self-contained structure. No nails could be used in the construction of any residence of the King. His safety was paramount.

There was no way for the bird to have escaped, but somehow it had. And if it hadn't been for that incontrovertible fact, the fact that gave credence to Lady Ahn's assertion that someone had entered the building during the night, Chin Ga So would have been certain that Lady Ahn had herself killed the King.

She certainly had good reason to. Chin kept a dossier on all the King's concubines and knew well her background. She was from a poor farming family in the southern Kingdom of Paekche that had been robbed

of their lands when the armies of Silla invaded and
conquered some of their northern provinces. Paekche's
land holdings were sizeably reduced, but they, along
with the northern Kingdom of Koguryo which also
shared this rich peninsula of Asia, were constantly
plotting to overthrow the exalted Lord of Silla.

She was also known to be athletic and strong, having actually worked for a while in her childhood as a
common farm laborer. As she grew older her family realized the much greater value of her incomparable
beauty, and she was sold to the Royal Court.

The piece of twine that Chin had found around the
King's neck was just slightly longer than the length of
both his outstretched hands; from small finger to
thumb, from thumb to small finger.

The same size, he knew from experience, as Lady
Ahn's willowlike waist.

But the escaped bird proved that Lady Ahn's story
was true and that someone had indeed invaded the inner sanctum of the King's chambers and killed him in
his sleep. Chin's thorough investigation was making it
apparent to everyone in court that the only means of
access would have been through the front door. Besides Chin, only the Royal Keeper of the Keys could
provide that access.

But as to the number of powerful people in court
who could coerce the Keeper of the Keys into doing
their bidding—that number was limitless.

Chin rubbed his hands together and couldn't stop a
rivulet of spittle from escaping onto his long gray
beard.

He ordered the Keeper of the Keys tortured.

He also instructed the Royal Truth Seeker to be
careful with him and not to take his confession until
later. Chin would decide who, from amongst his enemies at court, he would accuse as the accomplice in the
King's murder.

One of the scullery maids approached Chin Ga So,
bowed deeply, and requested permission to clean the
King's room. Chin nodded absently, thinking about his

enemies at court, and thinking about how his plot to murder the King had been usurped by someone else.

Another assassin.

Maybe someone more ruthless than he.

The old woman carried the food tray out, rattling the chinaware in her nervousness. Walking slowly and still stroking his long gray beard, Chin Ga So followed her across the footbridge and into the washroom behind the King's kitchen.

The scrubwomen and cooks gasped in astonishment when he entered.

"Put down that tray!" he bellowed.

The woman dropped it clattering to the wash counter and clutched her stomach, backing up and bowing like a foraging hen.

"All of you, out!" The workers tumbled over themselves getting out of the room. "Except for you." He pointed at the maid who had carried the tray. He recognized her from somewhere.

"You're from Paekche, aren't you?"

The woman's skin went as white as one of the plucked ducks hanging by their webbed feet along the back wall.

"You are Lady Ahn's personal servant." It wasn't a question. Chin remembered her now.

He turned to the tray and lifted some of the porcelain lids that covered the various bowls and dishes. There was bean curd with shoots of green onions in a red sauce, a delicately flavored bean-sprout soup, and, of course, two bowls of rice.

The glutinous white rice was packed evenly into the bowls, the surfaces perfectly symmetrical and rounded as if they had been pressed down with the curved contours of a very large spoon.

Not one grain was out of place.

A food presentation fit for a king.

Lovely and unblemished, the rice had been laced with the strongest poison known to civilized man.

If he allowed the greedy servants to eat it, they would all die. Worse, his plot would be revealed, and he and the Royal Food Taster would suffer a painful and ignominious death.

Chin fumbled with the food. He didn't throw it into the garbage, the servants would just sell it later to the poor people of Kyongju, but into the night soil container, so as to fertilize the rich fields of the Kingdom of Silla.

It was when he turned over the second bowl of rice that he saw the small, crushed body.

The bird.

Then he heard the scream.

When he got to her quarters, the ladies-in-waiting were running about and crying, and the Royal Physician was already being summoned to the scene.

Shin, the Royal Food Taster, caught Chin at the entrance to Lady Ahn's small compound and dragged him by the elbow off into the shadows of the Secret Garden.

"She must have eaten some of the food," he said. "Blood is seeping from her eyes and her nose, just as it would from my poison."

"But it took so long," Chin said.

"Maybe she ate very little. She is known," Shin said, "to eat little more than a bird."

Chin stroked his long gray beard for a moment, looked up suddenly at Shin, the Royal Food Taster, and then burst into uproarious laughter.

Lady Ahn must have hidden the remains of the crushed bird under the unblemished rice in hopes of fooling any investigator into believing that someone had entered the room. To make space enough for it, she had been forced to eat some of the poisoned rice, put the bird in the bottom of the bowl, and then make it look as if the food had not been touched.

Afterwards she rammed her head into the post to complete the facade.

She must have known that someone with the key to the front door, and the loyalty of the guards—through threat or bribery—would have been able to enter the chamber. That could be any number of powerful people at court, and after the death of the King, those in nominal but temporary power would seize upon their chance to root out their enemies and thereby improve their position at court.

After realizing the possibilities for gain, any rational investigator would not probe too deeply into the death of the King.

She hadn't counted on the obstinacy of Chin Ga So—or the poisoned rice.

He would have the scullery maid killed, Chin thought, for some trivial offense, and then the only person in the world besides himself who would have knowledge of the plot would be Shin the Royal Food Taster.

"Maybe she ate only enough," Chin said, laughing and slapping Shin on the back, "to hollow out a coffin for a bird. A coffin of rice!"

He laughed and laughed until slowly Shin's wrinkled face began to relax and his eyes got very wide and then he began to laugh, too. They were doubled over and almost crying in their mirth and so glad to have had someone do their dirty work for them and then slowly Chin Ga So stood up, wiped his eyes with the back of his hand, and as quick as a white crane darting for a fish, he pulled out his shimmering metal sword and decapitated Shin the Royal Food Taster.

The Gourmet Kidnaper
by Jack Ritchie

We were not notified of the kidnaping until after the
ransom had been paid and the victim returned unharmed, which took the immediacy out of it.

"How much was paid?" Ralph asked.

"Fifty thousand dollars," Cunningham said.

I pondered. Only fifty thousand dollars? That seemed
like a rather conservative figure for this day and age,
considering that Albert Cunningham's visible estate
consisted of acres of wooded and landscaped grounds, a
tremendous house, and a covey of functional and recre-
ational outbuildings.

We were in a drawing room considerably larger than
my entire apartment and twice as high. Cunningham
and his daughter, Stephanie, sat side by side on a sofa
opposite.

Cunningham commenced the details. "Monday evening I returned from the city at around eight and
stopped my car at the chain we keep across the driveway. Just as I was about to unhitch it, a man stepped
out of the darkness of some bushes and pointed a gun
at me."

"Could you describe him?" Ralph asked.

"Everything about him seemed about average, except for his full beard. That, of course, I later saw, in
a better light, was false."

I grasped the significance of the beard. "Obviously a
disguise."

Cunningham studied me for a moment, then continued, "He led me down the road a hundred yards or so
to another automobile parked at the side of the road."

"Did you get the license number?" Ralph asked, with the faintest of hope.

"I'm afraid not. It was too dark. He then ordered me to lie down on the rear floor of the car where he tied and blindfolded me."

"Was there anyone else in the car?"

"No. My kidnaper appeared to be alone. He drove for more than an hour before he finally stopped."

I nodded sagaciously. "The time of travel is unlikely to give us any true indication of exactly how far he took you from here. He could have made all kinds of devious turns so that you would have no idea of his true route."

Cunningham agreed. "When he finally stopped the car, he untied me, but left me blindfolded. He guided me into a building and down some stairs. When he removed my blindfold, I found that I was in a room approximately twelve by ten feet, its walls consisting of cinder blocks. There were no windows and only one door—a rather heavy one with metal sheathing and which, of course, was kept locked."

"What were the furnishings of this room?" I asked.

"Just a cot, a small table, a chair, and a small electric heater."

"Any reading materials?" I asked.

"No. I spent my time lying on the cot."

"A pity," I said. "You should have requested reading materials. Magazines, specifically."

Naturally they looked at me.

I chuckled. "It is entirely possible that the kidnaper subscribes to magazines, as almost all of us non-kidnapers do. And in an unthinking moment he might have gathered together an armful of his old magazines and brought them to you, forgetting that his mailing address would be on the cover of each one. Had he done this, we would now know his name, address, and the expiration dates of his magazines."

Stephanie Cunningham smiled benevolently. "On the other hand, if my father had been given the magazines, perhaps the kidnaper would belatedly have real-

ized that there were address labels on their covers and
that he would then have to kill him to protect his iden-
tity."

She smiled at her father now. "Daddy, do you realize
that you very likely saved your own life by not asking
for magazines?"

I cleared my throat. "Did you hear any noises?
Sounds which might enable you to pinpoint your place
of confinement? The whistle of a train on a regular
schedule? The roar of airplanes? The howling of
dogs?"

"No. Nothing at all, as far as I can recall."

"How long were you kept in this room?" Ralph
asked.

"Three days and almost four nights. I never set foot
out of that room until Friday morning at about five
A.M. when he drove me out into the country and left
me tied and blindfolded beside a road. I easily managed to free myself in five minutes and walked to a
farmhouse where I phoned Stephanie. She came and
picked me up about an hour later."

I drew Ralph to the other side of the room where
they could not overhear us.

"Ralph, I don't know what the motive is, but this
whole thing could be a fraud. The man was never kidnaped."

"What makes you say that, Henry?"

"The contents of the room."

"What about the contents of the room?"

"Cunningham claims that he was confined to that
room for three days and four nights. He also claims
that he never left the room for any purpose whatsoever.
Yet he made no mention of sanitary facilities. Surely
during the course of three days and four nights, he
must have had to ..." I delicately left the sentence
hanging in the air.

Ralph thought about that, but not for long. "I'll ask
him if there was a lavatory."

"Ralph," I cautioned, "if you put the question to him
direct, he will, of course, realize the flaw in his fabri-

cation and quickly create a mythical bathroom for his chimerical place of detention. No, Ralph, I will cleverly question him and back him into a corner."

We rejoined the Cunninghams.

Cunningham spoke first. "By the way, I forgot to mention that there was a chemical toilet in a corner of the room. One of those things that people put in their fishing and hunting cabins."

I cleared my throat. "There is one thing that bothers me. You say that you were dropped off in the countryside after five A.M. this morning. You walked to the nearest farmhouse and phoned. Your daughter picked you up an hour later, which means that it also must have taken her approximately that long to return here. In other words, you got back home before seven this morning, yet you did not phone the police until after eleven."

There was silence on the part of Cunningham and then he sighed. "To tell you the truth, I wasn't at all certain whether I should call the police or not. He really wasn't such a bad fellow at all. Quite polite, and he kept reassuring me that I had nothing at all to worry about. He said that even if the ransom were not paid, he would still release me unharmed at the end of the week."

I shrugged. "Undoubtedly a ploy to neutralize any attempt to escape."

"Perhaps," Cunningham said. "However, he also urged me to think of the fifty thousand dollars as a loan. He would pay it all back some day, plus any reasonable amount of interest I might choose to impose."

Cunningham sighed. "When I got home I gave the matter considerable thought. I wondered whether I really should create additional trouble for the man. He might legitimately and desperately need the money. And, after all, what is fifty thousand dollars?"

Ralph and I looked at each other.

"To me," Cunningham added.

Stephanie smiled. "We finally decided that perhaps it was our duty as citizens to report the matter to the

police, on the assumption that no matter what the mit-
igating circumstances, kidnaping is still an anti-social
act." She glanced at her watch. "It is high noon and
feeding time. Would you care to join us?"

"Well," Ralph said, "maybe some coffee."

In the dining room, however, places had already
been set for Ralph and me and we did not protest.

I buttered a slice of white bread. "You say that this
man wore a false beard? You never saw him without
it?"

"Never. I wouldn't be able to identify him without
it. However . . ."

I pounced. "However what?"

"Well, there *was* something slightly familiar about
him. Something about his eyes and his forehead. And
yet I am positive that I never saw him before in my
life."

"Are you certain that your kidnaper was a man?" I
asked. "After all, a beard can be quite comprehensive."

Cunningham selected a slice of rye bread. "He wore
a T-shirt occasionally."

Ralph put marmalade on his white bread. "There
was just this one man? He didn't have any accom-
plices?"

"If he did, I didn't see them."

Stephanie took her white bread without butter or
marmalade.

That made it three white. One rye. Why did it strike
me that there could be something of significance in
that?

Stephanie supplied further information. "I got the
phone call at about midnight. The man told me that
he'd kidnaped my father and he wanted fifty thousand
dollars for his return. Small bills, naturally. He said
he'd give me three days to get it together and then he
would phone again and give me directions on how to
get the money to him. I was not to call the police or he
would kill Dad."

Cunningham corroborated. "He apologized to me for

having to make the threat, but felt that in a situation like this it was *de rigueur*."

Stephanie agreed. "I got the money together and he phoned again Thursday night, which was yesterday. He told me to put the money into a briefcase and drive west on Highway 94 until I got to the turnoff ramp for Ionia. At the bottom of the ramp I would find an arterial stop sign. I was to leave the briefcase in the tall grass beside it. And I did. Then I found the entrance ramp and went back up onto Highway 94. Actually, I saw the kidnaper pick up the money. He must have been waiting."

I frowned thoughtfully. "You mean that you actually saw the briefcase being picked up?"

"Yes. From up on the highway. I looked back down and the ramp is lighted, you know. And I saw this bearded man appear, pick up the briefcase, and scoot toward a car parked at the side of the road."

"Did you, by any remote chance, follow him? At least long enough to get his license number?"

"No. I didn't want to do anything that might alarm him. After all, he still had my father."

I turned to Cunningham. "Did this kidnaper seem to be intelligent?"

He blinked. "Well, I didn't give him an I.Q. test, but from what talk we had I'd say he could easily hold his own."

I addressed Stephanie. "Who else besides you knew about the kidnaping?"

"No one. I didn't even tell the servants. As far as they're concerned, my father was simply off on a business trip."

My eyes went to the bit of rye bread in Cunningham's fingers. "During your days of confinement, what were you fed? Hamburgers? Hot dogs? TV-dinners?"

"No. As a matter of fact, the meals I was served were actually delicious. My kidnaper was a superb cook. I ate everything brought to me."

"You kidnaper cooked those meals for you? How do you know?"

"He told me. I mean after Wednesday's *Weiner Schnitzel* I offhandedly said, 'Give my compliments to the cook,' and he told me that he did all the cooking himself."

"Mr. Cunningham, are you allergic to white bread?"

"No."

"Then you eat rye bread by choice?"

"Yes. I just don't like the taste of white bread." He thought for a moment. "But I do happen to be allergic to tomatoes. They make me break out in a rash."

I was on the scent. "You mentioned that during your confinement you ate everything presented to you. Did that include white bread?"

"There was no white bread. Just rye."

I nodded relentlessly. "You had three breakfasts, three luncheons, and three dinners?"

"Yes."

"And at these luncheons and dinners, were you served a salad?"

"Yes."

"The same salad every time?"

"No. They were varied."

"And in any of these six salads, did you find a single shred or bit of tomato?"

"No."

"Ha," I said. "And you were served rye bread? Not white?"

"Rye bread."

"Did you *request* this rye bread?"

"No. It came with the food."

"No white bread was ever offered instead of rye?"

"No."

I smiled triumphantly. "Mr. Cunningham, we live in a white-bread society. White bread is automatically offered at every meal. And yet it was not offered to you even once. And further, despite being served six varied salads, not one of them contained so much as a sliver of tomato." I rubbed my hands. "All the pieces are beginning to fit together."

"That's nice," Stephanie said.

I nodded. "First of all, does it not strike you as rather odd that the kidnaper would leap out of the bushes to claim the ransom money practically as the depositor's taillights were disappearing into the darkness? Should he not have cautiously waited for at least a little while, on the possibility that this might be a police trap? How did he *know* that the police had not been called into the case?"

None of them, of course, had the answer.

I smiled grimly. "He *knew* that the police had not been brought into the case because his *accomplice* had given him that information. And that accomplice is in this very house."

There was an awed silence and then Stephanie said, "But the only person in this house who knew about the kidnaping and that I did not call the police is me. Are you saying that I had a part in this kidnaping just because I get a miserly allowance and need the extra spending money desperately?"

Cunningham smiled fondly. "I've arranged that Stephanie gets no substantial amount of money from me until she's thirty and has accomplished something in this world on her own. I think it builds character, or it should."

Stephanie pursued her point. "Are you insinuating that just because my father said that the kidnaper looked vaguely familiar—despite that itchy false beard—that he might have been one of my numerous boy friends and that we are were in cahoots?"

"Tut, tut," I said charitably. "I have other fish to fry. Let me reconstruct the 'compliments to the cook' incident. When you uttered those words, Mr. Cunningham, did your kidnaper not *blink* first, and then, quickly recovering, say that *he* did the cooking?"

"What are you getting at, Henry?" Ralph asked.

I nailed it down. "This kidnaper knew Mr. Cunningham's eating preferences and allergies. He did not have to be told."

Ralph was not impressed. "So he did a little research on Cunningham before he pulled the snatch."

I shook my head. "That simply doesn't wash, Ralph. What kidnaper would risk his precious anonymity by going about asking the food idiosyncracies of his intended victim? If he were so concerned about the matter, it is much more likely that he would ask his victim *after* he had kidnaped him. Mr. Cunningham, who knows that you eat only rye bread and are allergic to tomatoes?"

"I suppose a lot of my friends might. After all, I've led a full life."

"Your meals were served piping hot?"

"Yes."

I chuckled. "Do you know *why* your kidnaper blinked and suddenly volunteered the information that *he* was the one who did the cooking?"

Cunningham rubbed his jaw. "I still don't remember the blink."

"I assure you, sir, there *was* a blink. And for a very good reason. When you offered your compliments to the cook, your kidnaper suddenly realized that there existed the possibility that you might *recognize* the cooking. And he wanted to thwart that immediately."

"Recognize the cooking?"

I nodded. "Are you familiar with your own basement? Your own cellars?"

"Not particularly. I suppose there are probably some parts of this house where I've never set foot."

"I thought as much. It is my contention that when you were bound and blindfolded, you were driven in a great circle and brought directly *back to your own home* and led to a place of confinement in your own cellars."

There was a respectful silence and then Ralph said, "How do you arrive at that, Henry."

"The kidnaper had to have an accomplice. Someone who *knew* what Mr. Cunningham did and did not eat. Someone who could prepare delicious meals and see that they were served piping hot. And being here on the premises, the kidnaper would have *known* that the police had not been called into the case and that it was safe to pick up the money."

My smile wrapped things up. "I do not know her name. I have never seen her before, but I'll wager that if you step into your own kitchen, you will find your cook dreaming about what she will do with her share of fifty thousand dollars."

Cunningham's face became extremely thoughtful.

I rose. "Shall we interrogate the cook? What is her name, by the way?"

"Matilda," Cunningham said. He seemed to pull himself together. "There is just one thing wrong with your theory, Sergeant Turnbuckle."

"What is that?"

"The meals I ate in that basement room were absolutely delicious. And the simple fact is that our Matilda is a terrible cook."

Stephanie confirmed that. "Frankly we would fire her, but she's such a dear soul and she means well and tries her best."

I looked down at my plate. Here, while I had been talking, I had also been wrestling with a portion of stubborn Swiss steak. Also the mashed potatoes were lumpy and watery. The broccoli was definitely dead. There was no question about it, Matilda was a dreadful cook.

I sipped some coffee, which was bitter. "On the other hand, for those three days, Matilda may very cleverly have cooked superb meals just to throw us off the track."

Ralph had had enough to eat too. "I guess we'll be getting back to headquarters now."

In our car I brooded. "It is still possible that this kidnaping never took place at all. Or, if it did, Stephanie may indeed have had a part in it. We will have to observe if she spends above her allowance, whatever that is."

On Monday, a little after quitting time, Ralph had already gone home, when the phone at our desk rang. I glanced about hoping someone else would answer it, but no one was available. I picked up the receiver.

It was Stephanie Cunningham. "How is the case going?"

"We are diligently pursuing the matter. Something may break at any moment."

"Just as I thought. You're hopelessly stymied. How about coming over to our place for dinner tonight?"

A thought came to me. It had never been officially ascertained whether Stephanie herself might not secretly be a magnificent cook. Perhaps if I craftily got her to prepare a—

"We're starting to invite people over for dinner again," Stephanie said. "We've got a new cook and he's absolutely superb."

"He?"

"Yes. Father had a little talk with Matilda after you left and accidentally discovered that she had a brother who's a chef in a Sheboygan restaurant. So he drove right up there and hired him."

"What about Matilda?"

"We're not throwing her out into the cold. She'll be his assistant or whatever. Franz was just about to open a restaurant up there, but Daddy somehow persuaded him to come and work for us. Daddy claims that Franz is so good he's already paid him two years' salary in advance."

At the Cunninghams residence I found the occasion to peek into the kitchen.

I saw a short stocky man with blondish hair and a slightly bulging forehead, presiding cheerfully over steaming pots on the kitchen range.

I also saw a short stocky woman with blondish hair and a slightly bulging forehead, amiably chopping onions.

I pictured them both wearing beards. Yes, the bulging foreheads would suggest a certain filial relationship, which had, however, escaped Cunningham's attention until my words had created a comparison.

Had Matilda been Franz's accomplice?

I doubted it. Otherwise she would not have been so free to volunteer that she had a brother in Sheboygan.

But she and Franz had probably exchanged visits now and then, during which time Franz had learned of Cunningham's food preferences. And during the kidnaping itself—and Franz had probably taken Cunningham to some Sheboygan area cellar—he had undoubtedly phoned Matilda daily and learned in casual conversation that no member of the household staff was aware of the kidnaping and that obviously therefore the police had not been called into the case.

Had Cunningham presented Franz with an ultimatum? Exposure or kitchen service?

And could I now get Cunningham to testify against his new jewel of a cook? Do people who go to great lengths to find good cooks volunteer to send them to prison?

Of course not.

Ah, well.

At dinner I found the beef with Chinese black mushrooms absolutely delicious.

My Compliments
to the Chef

by Marge Blaine

I was a cook. A *chef extraordinaire*. One of those people who knows which comes first, the chicken or the egg. It's the chicken, of course. You save the eggs for dessert—in a soufflé perhaps.

Who would have thought, when I first opened my restaurant, that it would become so big a success? Or that it would lead to my becoming involved with the man in the black suit. Certainly not me! I'd never quite believed that people like Big Charlie even existed.

Cooking's been my passion for years. There are pictures of me at five or six, my braids pinned to the top of my head, standing on a stool so I can reach the stove, stirring a *sauce bechamel*. While I was still in my teens I took over all the family parties—Christmas, Thanksgiving, birthdays—planning and preparing food for more than a dozen people. That's when I began creating my own recipes—flaky desserts, smooth sauces, unusual combinations of flavors and textures.

Then there were the courses at the Cordon Bleu in Paris where I was the youngest student ever accepted. And my stint as a *sous-chef* at the four-star Paris Nuit. (I could tell you unbelievable tales about what goes on in their kitchen, only that's another story.) Afterward I was offered my choice of positions in France—in Paris, on the Riviera, and in the old walled city of Carcassonne. But I'd been away from my own country too long. I wanted to come back, to see if I could make it on my own turf.

The trip home was triumphant. I had free passage on the QEII in exchange for a series of lecture-demonstrations on the Nouvelle Cuisine. The audiences—middle-aged, mostly women—oohed and aahed over my garnishes and took notes assiduously. The talks, including preparation, took no more than three or four hours a day. For the rest of the time I was free.

That's when I met Mike. He was on his way back to the States too, after two years in the Peace Corps in North Africa. You might say it was love at first sight. It was certainly something at first sight. And not just because each of us had been relatively isolated for several years. We spent every available minute together, Mike joining the cooking group even though he didn't know a Cuisinart from a boning knife. We shared a table for two for late breakfasts—and my first-class cabin. By the end of the voyage we knew we belonged together forever.

We had some adjusting to do once we got back—looking for an apartment, becoming reacquainted with our families, getting married. Mike went to work for the Welfare Department. He said it wasn't much different from being in Africa, only here his clients had television sets so they could see what they were missing!

It was harder for me to find a job than I'd expected, given my qualifications. Most kitchens were still male bastions. In one place they even offered to hire me as a waitress! Me, who'd prepared soufflés for Princess Grace. Finally I was taken on as Pastry Assistant at Les Moules.

But my goal was not to become Pastry Chef or even Head Chef at a place like Les Moules. No, it was to open my own restaurant. Small yet elegant. Where I could experiment with food, create new dishes, earn my living the way I most enjoyed.

Fortunately Mike shared my dream. We saved frantically that first year, putting everything we could into our "restaurant fund." In our free time we explored the city, getting a feeling for its neighborhoods and people. And we began scouting for a location—off the beaten track so the rent would be affordable. Yet accessible enough so we could build a clientele. We dogged realtors, followed newspaper ads, checked out any promising lead.

There was the "long-established neighborhood restaurant" which turned out to be a bar and grill. The fast-food joint that touted "modern structure, plenty of free parking." Another had wall-to-wall cockroaches.

Then we found it. In one of those neighborhoods euphemistically called "changing." We just hoped it was changing for the better, not worse. There were still plenty of tenements and some deserted stores in the area, but there was an art school a few blocks away. And professionals were buying the shabby yet well-built rooming-houses, turning them back into elegant townhouses.

Let me pass briefly over the hassles of trying to open—workmen who didn't show up when they promised, the supplier who "forgot" to deliver the stoves.

Still, I was buoyed along by the excitement. I searched out the best sources for produce, meat, and fresh fish. And I haunted the small neighborhood antique shops. The décor was going to be as distinctive as the menu.

Finally we installed the sign on top of our front window. *RESTAURANT ROCHELLE,* it read, in ornate gold lettering. I'd thought we should call it Restaurant Rosalinda or Café Claudine to give it a French air, only Mike wouldn't hear of it. He insisted it be named after the chef. Why hadn't my parents thought of how my name would look on a marquee before they called me Rochelle!

Mike took a leave of absence from the Welfare Department. With him as manager and me as cook we'd be able to manage with a part-time assistant and one waitress—we hoped. It was all we could afford, even if things went well. And if they didn't? I tried not to think about that.

We found that our clientele consisted of three main types—older people, students, and the professionals from the area. The older people complained most and complimented least. The students stuck to tight budgets but tended to be appreciative. The professional people, couples in their thirties for the most part, spent more freely than the others, and fortunately, patronized us more often.

That's why I noticed the man in the black suit as soon as he came in. It was just before we opened one evening and I was checking the tables as I always did, to make sure everything was in place.

He was a tall beefy man in his fifties, stylishly dressed, but with an odd look about him. Perhaps it was the hat. I thought he'd come to the wrong place. He stood alone, at the entrance to the dining room, smoking a cigar, oblivious of the sign: *THANK YOU FOR NOT SMOKING IN THE DINING ROOM.*

One of my decisions had been to ban smoking. I hate restaurants where drifting smoke spoils the food. We'd set up a lounge in the lobby where people could smoke or have a glass of wine. So far it had worked out extremely well.

"Excuse me, sir," I said, walking toward him. "Smoking's not permitted in the dining room."

He seemed not to have heard. "I want to see the owner," he demanded in a deep harsh voice. He had broad shoulders, accentuated by the cut of his suit.

"I'm sorry, but there's no smoking in here. We'll have to go to the lounge."

He shoved the cigar into a corner of his mouth and glared at me. "Listen, I said the owner."

"I'm the owner," I told him, trying to keep my voice pleasant. It doesn't do to alienate anyone in this line of work, potential customer or not. "Let's go into the lobby—or my office." I turned, hoping he'd follow. I didn't have many options if he didn't.

I sat down behind my desk and pushed an ashtray toward him, putting my hands in my lap so he wouldn't see that they were shaking.

"Yes. What do you want?" I asked.

"You really the owner?"

I nodded.

"Pleased to meet'cha." He grimaced in what was probably meant to be a smile. "I seen all the work going on. Want to wish you luck in the new place. You've been open what now, three-four weeks?"

"Four weeks on Sunday," I told him. "Do you live nearby?"

He stuck the cigar back into his mouth, puffed, and blew the smoke out, angling it slightly away from me, yet in my general direction. "Yeah, I live here. Lived here all my life. You mean no one's told you about Big Charlie?"

"No." I shook my head. The smell of the cigar was making me queasy. Or it might have been his flat unemotional tone. I didn't think any longer that his visit was a mistake.

"Well, I'm Big Charlie." he said. "This is my area. I keep tabs on all the people—me and my boys. We lend a little money here and there. Watch the businesses on the street. Make sure no one breaks the windows or holds you up on your way to the bank at ten thirty at night."

I shivered. How did he know I made a deposit at ten thirty? He must have been following me. Or had one of his "boys" on my trail.

He smiled again. "So we've been watching your place, waiting to see how you'd make out. A nice young couple, starting a new venture. I like to see that happen. And I've heard the food here's pretty good. Unusual but good. I'll have to try it sometime."

"I hope you will," I told him, proud owner to the core.

"Now, we wouldn't want anything to happen," he said. "Broken window, broken arm, explosion in the kitchen, would we?"

"Of course not!"

"No. It would slow down business, just when you're getting started. Might even put you out of business if enough went wrong. That's what happened to the shoemaker over on Fifth Street."

I shivered again. Pictures of me with a broken arm

or leg—or even with broken fingers—flashed through my mind. And what if they hurt Mike?

"So we'll keep an eye out," he told me. "I'll assign someone to you, special. Your windows stay good. No robberies. No trouble of any kind. Any trouble you bring it straight to me, Big Charlie. It's all part of the deal."

The smell of cigar smoke combined with what he was saying were making me feel dizzy. He was strongarming me, here in my own restaurant. Big Charlie wanted to protect me all right—protect me from him! That's all I needed, an extortionist for a partner; we could barely manage the way things were.

"Ummm. How much would this cost?" I asked timidly.

He leaned back in the chair. "Five hundred a month."

I gasped. "I can't pay that!"

"Of course you can. Maybe not right away. But once you get on your feet, sure. Listen, I'm not going to interfere with your business. I'll give you a couple of weeks—start collecting the end of next month. How's that?"

In another month we might be on our feet, sure, I thought. But the most we figured we would clear was one or two thousand a month. Five hundred would drain us. We'd never show a profit. I needed time to think, to decide what to do about Big Charlie's threat. I couldn't afford to make a mistake. But he sat there, making no move to leave.

Finally I got up. "I have to get back to the kitchen now—my helper can't handle it alone. Are you staying for dinner?"

He stood too, taking another puff of his cigar. "Maybe I will. See if the food's as good as they say."

"Leave the cigar here, please," I told him firmly. "You can't smoke in the dining room."

Mike could see that I was upset. He raised his eyebrows quizzically as I passed, but there was no time to tell him what had happened. For the next two hours I sautéed, puréed, whipped, and stirred, Big Charlie never far from my thoughts. What could I do about his threat? Pay? Risk an accident? No solution came to mind.

As I worked I kept an eye on the dining room. Big Charlie did enjoy the meal. He nodded over the *Daurade Farci Aux Amandes* and smiled (a grim smile to be sure) when he tasted the *Tarte aux Pommes*.

When coffee was served, I saw his hand stray to his jacket pocket as if for a cigar, only he caught himself and brought his hand away empty. I took his check to his table myself.

"How was everything?" I asked.

"Very good. Excellent food. I'll be back." He pulled out a hefty bankroll, held by a gold clip, and paid the bill, leaving an enormous tip for Marie. She'd be pleased at any rate.

Everyone has a different way of dealing with problems. You might think, being in the line of work I am, that I'd eat. Or break dishes. I know some chefs who throw knives. But when I'm upset I cook. So in a way Big Charlie's threat was good for business. I came up with three variations on my basic paté the next day. But no solution to my dilemma.

The next time Big Charlie came in I took his order myself, a practice I followed with extremely difficult or especially favored customers. I suggested the veal, one of my new specialties. It was called *Escalopes de Veau Chasseau*, but privately I thought of it as *Escalopes de Veau Grand Charles* because he'd been on my mind when I'd created it.

"Delicious," Big Charlie told me when he'd finished eating. "I never tasted anything quite like that before. What was it?"

"Veal," I told him, "in a mushroom, tomato, and wine sauce with my own combination of herbs."

"Aaaah. Mama used to make that. Only she called it *Scallopini*. I never liked it when I was a boy. But the way you make it . . ." He kissed two fingers and held them in the air. "Reasonable prices, too." He leaned toward me. "You could charge more here, you know.

Two-three dollars more a plate. You wouldn't have any trouble paying up then."

"I can't." I shook my head. "We wouldn't attract the same crowd. The students would never be able to afford it. Things would change and I don't want them to."

"You think about it," he said, sounding almost fatherly. "You have until next month, remember?"

"I know. How could I forget?"

Big Charlie started coming in regularly, twice a week. I didn't want to see him, much less feed him. On the other hand, I was proud of my cooking. And I enjoyed his appreciation.

Still, fantasies of how to get rid of him occupied me on and off during the day. I'd find the perfect, undetectable poison and slip it into his espresso. Stab him behind the ear with a stiletto. I who couldn't bring myself to set a mousetrap! How could I kill a man?

The tension kept me on my toes in the kitchen, though. During that second week I turned out one inventive dish after another to the delight of my regulars. We hadn't planned to invite the critics yet, but someone must have tipped them off. It could have been the junior editor of *The Times*. Or maybe Big Charlie sent them. In any case, once the write-ups appeared, there was no denying our success. You couldn't get in without a reservation.

Still, profits were limited. They'd always be unless we raised our prices, cut down on the quality of food, or pushed the tables closer together. If we paid off Big Charlie, he'd come out ahead. It made me furious to think of his walking off with most of our profits.

We'd gone over our options again and again. There had to be a way out—if only we could think of it. But Mike was leaving the final decision up to me. "You're the cook," he said. "The owner. You're Rochelle. Either we pay or we don't pay. We could sell the restaurant, you know. I can always go back to the Welfare Department. You'll get another job. We won't starve.

It'll be easier than running this place. And safer than ending up in the river in a hunk of cement."

"But we can't give it up. Not after all our work, all our planning. The restaurant's exactly the way I dreamed it would be. I can't lose it!"

"Then we'll pay him what he asks, honey." Mike held me tenderly. He was a man in a million. "It isn't worth getting hurt for. And he's a guy who'll do what he says. I can smell it."

On Friday I served a shoulder of lamb stuffed with rosemary-flavored wild rice. And I found the answer to a problem that had eluded me for years—the perfect substitute for truffles.

I didn't see Big Charlie come in. I didn't even know he was there until the new waitress we'd had to hire whispered, "There's someone who says he wants to see you out front."

Big Charlie was sitting at a table for four that I knew had been reserved for one of the art teachers. He leered at me as I approached. "It looked as if I wouldn't get a table tonight," he said. "You're doing very well."

"How did you? I thought we were booked up."

"You were. But I found some twerp who was willing to settle for twenty bucks instead of a table. Simple, my dear. Money. Money always wins out. Money and power."

I felt myself steaming. He had them both. Money and power. Enough for his needs. More than enough. Five hundred dollars a month wouldn't make a bit of difference to him—not the way it would to us.

"My compliments to the chef. You're getting better and better." He waved his arm around the room. "A big success. Every table filled. People lining up to get in."

"Yes. We're doing all right. But it took years of training. And we don't make as much as you might think in a restaurant. There are all kinds of expenses."

"I know. I know. Don't you think I costed it before I gave you a price? You can manage the five hundred. Maybe not easily, but you can manage."

I stalked into the kitchen and began mincing parsley with a vengeance. Money didn't mean anything to him. I didn't mean anything to him. He just wanted to control me, run my restaurant. I'd be working for Big Charlie instead of for myself. I almost wished I was one of those knife-throwing chefs—I'd show him a thing or two.

The waitresses finished cleaning up and left. I told Mike to go on home, I needed to work late. I started preparations for an aspic, *Hue de Saumon au Citron et au Poivre Vert*, a time-consuming dish, but I needed to think. Maybe I could figure out a plan while waiting for the layers to jell. There had to be something we hadn't thought of, some way to keep the money and stay safe.

Finally, as I was shaving thin slices of lemon for the garnish, I came up with a fantastic plan. Only I didn't know if I could pull it off. A lot depended on Big Charlie. But more depended on me, whether I could make him knuckle under, the way he wanted me to.

Big Charlie made a reservation for late Friday night, the date the money was due. I was so nervous all week that I outdid myself, creating two new dessert soufflés, one with pears, the other with oranges and Cointreau. And I planned to serve *Truite en Papillote a L'Aneth et au Citron*, an impressive dish.

On Friday I waited until Big Charlie had finished his coffee, then brought his check to his table. "Ready for me?" he asked.

I nodded. "Come into my office," I said. "It's more private there."

I sat down behind my desk, put his check face down in front of me, and waited until he was seated. I was nervous, yet strangely at ease now that the time had come.

"You can smoke in here if you like," I told him.

He took a cigar from an inner pocket, snipped off one end, and lit it up. "Well," he said between puffs. "Let's have the money."

I watched the smoke drifting past me, steadying myself for what I had to say.

"Was everything all right tonight?" I asked.

"Of course. I already told you. You make the best food I've ever had. And it's comfortable here, too. Not like them snooty places uptown. Why else do you think I come here twice a week regular? I've never eaten so well in my life."

I was hoping he'd say that—counting on it, as a matter of fact. I tried to play on his sympathies. "Listen. You know we work hard here, Mike and I. Harder than when we had regular jobs. I'm at the market most mornings before six. And I'm here till long after midnight."

"But you love it."

"That's true. But you'll be bleeding us, skimming the cream from the milk, taking the meringue off the top of the pie."

Big Charlie shrugged. "Hey! It's my business."

"Please." I tried one more time. "Can't you let us off?"

"Are you kidding? If word got around that Big Charlie let anyone off the hook—" He made a slicing motion across his neck. "That would be it. I can't, even if I wanted to."

I knew then he'd never change his mind. "All right," I said. "I guess we'll have to pay—somehow."

I handed him the check. He turned it over, looked at the amount I'd put down, and turned red.

"Eighty-five dollars!" he exploded. "What's that for? The bill's usually twenty, maybe twenty-five bucks. What's going on?"

"A special bill for a special customer," I explained, hoping he couldn't hear the pounding of my heart. "I'm going to have extra expenses from now on that have to be covered."

He did a quick calculation. "Eighty-five dollars a meal, that's a hundred and seventy a week—about seven hundred bucks a month. You mean you're making it up on *me*?"

I nodded.

Big Charlie slammed his hand on the table and stood up. I thought he might hit me. Instead he began pacing back and forth. He could only manage two steps in either direction in my small office. Big Charlie said something in a language I didn't understand, then he slammed his fist on my desk and made a roaring sound. At first I thought it was anger, then I realized he was laughing.

"All right. All right," he sputtered. "I'll pay the bill, all the bills, every time I'm here. Only tell me. How come it's eighty-five dollars, seven hundred a month, instead of five? You only have to pay me five, right?"

"Yes," I told him sweetly. "I need five hundred for protection money. But you still have to pay for your dinner, don't you?"

Big Charlie put a hundred-dollar bill on my desk, shook his head and started toward the door. "See you on Tuesday," he said. "And make sure there's a table for me—a good one. Tell any twerp who's waiting, 'Big Charlie's first.' Remember, my usual days, Tuesday and Friday."

"I'll remember." He'd better keep coming, I told myself. Knowing that Big Charlie would be around regularly would keep me on my toes, nervous enough to assure perfection. I had to keep him as a satisfied customer.

Lamb to the Slaughter
by Roald Dahl

The room was warm and clean, the curtains drawn, the two table lamps alight—hers and the one by the empty chair opposite. On the sideboard behind her, two tall glasses, soda water, whiskey. Fresh ice cubes in the Thermos bucket.

Mary Maloney was waiting for her husband to come home from work.

Now and again she would glance up at the clock, but without anxiety, merely to please herself with the thought that each minute gone by made it nearer the time when he would come. There was a slow smiling air about her, and about everything she did. The droop of the head as she bent over her sewing was curiously tranquil. Her skin—for this was her sixth month with child—had acquired a rather wonderful translucent quality; the mouth was soft, and the eyes, with their new placid look, seemed larger, darker than before.

When the clock said ten minutes to 5, she began to listen, and a few moments later, punctually as always, she heard the tires on the gravel outside, and the car door slamming, the footsteps passing the window, the key turning in the lock. She laid aside her sewing, stood up, and went forward to kiss him as he came in.

"Hullo, darling," she said.

"Hullo," he answered.

She took his coat and hung it in the closet. Then she walked over and made the drinks, a strongish one for him, a very weak one for herself; and soon she was back again in her chair with the sewing, and he in the other opposite, holding the tall glass with both his hands, rocking it so the ice cubes tinkled against the side.

For her this was always a blissful time of day. She knew he didn't want to speak much until the first drink was finished, and she, on her side, was content to sit quietly, enjoying his company after the long hours alone.

She loved to luxuriate in the presence of this man, and to feel—almost as a sunbather feels the sun—that warm male glow that came out of him to her when they were alone together. She loved him for the way he sat loosely in a chair, for the way he came in a door, or moved slowly across the room with long strides. She loved the intent, far look in his eyes when they rested on her, the funny shape of the mouth, and especially the way he remained silent about his tiredness, sitting still with himself until the whiskey had taken some of it away.

"Tired, darling?"

"Yes," he said. "I'm tired." And as he spoke, he did an unusual thing. He lifted his glass and drained it in one swallow although there was still half of it, at least half of it, left. She wasn't really watching him, but she knew what he had done because she heard the ice cubes falling back against the bottom of the empty glass when he lowered his arm. He paused a moment, leaning forward in the chair, then he got up and went slowly over to fetch himself another.

"I'll get it!" she cried, jumping up.

"Sit down," he said.

When he came back, she noticed that the new drink was dark amber with the quantity of whiskey in it.

"Darling, shall I get your slippers?"

"No."

She watched him as he began to sip the dark yellow drink, and she could see little oily swirls in the liquid because it was so strong.

"I think it's a shame," she said, "that when a policeman gets to be as senior as you, they keep him walking about on his feet all day long."

He didn't answer, so she bent her head again and went on with her sewing; but each time he lifted the drink to his lips, she heard the ice cubes clinking against the glass.

"Darling," she said. "Would you like me to get you some cheese? I haven't made any supper because it's Thursday."

"No," he said.

"If you're too tired to eat out," she went on, "it's still not too late. There's plenty of meat and stuff in the freezer, and you can have it right here and not even move out of the chair."

Her eyes waited on him for an answer, a smile, a little nod, but he made no sign.

"Anyway," she went on, "I'll get you some cheese and crackers first."

"I don't want it," he said.

She moved uneasily in her chair, the large eyes still watching his face. "But you *must* have supper. I can easily do it here. I'd like to do it. We can have lamb chops. Or pork. Anything you want. Everything's in the freezer."

"Forget it," he said.

"But, darling, you *must* eat! I'll fix it anyway, and then you can have it or not, as you like."

She stood up and placed her sewing on the table by the lamp.

"Sit down," he said. "Just for a minute, sit down."

It wasn't till then that she began to get frightened.

"Go on," he said. "Sit down."

She lowered herself back slowly into the chair, watching him all the time with those large, bewildered eyes. He had finished the second drink and was staring down into the glass, frowning.

"Listen," he said. "I've got something to tell you."

"What is it, darling? What's the matter?"

He had now become absolutely motionless, and he kept his head down so that the light from the lamp beside him fell across the upper part of his face, leaving the chin and mouth in shadow. She noticed there was a little muscle moving near his left eye.

"This is going to be a bit of a shock to you, I'm afraid," he said. "But I've thought about it a good deal, and I've decided the only thing to do is tell you right away. I hope you won't blame me too much."

And he told her. It didn't take long, four or five minutes at most, and she sat very still through it all, watching him with a kind of dazed horror as he went farther and farther away from her with each word.

"So there it is," he added. "And I know it's kind of a bad time to be telling you, but there simply wasn't any other way. Of course, I'll give you money and see you're looked after. But there needn't really be any fuss. I hope not, anyway. It wouldn't be very good for my job."

Her first instinct was not to believe any of it, to reject it all. It occurred to her that perhaps he hadn't even spoken, that she herself had imagined the whole thing. Maybe, if she went about her business and acted as though she hadn't been listening, then later, when she sort of woke up again, she might find none of it had ever happened.

"I'll get the supper," she managed to whisper, and this time he didn't stop her.

When she walked across the room, she couldn't feel her feet touching the floor. She couldn't feel anything at all—except a slight nausea and a desire to vomit. Everything was automatic now—down the steps to the cellar, the light switch, the freezer, the hand inside the cabinet taking hold of the first object it met. She lifted it out, and looked at it. It was wrapped in paper, so she took off the paper and looked at it again.

A leg of lamb.

All right then, they would have lamb for supper.

She carried it upstairs, holding the thin bone-end of it with both her hands, and as she went through the living-room, she saw him standing by the window with his back to her.

"For God's sake," he said, hearing her, but not turning round, "don't make supper for me. I'm going out."

At that point Mary Maloney simply walked up behind him, and without any pause, she swung the big frozen leg of lamb high in the air and brought it down as hard as she could on the back of his head.

She might just as well have hit him with a steel club.

She stepped back a pace, waiting, and the funny thing was that he remained standing there for at least four or five seconds, gently swaying. Then he crashed to the carpet.

The violence of the crash, the noise, the small table overturning, helped bring her out of the shock. She came out slowly, feeling cold and surprised, and she stood for a while, blinking at the body, still holding the ridiculous piece of meat tight with both hands.

All right, she told herself. So I've killed him.

It was extraordinary, now, how clear her mind became all of a sudden. She began thinking very fast. As the wife of a detective, she knew quite well what the penalty would be. That was fine. It made no difference to her. In fact, it would be a relief. On the other hand, what about the child? What were the laws about murderers with unborn children? Did they kill them both— mother and child? Or did they wait until the tenth month? What did they do?

Mary Maloney didn't know. And she wasn't going to take a chance.

She carried the meat into the kitchen, placed it in a pan, turned the oven on high, and shoved it inside. Then she washed her hands, and ran upstairs to the bedroom. She sat down before the mirror, tidied her hair, touched up her lips and face. She tried a smile. It came out rather peculiar. She tried again.

"Hullo, Sam," she said brightly, aloud.

The voice sounded peculiar, too.

"I want some potatoes, please, Sam. Yes, and I think a can of peas."

That was better. Both the smile and the voice were

coming out better now. She rehearsed it several times more. Then she ran downstairs, took her coat, went out the back door, down the garden, into the street.

It wasn't 6 o'clock yet and the lights were still on in the grocery shop.

"Hullo, Sam," she said brightly, smiling at the man behind the counter.

"Why, good evening, Mrs. Maloney. How're *you*?"

"I want some potatoes, please, Sam. Yes, and I think a can of peas."

The man turned and reached up behind him on the shelf for the peas.

"Patrick's decided he's tired and doesn't want to eat out tonight," she told him. "We go out Thursdays, and now he's caught me without any vegetables in the house."

"Then how about meat, Mrs. Maloney?"

"No, I've got meat, thanks. I got a nice leg of lamb from the freezer."

"Ah."

"I don't much like cooking it frozen, Sam, but I'm taking a chance on it this time. You think it'll be all right?"

"Personally," the grocer said, "I don't believe it makes any difference. You want these Idaho potatoes?"

"Oh, yes, that'll be fine. Two of those."

"Anything else?" The grocer cocked his head on one side, looking at her pleasantly. "How about afterward? What you going to give him for afterward?"

"Well—what would you suggest, Sam?"

The man glanced around his shop. "How about a nice big slice of cheesecake? I know he likes that."

"Perfect," she said. "He loves it."

And when it was all wrapped and she had paid, she put on her brightest smile and said, "Thank you, Sam. Good night."

"Good night, Mrs. Maloney. And thank *you*."

And now, she told herself as she hurried back, all she was doing now was returning home to her husband and he was waiting for his supper; and she must cook it good, and make it as tasty as possible because the poor man was tired; and if, when she entered the house, she happened to find anything unusual, or tragic, or terrible, then naturally it would be a shock and she'd become frantic with grief and horror. Mind you, she wasn't *expecting* to find anything. She was just going home with the vegetables: Mrs. Patrick Maloney going home with the vegetables on Thursday evening to cook supper for her husband.

That's the way, she told herself. Do everything right and natural. Keep things absolutely natural and there'll be no need for any acting at all.

Therefore, when she entered the kitchen by the back door, she was humming to herself, and smiling.

"Patrick!" she called. "How are you, darling?"

She put the parcel down on the table, and went through into the living room; and when she saw him lying there on the floor with his legs doubled up and one arm twisted back underneath his body, it really was rather a shock.

All the old love and longing for him welled up inside her, and she ran over to him, knelt down beside him, and began to cry her heart out. It was easy. No acting was necessary.

A few minutes later she got up and went to the phone. She knew the number of the police station, and when the man at the other end answered, she cried to him, "Quick! Come quick! Patrick's dead!"

"Who's speaking?"

"Mrs. Maloney. Mrs. Patrick Maloney."

"You mean Patrick Maloney's dead?"

"I think so," she sobbed. "He's lying on the floor and I think he's dead."

"Be right over," the man said.

The car came very quickly, and when she opened the front door, two policemen walked in. She knew them both—she knew nearly all the men at that precinct—and she fell right into Jack Noonan's arms, weeping hysterically. He put her gently into a chair, then went over to join the other one, who was called O'Malley, kneeling by the body.

"Is he dead?" she cried.

"I'm afraid he is. What happened?"

Briefly, she told her story about going out to the grocer and coming back to find him on the floor.

While she was talking, crying and talking, Noonan discovered a small patch of congealed blood on the dead man's head. He showed it to O'Malley, who got up at once and hurried to the phone.

Soon, other men began to come into the house. First a doctor, then two detectives, one of whom she knew by name. Later, a police photographer arrived and took pictures, and a man who knew about fingerprints. There was a great deal of whispering and muttering beside the corpse, and the detectives kept asking her a lot of questions. But they always treated her kindly. She told her story again, this time right from the beginning, when Patrick had come in, and she was sewing, and he was tired, so tired he hadn't wanted to go out for supper. She told how she'd put the meat in the oven—"it's there now, cooking"—and how she'd slipped out to the grocer for vegetables, and come back to find him lying on the floor.

"Which grocer?" one of the detectives asked.

She told him, and he turned and whispered something to the other detective, who immediately went outside into the street.

In fifteen minutes, he was back with a page of notes, and there was more whispering, and through her sobbing she heard a few of the whispered phrases— ". . . acted quite normal . . . very cheerful . . . wanted to give him a good supper . . . peas . . . cheesecake . . . impossible that she . . ."

After a while the photographer and the doctor departed, and two other men came in and took the corpse away on the stretcher. Then the fingerprint man went away. The two detectives remained, and so did the two policemen. They were exceptionally nice to her, and Jack Noonan asked if she wouldn't rather go some-

where else, to her sister's house perhaps, or his own
wife who would take care of her and put her up for the
night.

No, she said, she didn't feel she could move even a
yard at the moment. Would they mind awfully if she
stayed just where she was until she felt better. She
didn't feel too good at the moment, she really didn't.

Then hadn't she better lie down on the bed? Jack
Noonan asked.

No, she said. She'd like to stay right where she was,
in this chair. A little later, perhaps, when she felt better, she would move.

So they left her there while they went about their
business, searching the house. Occasionally, one of the
detectives asked her another question. Sometimes Jack
Noonan spoke to her gently as he passed by. Her husband, he told her, had been killed by a blow on the
back of the head administered with a heavy blunt instrument, almost certainly a large piece of metal. They
were looking for the weapon. The murderer may have
taken it with him, but on the other hand, he may've
thrown it away or hidden it somewhere on the premises.

"It's the old story," he said. "Get the weapon, and
you've got the man."

Later, one of the detectives came up and sat beside
her. Did she know, he asked, of anything in the house
that could've been used as the weapon? Would she
mind having a look around to see if anything was
missing—a big monkey wrench or a heavy metal vase.

They didn't have any heavy metal vases, she said.

"Or a big monkey wrench?"

She didn't think they had a big monkey wrench. But
there might be some things like that in the garage.

The search went on. She knew that there were other
policemen in the yard all around the house. She could
hear their footsteps on the gravel outside, and sometimes she saw the flash of a torch through a chink in
the curtains. It began to get late, nearly 9, she noticed
by the clock on the mantel. The four men searching the

rooms seemed to be growing weary, a trifle exasperated.

"Jack," she said, the next time Sergeant Noonan went by, "would you mind giving me a drink?"

"Sure I'll give you a drink. You mean this whiskey?"

"Yes, please. But just a small one. It might make me feel better."

He handed her the glass.

"Why don't you have one yourself," she said. "You must be awfully tired. Please do. You've been very good to me."

"Well," he answered. "It's not strictly allowed, but I might take just a drop to keep me going."

One by one, the others came in and were persuaded to take a little nip of whiskey. They stood around rather awkwardly with the drinks in their hands, uncomfortable in her presence, trying to say consoling things to her. Sergeant Noonan wandered into the kitchen, came out quickly, and said, "Look, Mrs. Maloney. You know that oven of yours is still on, and the meat still inside?"

"Oh *dear* me!" she cried. "So it is!"

"I better turn it off for you, hadn't I?"

"Will you do that, Jack? Thank you so much."

When the sergeant returned the second time, she looked at him with her large, dark, tearful eyes. "Jack Noonan," she said.

"Yes?"

"Would you do me a small favor—you and these others?"

"We can try, Mrs. Maloney."

"Well," she said. "Here you all are, and good friends of dear Patrick's too, and helping to catch the man who killed him. You must be terribly hungry by now because it's long past your suppertime, and I know Patrick would never forgive me, God bless his soul, if I allowed you to remain in his house without offering you decent hospitality. Why don't you eat up that lamb that's in the oven? It'll be cooked just right by now."

"Wouldn't dream of it," he said.

"Please," she begged. "Please eat it. Personally I couldn't touch a thing, certainly not what's been in the house when he was here. But it's all right for you. It'd be a favor to me if you'd eat it up. Then you can go on with your work again afterward."

There was a good deal of hesitating among the four policemen, but they were clearly hungry, and in the end she was able to persuade them to go into the kitchen and help themselves.

The woman stayed where she was, listening to them through the open door, and she could hear them speaking among themselves, their voices thick and sloppy because their mouths were full of meat.

"Have some more, Charlie?"

"No. Better not finish it."

"She *wants* us to finish it. She said so. Be doing her a favor."

"Okay, then. Give me some more."

"That's a hell of a big club the guy must've used to hit poor Patrick," one of them was saying. "The doc says his skull was smashed all to pieces just like from a sledge hammer."

"That's why it ought to be easy to find."

"Exactly what I say."

"Whoever done it, they're not going to be carrying a thing like that around with them longer than they need."

One of them belched.

"Personally, I think it's right here on the premises."

"Probably right under our noses. What you think, Jack?"

And in the other room, Mary Maloney began to giggle.

A Dry Manhattan Story
by Alan Gordon

"Tell me a story, Vince."

It was ten o'clock, shutdown time at the airport, and Litelli and Lopez were making a final tour of the security checkpoints in the main terminal before turning it over to the night shift. A few late flights were still straggling in, and Customs had phased down to just a few personnel. The shops and restaurants had closed, and the bums and panhandlers were settling down for the night. As head of security, Litelli had come to an informal accommodation with those who made the airport their home: He wouldn't give them trouble as long as they behaved and allowed his people to search them periodically for drugs and weapons. Lopez had just finished frisking Downtown Louie. He was clean, and she flipped him a quarter so he could watch the news on a pay-TV before falling asleep in an upright position on one of those hard plastic chairs.

The storytelling was a private ritual for Litelli and Lopez. They would be checking the burglar gates on the shops, and whenever they passed the candy store, Lopez would glance quickly at a heart-shaped box of chocolates. Her normally steel-hard eyes would soften at some private memory that Litelli swore he would never ask her about, and then some thirteen to fifteen steps later, she would ask him for some war-story from his days on the force.

"Okay," he said, racking his brain. "This one you haven't heard. This is from when I was a detective second grade, working out of the Three-Oh. You know the Three-Oh?"

"Not too well. I was downtown, mostly."

"Well, this was about fifteen years ago, and I had only been a detective for maybe eight months. There were four of us on the two-to-ten: me, Barry Dunwell, Jamie O'Donohugh, and Jerry Elfman."

"Jerry the Elf? I never knew you worked with him."

"You heard of him?"

She barked a quick, derisive laugh. "There is more stuff written about Jerry the Elf in department ladies' rooms than anyone else. He must have hit on half the female cadets when he was instructing at the academy."

"Yeah, well, so you can imagine what he was like when he was actually young enough to do anything with them. Anyway, we used to go after work to a local bar called Lenny's to wind down, compare notes . . ."

"Drink, chase women . . ."

"That too, although I was a nice married man back then. The place was a neighborhood bar, no margaritas in designer colors, just your basic domestic beer and hard liquor joint. Everybody knew everybody, and Tom, the bartender, knew everybody and their drink. He'd start pouring the moment he saw you come in so you didn't have to waste time ordering. Expert bartender, the best ever. There was a pool table, dart board, pinball machine, and a jukebox with Irish music and Sinatra on it, nothing else. We'd drink, schmooze, solve the problems of mankind, and call it a night. Sometimes one of the guys would get lucky, sometimes not. Then Lois Moorehouse showed up."

Litelli closed his eyes, visualizing the smoke, the noise, the fumes fighting the aromas, and remembered the night she came in. They were arguing over whether the Mets would repeat or not when Jerry the Elf's entire body stiffened in the direction of the bar like a pointer picking up a scent. A new woman, guessed Litelli as he turned to look. She was about twenty-five, with the blowsy elegance of a beautiful woman who had been in bars long before she was old enough to drink legally. She slid onto the bar stool with the practiced ease of someone who knew how to show off her legs to an appreciative room. And the room was certainly getting appreciative fast as a multitude of male murmurs eddied about, colliding and spinning off each other until there was a dull roar of "Check this one out."

But no one was faster in these situations than Jerry the Elf. Quicker than thought, he was sitting next to her, id firmly in control.

"May I buy you a drink?" he said, using the most obvious approach.

"Thank you," she said with a smile that would have melted an iceberg. "A Manhattan, dry, with rye. And with a twist of lime."

"Lime?" said Tom. "Most take 'em with lemon."

"I am not most people," she said, turning the smile on the barkeep, only this one would have brought the iceberg back. Tom shrugged and fixed the drink, and she turned her attentions back to the Elf. He talked, she laughed in all the right places, and some heavy betting started going down.

"Think she's a pro?" muttered Dunwell.

"Nah, she'd be too obvious," commented Litelli.

"Five bucks says the Elf goes home with her," said O'Donohugh.

"That's a sucker bet," said Dunwell. "She may not be a pro, but she came in here looking for action."

"Yeah," agreed Litelli. "Watch the two of 'em, it's hard to tell which one's the bait and which one's the fish. Well, gentlemen, it's been a lousy day, so naturally I'm going home to my wife. See you tomorrow."

"So, did the Elf score?" asked Lopez.

"The Elf not only scored, he fell for her. Every night he'd wait for her, then order her drink. 'A Manhattan for the lady, Tom, dry, with rye, and with a twist of lime, not lemon.' Tom would keep on arguing about the lime, she'd keep on drinking, and the rest of us just sat and envied him being with this woman."

"The Elf in love. Hard to believe."
"Of course it didn't last."

Two weeks later, the Elf spent the entire day moping at his desk. When they got to the bar, to their surprise he sat with them at their regular table.

"No Lois tonight?" asked Dunwell.

"Nope," spat the Elf. The other three glanced around the table, wondering who should ask the next question. Litelli took a deep breath and prepared to duck. "What happened, Jerry?"

The Elf slammed his glass down. "She dropped me. No explanation, just it's been great, it's been fun, you've been lovely, now you're done. I say, what about being in love? and she laughs. What the hell happened? I don't know, just that I'm out."

Tom appeared out of nowhere with a refill. "On the house," he said. Tom was like that.

Just then, Lois Moorehouse entered the bar. Without even glancing in Jerry's direction, she sauntered by the pool table, sized up the players, and sunk her hooks into the tallest one, a guy named Cater. Mesmerized, he followed her to the bar, and said, "A dry Manhattan, Tom. With rye."

"And with a twist, Tom," she added.

"I know, Miss Moorehouse," growled Tom. "Lime, not lemon."

And Cater started talking to her, and she let him think the whole thing was her idea, and the four detectives just stared.

"Gotta go," Dunwell said finally.

"Me too," said O'Donohugh.

"C'mon, Jerry," said Litelli, and laying a firm grip on the Elf's arm, he half-led, half-dragged him out of there.

The Elf kept staring at the bar. Dunwell flagged a cab, and the three of them forced the Elf inside.

"I'll see that he gets home," said Dunwell, climbing in after him.

* * *

"Then two weeks later?" guessed Lopez.
"You catch on fast."

Two weeks later, the four detectives entered the bar and saw a cluster of pool players hovering around Cater, who was crying into the latest of a series of beers. As they sat down, Tom made the rare gesture of bringing their drinks to their table himself rather than giving them to the waitress.

"What happened to Cater?" asked Dunwell.

"Same thing that happened to Jerry. She dumped him, no explanation. He's broken up over it. Can't even sink a sitting duck at the table. Keeps scratching, and you know Cater doesn't do that."

"The bitch," muttered Jerry. "I haven't been able to think straight since she did it to me."

"A lot of people are very angry about it," said Tom. "I just wish she would go somewhere else tonight."

On cue, the door opened, and a hush fell over the room as Lois Moorehouse came in. She ambled past the pool table and watched a dart game in progress.

Then she leaned over to one of the players and said, "Buy me a drink."

Cater stood up with a roar. "Nobody buys you a drink unless it's me. Give her the damn Manhattan, Tom, and don't forget the goddam twist of lime."

"Yeah, Tom," shouted Jerry, striding towards the dart players. "No lemon, just lime for the lady. Only I'm buying."

The chosen dart player turned around, clutching two darts in his hand. "Stay out of this, runt. The lady is with me."

"This is not a good situation," said Litelli, getting to his feet.

"Yeah," said Dunwell. "Three drunk, angry people, armed with darts, pool cues, and an off-duty gun."

"Plus all of their drunk, angry friends," added O'Donohugh.

Cater, the Elf, and the dart player glowered at each other in a decent rendition of the final confrontation in

The Good, the Bad, and the Ugly, then charged, bellowing, up to the bar. Three heads cracked together, followed by the smash of a pool cue, the slash of a dart, and the flash of a badge. The badge was Litelli's, but nobody seemed to pay much attention to it. The various supporting factions piled onto the original combatants like they were looking for a loose football. The three detectives hauled the Elf out of the fight. Litelli looked up briefly to see Lois Moorehouse watching calmly, an amused smile on her face. Litelli turned his attention back to the Elf, who was frantically trying to reach his .38 while Dunwell and O'Donohugh pinioned his arms. Dunwell yelled, "Do it!" and Litelli swung his fist into the Elf's jaw. He only needed to hit him once. The Elf sagged into his brother officers' arms.

"Shouldn't someone call the police?" screamed one of the pool players.

"Excuse me, we're here," shouted Litelli, and three badges waved in the air. Surprisingly, this had the desired effect. The fighting ceased, excepting one bottle smashing down on a dart player's head. Various people were bleeding from various places, but everyone seemed able to walk.

"Okay, I suggest that we all call it a night," said Litelli. "Anyone hurt bad? Nothing a Band-aid won't help? Good, go home. Nothing happened here."

The dart players left first, followed by Cater and company. The three detectives helped Tom right the tables and chairs, then picked up the Elf and headed home.

"So, what happened next?" asked Lopez.
"Patience. The good part is coming up."

Litelli and Dunwell were driving from an apartment burglary the next day when they caught the squeal. Corpse in car by the park. A uniform was maintaining crowd control as they arrived. The car was parked illegally in an access road used by the park's maintenance people. In the driver's seat was Lois Moorehouse, wearing the same outfit that she'd had on in the bar the previous evening. She was facing forward. Actually, only her body was facing forward. Her actual face was facing backward. Her final expression was one of peevishness.

"Whattaya think?" said Dunwell.

"Either her neck's broken or she doubled for Linda Blair in *The Exorcist*," said Litelli. "I'd say she's probably dead."

"You don't think the Elf, do ya?"

Litelli had been thinking just that. "We'll have to question him. If we don't, someone will start wondering why."

"Plus, it might have been him," said Dunwell.

"That too."

The Elf had called in sick that day. It hadn't surprised Litelli. His knuckles still ached from slugging him. When they knocked on his door, they heard some staggering footsteps, then some retching. When he finally opened it, he looked slightly worse than they expected.

"Hello," he said. "What's up?"

"Where'd you go after we brought you home last night?" said Litelli.

The Elf paled. "What happened? Who got what that you should be asking me about it?"

Litelli sighed. The Elf, even in his current condition, would not be an easy interrogation. "Lois was killed last night. Or sometime this morning. Did you go out after we brought you home?"

The Elf sat down on the front stoop, rubbing his eyes. "Yeah, I did. I headed back to the bar. I wanted to talk to her. I was mad. But I never made it there."

"Why not?" said Dunwell.

"I ran into Cater. He was gonna do the same thing. We started screaming about it at each other, then we started slugging each other, then I think we realized what a stupid situation it was. I started laughing, even while he was hitting me, and then he started laughing, and we sat there in the middle of the street and just howled."

"Then what?"

"We went to another bar and got blasted. We were together the whole time."

"But you split up, didn't you?" said Litelli.

"Nope," grinned the Elf. "He's in there, sleeping on the couch."

Litelli and Dunwell stared at each other, then went in to arouse the sleeping giant. Cater, once he had sufficiently cleared his head, confirmed the Elf's account.

"What time did you get back here?" asked Litelli.

"Dunno," said Cater. "I was wasted. I came in here and passed out."

"How much did you have to drink?"

Cater thought for a minute. "A lot," he concluded finally.

"How about you?" Litelli asked, turning to the Elf.

"Less than him. We came back here because he couldn't remember where he lived. I think about one."

"Okay, don't leave town," said Litelli.

Dunwell waited until they got outside to speak.

"Could've been either one. It's not really an alibi. One guy passes out, the other one heads back. Jerry could've gotten Cater extra drunk, or slipped him a mickey, used him for the alibi, and snuck out after he falls asleep."

"Cater could've done it to Jerry, too," said Litelli as they got into the car. "Or they both could've done it together. Motive, opportunity."

"Terrific. All we need is evidence, and you know Jerry's too smart to leave any. He'd put on gloves so there wouldn't be any fingerprints, and he'd strangle her so there'd be no bullet to trace."

"Yeah, only he's just a little guy. Cater's big enough to break her neck like that. He could do it easy. I think he's our guy. He's too big to drink so much he'd pass out."

"Or it could have been someone else entirely."

"Yeah," said Litelli. "Great thing about New York is that there's never a suspect shortage."

They spent the rest of the day checking on the other pool and dart players. All of them could account for their whereabouts. Then they went to Lenny's. Tom nodded as they came in. "Drinks? You're a little early tonight."

"No, thanks," replied Litelli. "You heard about Lois?"

"Sure," said Tom. "You want to know about what happened when you left?"

They nodded. "Well," said Tom. "Once the walking wounded headed out, there weren't too many people left. I gave her her drink, and Bess and I kept picking up the mess. She was talking to some guy, not a regular, he was drinking Budweisers. She may have left with him. About one A.M. He was about thirty, maybe five eleven, brown hair, flannel shirt, jeans, and that's all I can remember."

Litelli wrote it down, and they headed back to the precinct.

"So Lois walked out with her killer," commented Dunwell.

"Or someone else did it to her," said Litelli. "Lady like that stirs up a lot of emotions. Meets the wrong kind of people, or sometimes even the right kind of people turn wrong. We may not get this guy."

The autopsy report was on his desk when he got back. Lois Moorehouse had died of a broken neck. The stomach contents indicated that she had died at about two in the morning. She had eaten a cheeseburger ("'medium rare," the M.E. had scribbled in) with lettuce, tomato, pickle, and onion, a fruit salad with pieces of orange, grapefruit, cantaloupe, lemon, and pineapple in a syrup, and enough liquor to give her a blood alcohol content of .18. If she weren't dead, thought Litelli, we could have gotten her for driving while intoxicated. She'd have lost her license, but under the circumstances, not a bad tradeoff.

* * *

"*And then, I figured it out,*" *said Litelli. Lopez looked puzzled.*

"*Figured what out?*"

"*Who did it. I didn't have solid proof, but I knew who it was. Don't you get it?*" *He was grinning broadly. Lopez frowned, thinking. Then her face brightened.*

"*The fruit salad?*" *she said.*

"*Bingo,*" *said Litelli.*

Litelli and Dunwell went back to Lenny's that night. The regulars had stayed home, apparently, so there were just a few transients seated at a table by the door. The two detectives sat at the bar instead of their usual table. Tom placed their drinks in front of them.

"What I like about this place is the service," said Dunwell. "You mix them better than anyone, Tom."

"If you don't take pride in your work, why bother?" said Tom.

"Exactly," agreed Litelli. "Which is why it's frustrating for us on this Moorehouse case. You sure you didn't get a good look at the guy's face?"

"I'm sorry, Vince, but I really didn't."

Litelli finished his drink. "Another?" said Tom.

"Hm," pondered Litelli. "Maybe I'll try something different. What was in those Manhattans?"

"One part dry vermouth to two parts bourbon or rye, poured over ice and stirred, serve it up in a Manhattan glass."

"Sounds good. She liked it with lime?"

"That isn't a proper Manhattan," said Tom. "Lime ruins it. The proper garnish is lemon, or maybe an olive."

"You're quite the perfectionist, aren't you?" said Dunwell.

"Pride in my work, as I said."

"She must have driven you crazy," sympathized Litelli. "Coming in with that attitude, and then ordering the drink the wrong way."

"Well . . ." said Tom.

"And she kept harping on it, didn't she?" said Dunwell.

"Yes, she did," said Tom.

"Not to mention what she was doing to your regulars," said Litelli. "I mean, first Jerry, then Cater, and she was gonna take out the dart guy next."

Tom was sweating.

"And the fight she started," said Dunwell. "Nobody ever got into a fight here until she came into the place."

"You see, Tom," said Litelli, "we understand why you did it. This place is you, Tom. Once a bar stops being a place to go, it dies. This was really just a self-defense thing, wasn't it?"

"Yes," whispered Tom.

"Talk to us, buddy," said Dunwell. "You know we'll try to help you on this one."

"She had done this to me once before," Tom began haltingly. "Another bar, about five years ago. I loved her, but she dropped me, then kept coming to the bar with other men. She always ordered the Manhattans with the lime. She knew it drove me crazy. She drove our customers out. I lost the bar. Then I had to scrounge to save up enough to open this place. And just when it was going well, she showed up here a month ago. By accident, she told me, but she started playing the same games. I didn't want to lose this place, and I didn't want to see her destroying my customers. *My* customers. So, I waited for her, and I killed her."

He stopped, mixed a drink, a dry Manhattan, and topped it off with a slice of lemon. "It's really a great drink," he said, sipping it. "And the last thing I did before I killed her was I made her drink a real Manhattan. Just for the personal satisfaction, you see."

"We understand," said Litelli. "That's why, when I saw the lemon in the M.E.'s report, I knew you must have done it. No one puts lemon in a fruit salad. Could you come with us now, Tom?"

* * *

"And he came," said Litelli. "He really wasn't a violent guy. Just this one quirk. He copped to manslaughter, did eight years, and is out on parole. Unfortunately, convicted felons can't get bartenders' licenses."

"That's unfortunate?" said Lopez.

"He really was the best bartender I ever saw," said Litelli wistfully. "That's what tipped me off. He left his signature there. Not just the lemons. It was how she died. Just like her drink."

Lopez started laughing.

"With a twist," said Litelli.

"With a twist."

The Avenging Chance
by Anthony Berkeley

Roger Sheringham was inclined to think afterwards that the Poisoned Chocolates Case, as the papers called it, was perhaps the most perfectly planned murder he had ever encountered. The motive was so obvious, when you knew where to look for it—but you didn't know; the method was so significant when you had grasped its real essentials—but you didn't grasp them; the traces were so thinly covered, when you had realized what was covering them—but you didn't realize. But for a piece of the merest bad luck, which the murderer could not possibly have foreseen, the crime must have been added to the classical list of great mysteries.

This is the gist of the case, as Chief-Inspector Moresby told it one evening to Roger in the latter's rooms in the Albany a week after it happened:

On Friday morning, the fifteenth of November, at half-past ten in the morning, in accordance with his invariable custom, Sir William Anstruther walked into his club in Piccadilly, the very exclusive *Rainbow Club,* and asked for his letters. The porter handed him three and a small parcel. Sir William walked over to the fireplace in the big lounge hall to open them.

A few minutes later another member entered the club, a Mr. Graham Beresford. There were a letter and a couple of circulars for him, and he also strolled over to the fireplace, nodding to Sir William, but not speaking to him. The two men only knew each other very slightly, and had probably never exchanged more than a dozen words in all.

Having glanced through his letters, Sir William opened the parcel and, after a moment, snorted with disgust. Beresford looked at him, and with a grunt Sir William thrust out a letter which had been enclosed in the parcel. Concealing a smile (Sir William's ways were a matter of some amusement to his fellow-members), Beresford read the letter. It was from a big firm of chocolate manufacturers, Mason & Sons, and set forth that they were putting on the market a new brand of liqueur-chocolates designed especially to appeal to men; would Sir William do them the honor of accepting the enclosed two-pound box and letting the firm have his candid opinion on them?

"Do they think I'm a blank chorus-girl?" fumed Sir William. "Write 'em testimonials about their blank chocolates, indeed! Blank 'em! I'll complain to the blank committee. That sort of blank thing can't blank well be allowed here."

"Well, it's an ill wind so far as I'm concerned," Beresford soothed him. "It's reminded me of something. My wife and I had a box at the Imperial last night. I bet her a box of chocolates to a hundred cigarettes that she wouldn't spot the villain by the end of the second act. She won. I must remember to get them. Have you seen it—*The Creaking Skull?*"

Sir William had not seen it, and said so with force.

"Want a box of chocolates, did you say?" he added, more mildly. "Well, take this blank one. I don't want it."

For a moment Beresford demurred politely and then, most unfortunately for himself, accepted. The money so saved meant nothing to him for he was a wealthy man; but trouble was always worth saving.

By an extraordinarily lucky chance neither the outer wrapper of the box nor its covering letter were thrown into the fire, and this was the more fortunate in that both men had tossed the envelopes of their letters into the flames. Sir William did, indeed, make a bundle of the wrapper, letter, and string, but he handed it over to Beresford, and the latter simply dropped it inside the fender. This bundle the porter subsequently extracted and, being a man of orderly habits, put it tidily away in the waste-paper basket, whence it was retrieved later by the police.

Of the three unconscious protagonists in the impending tragedy, Sir William was without doubt the most remarkable. Still a year or two under fifty, he looked, with his flaming red face and thick-set figure, a typical country squire of the old school, and both his manners and his language were in accordance with tradition. His habits, especially as regards women, were also in accordance with tradition—the tradition of the bold, bad baronet which he undoubtedly was.

In comparison with him, Beresford was rather an ordinary man, a tall, dark, not unhandsome fellow of two-and-thirty, quiet and reserved. His father had left him a rich man, but idleness did not appeal to him, and he had a finger in a good many business pies.

Money attracts money: Graham Beresford had inherited it, he made it, and, inevitably, he married it, too. The daughter of a late shipowner in Liverpool, with not far off half a million in her own right. But the money was incidental, for he needed her and would have married her just as inevitably (said his friends) if she had not had a farthing. A tall, rather serious-minded, highly cultured girl, not so young that her character had not had time to form (she was twenty-five when Beresford married her, three years ago), she was the ideal wife for him. A bit of a Puritan perhaps in some ways, but Beresford, whose wild oats, though duly sown, had been a sparse crop, was ready enough to be a Puritan himself. To make no bones about it, the Beresfords succeeded in achieving that eighth wonder of the modern world, a happy marriage.

And into the middle of it there dropped, with irretrievable tragedy, the box of chocolates.

Beresford gave them to her after lunch as they sat over their coffee, with some jesting remark about paying his honorable debts, and she opened the box at once. The top layer, she noticed, seemed to consist only of kirsch and maraschino. Beresford, who did not believe in spoiling good coffee, refused when she offered him the box, and his wife ate the first one alone. As she did so she exclaimed in surprise that the filling seemed exceedingly strong and positively burned her mouth.

Beresford explained that they were samples of a new brand and then, made curious by what his wife had said, took one too. A burning taste, not intolerable but much too strong to be pleasant, followed the release of the liquid, and the almond flavoring seemed quite excessive.

"By Jove," he said, "they are strong. They must be filled with neat alcohol."

"Oh, they wouldn't do that, surely," said his wife, taking another. "But they are very strong. I think I rather like them, though."

Beresford ate another, and disliked it still more. "I don't," he said with decision. "They make my tongue feel quite numb. I shouldn't eat any more of them if I were you. I think there's something wrong with them."

"Well, they're only an experiment, I suppose," she said. "But they do burn. I'm not sure whether I like them or not."

A few minutes later Beresford went out to keep a business appointment in the City. He left her still trying to make up her mind whether she liked them, and still eating them to decide. Beresford remembered that scrap of conversation afterwards very vividly, because it was the last time he saw his wife alive.

That was roughly half-past two. At a quarter to four Beresford arrived at his club from the City in a taxi, in a state of collapse. He was helped into the building by the driver and the porter, and both descried him subsequently as pale to the point of ghastliness, with staring eyes and livid lips, and his skin damp and clammy. His mind seemed unaffected, however, and when they had got him up the step he was able to walk, with the porter's help, into the lounge.

The porter, thoroughly alarmed, wanted to send for a doctor at once, but Beresford, who was the last man in the world to make a fuss, refused to let him, saying that it must be indigestion and he would be all right in a few minutes. To Sir William Anstruther, however, who was in the lounge at the time, he added after the porter had gone:

"Yes, and I believe it was those infernal chocolates you gave me, now I come to think of it. I thought there was something funny about them at the time. I'd better go and find out if my wife—" He broke off abruptly. His body, which had been leaning back limply in his chair, suddenly heaved rigidly upright; his jaws locked together, the livid lips drawn back in a horrible grin, and his hands clenched on the arms of his chair. At the same time Sir William became aware of an unmistakable smell of bitter almonds.

Thoroughly alarmed, believing indeed that the man was dying under his eyes, Sir William raised a shout for the porter and a doctor. The other occupants of the lounge hurried up, and between them they got the convulsed body of the unconscious man into a more comfortable position. Before the doctor could arrive a telephone message was received at the club from an agitated butler asking if Mr. Beresford was there, and if so would he come home at once as Mrs. Beresford had been taken seriously ill. As a matter of fact, she was already dead.

Beresford did not die. He had taken less of the poison than his wife, who after his departure must have eaten at least three more of the chocolates, so that its action was less rapid on Beresford and the doctor had time to save him. As a matter of fact it turned out afterwards that he had not had a fatal dose. By about eight o'clock that night he was conscious; the next day he was practically convalescent.

As for the unfortunate Mrs. Beresford, the doctor

had arrived too late to save her, and she passed away very rapidly in a deep coma.

The police had taken the matter in hand as soon as Mrs. Beresford's death was reported to them and the fact of poison established, and it was only a very short time before things had become narrowed down to the chocolates as the active agent.

Sir William was interrogated, the letter and wrapper were recovered from the waste-paper basket, and, even before the sick man was out of danger, a detective-inspector was asking for an interview with the managing-director of Mason & Sons. Scotland Yard moves quickly.

It was the police theory at this stage, based on what Sir William and the two doctors had been able to tell them, that by an act of criminal carelessness on the part of one of Mason's employees, an excessive amount of oil of bitter almonds had been included in the filling-mixture of the chocolates, for that was what the doctors had decided must be the poisoning ingredient. However, the managing-director quashed this idea at once: oil of bitter almonds, he asserted, was never used by Mason's.

He had more interesting news still. Having read with undisguised astonishment the covering letter, he at once declared that it was a forgery. No such letter, no such samples had been sent out by the firm at all; a new variety of liqueur-chocolates had never even been mooted. The fatal chocolates were their ordinary brand.

Unwrapping and examining one more closely, he called the Inspector's attention to a mark on the underside, which he suggested was the remains of a small hole drilled in the case, through which the liquid could have been extracted and the fatal filling inserted, the hole afterwards being stopped up with softened chocolate—a perfectly simple operation.

He examined it under a magnifying glass and the Inspector agreed. It was now clear to him that somebody had been trying deliberately to murder Sir William Anstruther.

Scotland Yard doubled its activities. The chocolates were sent for analysis, Sir William was interviewed again, and so was the now conscious Beresford. From the latter the doctor insisted that the news of his wife's death must be kept till the next day, as in his weakened condition the shock might be fatal, so that nothing very helpful was obtained from him.

Nor could Sir William throw any light on the mystery or produce a single person who might have any grounds for trying to kill him. He was living apart from his wife, who was the principal beneficiary in his will, but she was in the South of France, as the French police subsequently confirmed. His estate in Worcestershire, heavily mortgaged, was entailed and went to a nephew; but as the rent he got for it barely covered the interest on the mortgage, and the nephew was considerably better off than Sir William himself, there was no motive there. The police were at a dead end.

The analysis brought one or two interesting facts to light. Not oil of bitter almonds but nitrobenzine, a kindred substance, chiefly used in the manufacture of aniline dyes, was the somewhat surprising poison employed. Each chocolate in the upper layer contained exactly six minims of it, in a mixture of kirsch and maraschino. The chocolates in the other layers were harmless.

As to the other clues, they seemed equally useless. The sheet of Mason's notepaper was identified by Merton's, the printers, as of their work, but there was nothing to show how it had got into the murderer's possession. All that could be said was that, the edges being distinctly yellowed, it must be an old piece. The machine on which the letter had been typed, of course, could not be traced. From the wrapper, a piece of ordinary brown paper with Sir William's address handprinted on it in large capitals, there was nothing to be learned at all beyond that the parcel had been posted at the post office in Southampton Street between the hours of 8:30 and 9:30 on the previous evening.

Only one thing was quite clear. Whoever had coveted Sir William's life had no intention of paying for it with his or her own.

"And now you know as much as we do, Mr. Sheringham," concluded Chief-Inspector Moresby, "and if you can say who sent those chocolates to Sir William, you'll know a good deal more."

Roger nodded thoughtfully.

"It's a brute of a case. I met a man only yesterday who was at school with Beresford. He didn't know him very well because Beresford was on the modern side and my friend was a classical bird, but they were in the same house. He says Beresford's absolutely knocked over by his wife's death. I wish you could find out who sent those chocolates, Moresby."

"So do I, Mr. Sheringham."

"It might have been anyone in the whole world," Roger mused. "What about feminine jealousy, for instance? Sir William's private life doesn't seem to be immaculate. I daresay there's a good deal of off with the old light-o'-love and on with the new."

"Why, that's just what I've been looking into, Mr. Sheringham, sir," retorted Chief-Inspector Moresby reproachfully. "That was the first thing that came to me. Because if anything does stand out about this business it is that it's a woman's crime. Nobody but a woman would send poisoned chocolates to a man. Another man would send a poisoned sample of whisky, or something like that."

"That's a very sound point, Moresby," Roger meditated. "Very sound indeed. And Sir William couldn't help you?"

"Couldn't," said Moresby, not without a trace of resentment, "or wouldn't. I was inclined to believe at first that he might have his suspicions and was shielding some woman. But I don't think so now."

"Humph!" Roger did not seem quite so sure. "It's reminiscent, this case, isn't it? Didn't some lunatic once send poisoned chocolates to the Commissioner of Police himself? A good crime always gets imitated, as you know."

Moresby brightened.

"It's funny you should say that, Mr. Sheringham, because that's the very conclusion I've come to. I've tested every other theory, and so far as I know there's not a soul with an interest in Sir William's death, whether from motives of gain, revenge, or what you like, whom I haven't had to rule out. In fact, I've pretty well made up my mind that the person who sent those chocolates was some irresponsible lunatic of a woman, a social or religious fanatic who's probably never even seen him. And if that's the case," Moresby sighed, "a fat chance I have of ever laying hands on her."

"Unless Chance steps in, as it so often does," said Roger brightly, "and helps you. A tremendous lot of cases get solved by a stroke of sheer luck, don't they? *Chance the Avenger.* It would make an excellent film title. But there's a lot of truth in it. If I were superstitious, which I'm not, I should say it wasn't chance at all, but Providence avenging the victim."

"Well, Mr. Sheringham," said Moresby, who was not superstitious either, "to tell the truth, I don't mind what it is, so long as it lets me get my hands on the right person."

If Moresby had paid his visit to Roger Sheringham with any hope of tapping that gentleman's brains, he went away disappointed.

To tell the truth, Roger was inclined to agree with the Chief-Inspector's conclusion, that the attempt on the life of Sir William Anstruther and the actual murder of the unfortunate Mrs. Beresford must be the work of some unknown criminal lunatic. For this reason, although he thought about it a good deal during the next few days, he made no attempt to take the case in hand. It was the sort of affair, necessitating endless inquiries,

that a private person would have neither the time nor
the authority to carry out, which can be handled only
by the official police. Roger's interest in it was purely
academic.

It was hazard, a chance encounter nearly a week
later, which translated this interest from the academic
into the personal.

Roger was in Bond Street, about to go through the
distressing ordeal of buying a new hat. Along the
pavement he suddenly saw bearing down on him Mrs.
Verreker-le-Flemming. Mrs. Verreker-le-Flemming
was small, exquisite, rich, and a widow, and she sat at
Roger's feet whenever he gave her the opportunity.
But she talked. She talked, in fact, and talked, and
talked. And Roger, who rather liked talking himself,
could not bear it. He tried to dart across the road, but
there was no opening in the traffic stream. He was
cornered.

Mrs. Verreker-le-Flemming fastened on him gladly.

"Oh, Mr. Sheringham! *Just* the person I wanted to
see. Mr. Sheringham, *do* tell me. In confidence. *Are*
you taking up this dreadful business of poor Joan
Beresford's death?"

Roger, the frozen and imbecile grin of civilized in-
tercourse on his face, tried to get a word in; without
result.

"I was horrified when I heard of it—simply horrified. You see, Joan and I were such *very* close friends.
Quite intimate. And the awful thing, the truly *terrible*
thing is that Joan brought the whole business on herself. Isn't that *appalling*?"

Roger no longer wanted to escape.

"What did you say?" he managed to insert incredu-
lously.

"I suppose it's what they call tragic irony," Mrs.
Verreker-le-Flemming chattered on. "Certainly it was
tragic enough, and I've never heard anything so terribly ironical. You know about that bet she made with
her husband, of course, so that he had to get her a box
of chocolates, and if he hadn't Sir William would

never have given him the poisoned ones and he'd have eaten them and died himself and good riddance? Well, Mr. Sheringham—" Mrs. Verreker-le-Flemming lowered her voice to a conspirator's whisper and glanced about her in the approved manner. "I've never told anybody else this, but I'm telling you because I know you'll appreciate it. *Joan wasn't playing fair.*"

"How do you mean?" Roger asked, bewildered.

Mrs. Verreker-le-Flemming was artlessly pleased with her sensation.

"Why, she'd seen the play before. We went together, the very first week it was on. She *knew* who the villain was all the time."

"By Jove!" Roger was as impressed as Mrs. Verreker-le-Flemming could have wished. "Chance the Avenger! We're none of us immune from it."

"Poetic justice, you mean?" twittered Mrs. Verreker-le-Flemming, to whom these remarks had been somewhat obscure. "Yes, but Joan Beresford of all people! That's the extraordinary thing. I should never have thought Joan *would* do a thing like that. She was such a *nice* girl. A little close with money, of course, considering how well-off they are, but that isn't anything. Of course it was only fun, and pulling her husband's leg, but I always used to think Joan was such a *serious* girl, Mr. Sheringham. I mean, ordinary people don't talk about honor and truth, and playing the game, and all those things one takes for granted. But Joan did. She was always saying that this wasn't honorable, or that wouldn't be playing the game. Well, she paid herself for not playing the game, poor girl, didn't she? Still, it all goes to show the truth of the old saying, doesn't it?"

"What old saying?" said Roger, hypnotized by this flow.

"Why, that still waters run deep. Joan must have been deep, I'm afraid." Mrs. Verreker-le-Flemming sighed. It was evidently a social error to be deep. "I mean, she certainly took me in. She can't have been quite so honorable and truthful as she was always pretending, can she? And I can't help wondering whether a girl who'd deceived her husband in a little thing like that might not—oh, well, I don't want to say anything against poor Joan now she's dead, poor darling, but she can't have been *quite* such a plaster saint after all, can she? I mean," said Mrs. Verreker-le-Flemming, in hasty extenuation of these suggestions, "I do think psychology is so very interesting, don't you, Mr. Sheringham?"

"Sometimes, very," Roger agreed gravely. "But you mentioned Sir William Anstruther just now. Do you know him, too?"

"I used to," Mrs. Verreker-le-Flemming replied, without particular interest. "Horrible man! Always running after some woman or other. And when he's tired of her, just drops her—biff!—like that. At least," added Mrs. Verreker-le-Flemming somewhat hastily, "so I've heard."

"And what happens if she refuses to be dropped?"

"Oh, dear, I'm sure I don't know. I suppose you've heard the latest?"

Mrs. Verreker-le-Flemming hurried on, perhaps a trifle more pink than the delicate aids to nature on her cheeks would have warranted.

"He's taken up with that Bryce woman now. You know, the wife of the oil man, or petrol, or whatever he made his money in. It began about three weeks ago. You'd have thought that dreadful business of being responsible, in a way, for poor Joan Beresford's death would have sobered him up a little, wouldn't you? But not a bit of it; he—"

Roger was following another line of thought. "What a pity you weren't at the Imperial with the Beresfords that evening. She'd never have made that bet if you had been." Roger looked extremely innocent. "You weren't, I suppose?"

"I?" queried Mrs. Verreker-le-Flemming in surprise. "Good gracious, no, I was at the new revue at the Pavilion. Lady Gavelstroke had a box and asked me to join her party."

"Oh, yes. Good show, isn't it? I thought that sketch *The Sempiternal Triangle* very clever. Didn't you?"

"The Sempiternal Triangle?" wavered Mrs. Verreker-le-Flemming.

"Yes, in the first half."

"Oh! Then I didn't see it. I got there disgracefully late, I'm afraid. But then," said Mrs. Verreker-le-Flemming with pathos, "I always do seem to be late for simply everything."

Roger kept the rest of the conversation resolutely upon theatres. But before he left her, he had ascertained that she had photographs of both Mrs. Beresford and Sir William Anstruther and had obtained permission to borrow them some time. As soon as she was out of view, he hailed a taxi and gave Mrs. Verreker-le-Flemming's address. He thought it better to take advantage of her permission at a time when he would not have to pay for it a second time over.

The parlor maid seemed to think there was nothing odd in his mission, and took him up to the drawing room at once. A corner of the room was devoted to the silver-framed photographs of Mrs. Verreker-le-Flemming's friends, and there were many of them. Roger examined them with interest, and finally took away with him not two photographs but six, those of Sir William, Mrs. Beresford, Beresford, two strange males who appeared to belong to the Sir William period, and lastly, a likeness of Mrs. Verreker-le-Flemming herself. Roger liked confusing his trail.

For the rest of the day he was very busy.

His activities would have no doubt seemed to Mrs. Verreker-le-Flemming not merely baffling but pointless. He paid a visit to a public library, for instance, and consulted a work of reference, after which he took a taxi and drove to the offices of the Anglo-Eastern Perfumery Company, where he inquired for a certain Mr. Joseph Lea Hardwick and seemed much put out on hearing that no such gentleman was known to the firm and was certainly not employed in any of their branches. Many questions had to be put about the firm and its branches before he consented to abandon the quest.

After that he drove to Messrs. Weall & Wilson, the well-known institution which protects the trade interests of individuals and advises its subscribers regarding investments. Here he entered his name as a subscriber, and explaining that he had a large sum of money to invest, filled in one of the special inquiry-forms which are headed *Strictly Confidential.*

Then he went to the *Rainbow Club,* in Piccadilly.

Introducing himself to the porter without a blush as connected with Scotland Yard, he asked the man a number of questions, more or less trivial, concerning the tragedy.

"William, I understand," he said finally, as if by the way, "did not dine here the evening before?"

There it appeared that Roger was wrong. Sir William had dined in the club, as he did about three times a week.

"But I understood he wasn't here that evening?" Roger said plaintively.

The porter was emphatic. He remembered quite well. So did a waiter, whom the porter summoned to corroborate him. Sir William had dined, rather late, and had not left the dining-room till about nine o'clock. He spent the evening there, too, the waiter knew, or at least some of it, for he himself had taken him a whisky-and-soda in the lounge not less than half an hour later.

Roger retired.

He retired to Merton's, in a taxi.

It seemed that he wanted some new notepaper printed, of a very special kind, and to the young woman behind the counter he specified at great length and in wearisome detail exactly what he did want. The young woman handed him the books of specimen pieces and asked him to see if there was any style there which would suit him. Roger glanced through them, remarking garrulously to the young woman that he had been recommended to Merton's by a very dear friend, whose photograph he happened to have on him at that moment. Wasn't that a curious coincidence? The young woman agreed that it was.

"About a fortnight ago, I think, my friend was in here last," said Roger, producing the photograph. "Recognize this?"

The young woman took the photograph, without apparent interest.

"Oh, yes. I remember. About some notepaper, too, wasn't it? So that's your friend. Well, it's a small world. Now this is a line we're selling a good deal of just now."

Roger went back to his rooms to dine. Afterwards, feeling restless, he wandered out of the Albany and turned up Piccadilly. He wandered round the Circus, thinking hard, and paused for a moment out of habit to inspect the photographs of the new revue hung outside the Pavilion. The next thing he realized was that he had got as far as Jermyn Street and was standing outside the Imperial Theatre. Glancing at the advertisements of *The Creaking Skull,* he saw that it began at half-past eight. Glancing at his watch, he saw that the time was twenty-nine minutes past that hour. He had an evening to get through somehow. He went inside.

The next morning, very early for Roger, he called on Moresby at Scotland Yard.

"Moresby," he said without preamble, "I want you to do something for me. Can you find me a taximan who took a fare from Piccadilly Circus or its neighborhood at about ten past nine on the evening before the Beresford crime, to the Strand somewhere near the bottom of Southampton Street, and another who took a fare back between those points? I'm not sure about the first. Or one taxi might have been used for the double journey, but I doubt that. Anyhow, try to find out for me, will you?"

"What are you up to now, Mr. Sheringham?" Moresby asked suspiciously.

"Breaking down an interesting alibi," replied Roger serenely. "By the way, I know who sent those chocolates to Sir William. I'm just building up a nice structure of evidence for you. Ring up my rooms when you've got those taximen."

He strolled out, leaving Moresby positively gaping after him.

The rest of the day he spent apparently trying to buy a second-hand typewriter. He was very particular that it should be a Hamilton No. 4. When the shop-people tried to induce him to consider other makes he refused to look at them, saying that the Hamilton No. 4 had been so strongly recommended to him by a friend, who had bought one about three weeks ago. Perhaps it was at this very shop? No? They hadn't sold a Hamilton No. 4 for the last three months? How odd.

But at one shop they had sold a Hamilton No. 4 within the last month, and that was odder still.

At half-past four Roger got back to his rooms to await the telephone message from Moresby. At half-past five it came.

"There are fourteen taxi-drivers here, littering up my office," said Moresby offensively. "What do you want me to do with 'em?"

"Keep them till I come, Chief-Inspector," returned Roger with dignity.

The interview with the fourteen was brief enough, however. To each man in turn Roger showed a photograph, holding it so that Moresby could not see it, and asked if he could recognize his fare. The ninth man did so, without hesitation.

At a nod from Roger, Moresby dismissed them, then sat at his table and tried to look official. Roger seated himself on the table, looking most unofficial, and swung his legs. As he did so, a photograph fell unnoticed out of his pocket and fluttered, face down-

wards under the table. Moresby eyed it but did not
pick it up.

"And now, Mr. Sheringham, sir," he said, "perhaps
you'll tell me what you've been doing?"

"Certainly, Moresby," said Roger blandly. "Your
work for you. I really have solved the thing, you know.
Here's your evidence." He took from his note-case an
old letter and handed it to the Chief-Inspector. "Was
that typed on the same machine as the forged letter
from Mason's, or was it not?"

Moresby studied it for a moment, then drew the
forged letter from a drawer of his table and compared
the two minutely.

"Mr. Sheringham," he said soberly, "where did you
get hold of this?"

"In a second-hand typewriter shop in St. Martin's
Lane. The machine was sold to an unknown customer
about a month ago. They identified the customer from
that same photograph. As it happened, this machine
had been used for a time in the office after it was re-
paired, to see that it was O.K., and I easily got hold of
that specimen of its work."

"And where is the machine now?"

"Oh, at the bottom of the Thames, I expect," Roger
smiled. "I tell you, this criminal takes no unnecessary
chances. But that doesn't matter. There's your evidence."

"Humph! It's all right so far as it goes," conceded
Moresby. "But what about Mason's paper?"

"That," said Roger calmly, "was extracted from
Merton's book of sample notepapers, as I'd guessed
from the very yellowed edges might be the case. I can
prove contact of the criminal with the book, and there
is a page which will certainly turn out to have been
filled by that piece of paper."

"That's fine," Moresby said, more heartily.

"As for that taximan, the criminal had an alibi.
You've heard it broken down. Between ten past nine
and twenty-five past—in fact, during the time when
the parcel must have been posted—the murderer took

a hurried journey to that neighborhood, going probably by 'bus or Underground, but returning, as I expected, by taxi, because time would be getting short."

"And the murderer, Mr. Sheringham?"

"The person whose photograph is in my pocket,"
Roger said unkindly. "By the way, do you remember
what I was saying the other day about Chance the
Avenger, my excellent film title? Well, it's worked
again. By a chance meeting in Bond Street with a silly
woman I was put, by the merest accident, in possession
of a piece of information which showed me then and
there who had sent those chocolates addressed to Sir
William. There were other possibilities, of course, and
I tested them, but then and there on the pavement I saw
the whole thing, from first to last."

"Who was the murderer, then, Mr. Sheringham?" re-
peated Moresby.

"It was so beautifully planned," Roger went on
dreamily. "We never grasped for one moment that we
were making the fundamental mistake that the murderer all along intended us to make."

"And what was that?" asked Moresby.

"Why, that the plan had miscarried. That the wrong
person had been killed. That was just the beauty of it.
The plan had *not* miscarried. It had been brilliantly
successful. The wrong person was *not* killed. Very
much the right person was."

Moresby gaped.

"Why, how on earth do you make that out, sir?"

"Mrs. Beresford was the objective all the time.
That's why the plot was so ingenious. Everything was
anticipated. It was perfectly natural that Sir William
should hand the chocolates over to Beresford. It was
foreseen that we should look for the criminal among
Sir William's associates and not the dead woman's. It
was probably even foreseen that the crime would be
considered the work of a woman!"

Moresby, unable to wait any longer, snatched up the
photograph.

"Good heavens! But Mr. Sherringham, you don't mean to tell me that . . . Sir William himself!"

"He wanted to get rid of Mrs. Beresford," Roger continued. "He had liked her well enough at the beginning, no doubt, though it was her money he was after all the time.

"But the real trouble was that she was too close with her money. He wanted it, or some of it, pretty badly; and she wouldn't part. There's no doubt about the motive. I made a list of the firms he's interested in and got a report on them. They're all rocky, every one. He'd got through all his own money, and he had to get more.

"As for the nitrobenzine which puzzled us so much, that was simple enough. I looked it up and found that beside the uses you told me, it's used largely in perfumery. And he's got a perfumery business. The Anglo-Eastern Perfumery Company. That's how he'd know about it being poisonous, of course. But I shouldn't think he got his supply from there. He'd be cleverer than that. He probably made the stuff himself. And schoolboys know how to treat benzol with nitric acid to get nitrobenzine."

"But," stammered Moresby, "but Sir William . . . He was at Eton."

"Sir William?" said Roger sharply. "Who's talking about Sir William? I told you the photograph of the murderer was in my pocket." He whipped out the photograph in question and confronted the astounded Chief-Inspector with it. "Beresford, man! Beresford's the murderer of his own wife.

"Beresford," he went on more mildly, "who didn't want his wife but did want her money. He contrived this plot, providing as he thought against every contingency that could possibly arise. He established a mild alibi, if suspicion ever should arise, by taking his wife to the Imperial, and slipped out of the theatre at the first intermission. (I sat through the first act of the dreadful thing myself last night to see when the intermission came.) Then he hurried down to the Strand, posted his parcel, and took a taxi back. He had ten minutes, but nobody would notice if he got back to the box a minute late.

"And the rest simply followed. He knew Sir William came to the club every morning at ten thirty, as regularly as clockwork; he knew that for a psychological certainty he could get the chocolates handed over to him if he hinted for them; he knew that the police would go chasing after all sorts of false trails starting from Sir William. And as for the wrapper and the forged letter he carefully didn't destroy them because they were calculated not only to divert suspicion but actually to point away from him to some anonymous lunatic."

"Well, it's very smart of you, Mr. Sheringham," Moresby said, with a little sigh, but quite ungrudgingly. "Very smart indeed. What was it the lady told you that showed you the whole thing in a flash?"

"Why, it wasn't so much what she actually told me as what I heard between her words, so to speak. What she told me was that Mrs. Beresford knew the answer to that bet; what I deduced was that, being the sort of person she was, it was quite incredible that she should have made a bet to which she already knew the answer. *Ergo,* she didn't. *Ergo,* there never was such a bet. *Ergo,* Beresford was lying. *Ergo,* Beresford wanted to get hold of those chocolates for some reason other than he stated. After all, we only had Beresford's word for the bet, hadn't we?

"Of course he wouldn't have left her that afternoon till he'd seen her take, or somehow made her take, at least six of the chocolates—more than a lethal dose. That's why the stuff was in those meticulous six-minim doses. And so that he could take a couple himself, of course. A clever stroke, that."

Moresby rose to his feet.

"Well, Mr. Sheringham, I'm much obliged to you, sir. And now I shall have to get busy myself." He scratched his head. "Chance the Avenger, eh? Well, I can tell you one pretty big thing Beresford left to

Chance the Avenger, Mr. Sheringham. Suppose Sir William hadn't handed over the chocolates after all? Supposing he'd kept 'em, to give to one of his own ladies?"

Roger positively snorted. He felt a personal pride in Beresford by this time.

"Really, Moresby! It wouldn't have had any serious results if Sir William had. Do give my man credit for being what he is. You don't imagine he sent the *poisoned* ones to Sir William, do you? Of course not! He'd send *harmless* ones, and exchange them for the others on his way home. Dash it all, he wouldn't go right out of his way to present opportunities to Chance.

"If," added Roger, "Chance really is the right word."

Food for Thought
by Victor Canning

The last time I'd seen Monsieur Pluvet was in the first November after the end of the war. It was outside a small hut in the hills behind Clambéry, in the Savoy. He looked glum and depressed—glum because it was snowing and he hated the cold, and depressed because even then, I guess, he was hating his job. He was in the Sûreté at Chambéry, and they had sent him out to piece together a family which a returning French soldier, in a fit of insane rage, had dismembered before cutting his own throat.

"Such an untidy man, *mon ami*," Pluvet had said, as we walked down to the village afterwards. "I prefer forgers. They never put you off your food."

And now here he was, four years later, the proprietor of *La Reine Inconnue,* a small inn well off the beaten track. His face was wreathed in smiles as he took my hand.

"Mon ami," he said. "What a pleasure!"

"My friend," I said, "What a surprise! The last time I saw you, you were about to become Inspector. Now I find you an innkeeper."

"Come into the office," Pluvet said. "We will have a *fine* together, and I'll tell them in the kitchen to prepare us a nice duck with orange sauce and some asparagus. *Caneton à l'orange*—it is the specialty of the house. People come from a long way for it. It is good you are here today, *mon ami,* for a duck is just too much for one person, but shared between two—it is just right!"

"So, you've given up crime for the cuisine?" I said,

as we sat together over our drink. "Do I smell a story in this?"

Pluvet smiled. In the old days it was quite an event if he smiled, but now it sat on his face as comfortably as a cat on a cushion. "Maybe. But deep here—" he patted his chest "—it was always what I wanted. Always I said to myself, 'Pluvet, you are a good detective, but Pluvet, you would be a better *hôtelier*.' Watching people explain themselves, tell lies, open up their dirty little secrets—all that makes me unhappy. Watching them eat—ah, that makes me happy! Also I earn more money making them happy. That makes me happier."

"How did you find this place?" I knew Pluvet. I knew a story was there, and I knew he meant me to dig for it.

"I come here one day. I see it. I like it. I buy it. Just like that. Simple."

Little by little I got it out of him. It wasn't hard. It was just a matter of patience. It wasn't any accident which had brought him to *La Reine Inconnue*. He'd come out here on a case—the murder of a Colonel Thery who had lived at Chambéry.

The Colonel was rich, retired, and a widower. He was also the president of a curious little club which had been formed in Chambéry by himself and four other men. They called themselves the Chambéry Club for Eating, Walking, and the Direct Observation of Nature. It was quite a mouthful of a name, but, as Pluvet said, when a party of old fellows get together a boyish, fanciful streak often develops in them. In Chambéry itself, they were known as the *Ga-Ga's*. Not that they were ga-ga, however. Each one had his head well screwed on, and they were all men of good position.

There was the Colonel, a hell of a bore apparently when you got him on the subject of Algeria; there was a lawyer, Avocat Rochelle, a plump little man with a mind like a razor blade; a Monsieur Delabord, who was a factory-owner; André Justand, a political writer whose books were well-known in France; and a Monsieur Sainte-Verde who ran a prosperous finance company of the kind which offers to advance money without security, but never does.

"These five," said Pluvet, "they have a little ritual which goes on almost every fortnight during Spring and Summer. Every other Sunday they hire a car and drive out from Chambéry and breakfast at some little village. Already on the map they have picked out a route over the hills to some other village where there is a good inn. After breakfast they set out. Each man walks alone by his own route, and each man must do the walk within a certain time and, as he goes, he must observe nature, make little notes of the birds and flowers he sees, collect specimens, and so on. When they meet in the evening, they have a good meal, compare their notes, and elect a winner on the basis of the variety and interest of the observations and specimens collected. Childish, no? *Mais oui*—but they like it, and they do it for years. Maybe for all the years they live these five come nearest to being human and worthy people on these Sundays. Until the Sunday comes when the Colonel is murdered."

"What happened?"

"Well, it is like this. This Sunday in August they drive out for breakfast to a little village called Boisne. They have arranged to walk over the hills from there to *La Reine Inconnue*. They have a little discussion about what they shall eat when they get here, but this time it is not a long discussion for the specialty of this house is known and they are all for duck. But there was some argument over the wine, I believe. Then they telephone here and order the dinner and—off they go like a lot of Boy Scouts.

"It is a very hot day. And remember, they are not so young, and this time they are all a little over their time limit when they reach here. When I say all, I mean all except the Colonel. The other four—Rochelle, Sainte-Verde, Delabord, and Justand—they sit outside drinking beer and waiting for the Colonel. But the Colonel does not come. Then the proprietor who was here be-

fore me calls out that the ducklings are ready, and they
go in and eat and joke a bit about the Colonel. He is
getting too old to keep up with them, no?

"At 10 o'clock when their car is come for them
there is still no Colonel and they are all alarmed now.
Well, it is not until the next morning that the Colonel
is found. A forest guard finds him up in the hills and
someone has knocked his head in with a rock and
robbed him. It is at this point, you understand, that I
come in. I have just been made Inspector. I must make
a good show. You know how it is. When you get pro-
motion all your friends watch you, waiting for you to
trip. And I have many friends."

"You never tripped in your life, Pluvet. You watch
your step too carefully."

"Maybe. But what kind of a life is that, watching
your boots all day long? Anyway, two days later we
pick up a young gypsy lad some miles from here. He
has the Colonel's watch, his ring, and some of the
money he has taken from the old boy's wallet. I take
him along with me. I talk to him. Maybe I talk a little
roughly with him, but all I get from him is that he is
passing through the hills and comes across the body
and he robs it. Robbing a dead body, you understand,
is less immoral than robbing a live one. Also it is
easier. This lad, he is too indignant at the fuss we make
over a simple robbery to understand the mess he is in.
And it is this, *mon ami,* which makes me think that
maybe he tells the truth. So—"

"You decided to look into the movements of the
other members of the club who were up in the hills?"

"*Naturellement.* They are all up there. Any of them
could have done it. But why? It is always that, you understand, which is harder than the how. All of them
knew which way the Colonel would walk because they
all agreed on their routes beforehand. Any one of them
could have slipped across and knocked his head in and
then gone back to his own route.

"You know," he went on, "in a small town—if you

dig deep enough—you can find a reason for any man murdering any other man. What do I find?"

"That they all have motives?"

"*Naturellement.* Take André Justand. He has a daughter who is in love with the Colonel's son. The son, he is in love with her—but the Colonel has refused to give his consent to the marriage. He has another and richer bride picked for his son. With the Colonel out of the way, the two can marry—and André Justand idolizes his daughter and would do anything for her.

"Then take Sainte-Verde. He is rich, but he is as mean as they come, and he has a wife who likes luxuries. What do I find? That when Sainte-Verde goes away from home sometimes, the Colonel was in the habit of entertaining his wife. You understand? Sainte-Verde may be mean, but he still does not like another man giving his wife a good time. You see, *mon ami,* what we find when we dig is not always pretty. Then there is Delabord. He is ambitious with his factory and the Colonel is refusing to sell him a piece of land which he wants for expansion. With the lawyer Rochelle it is even more simple. Poor Rochelle—he is in prison now. He has been embezzling his clients' money and the Colonel has found it out. They are old friends, but even so the Colonel—the soul of honor, you understand—will be forced to expose him unless he makes full restitution by a certain date. When I talked to Rochelle he admitted that the Colonel's death had come as a relief to him, although it had done him no good for his difficulties are now known. But he had expected more support from his old friend. He is a little simple, eh, to expect too much from friends?

"So, I talk to them all. I find out about them, and I have a feeling that among them is the murderer, and that the gypsy boy is just an unlucky intruder. But what am I to do? There is a great deal against the boy—unless I can discover the truth."

A girl put her head round the door. "*Patron, c'est servi.*"

"Come on, my friend, let us eat."

When you're in the newspaper trade you have to learn to put your curiosity on the shelf with your hat when you eat, otherwise you develop ulcers. We ate, and it was one of the best meals I'd had for a long time. There was no question that duck was the specialty of the house. It would have been the specialty of any house. But when we got to the *brie*—and what a cheese, as rich and ripe as a harvest moon—I came back to the attack.

"You haven't come to the point, Pluvet. How did you find this place?"

"During my inquiries, *mon ami.* I began to like the gypsy boy. I work hard for him, and for myself because I don't want to do an injustice to an innocent man on my first case as Inspector. So I go everywhere. I go to the little inn at Boisne where the party had their breakfast. I talk with everyone. Then I walk across the hills. I walk all five routes, and you know how I hate to walk. And then I come down here and talk to everyone. That is how I find the place is for sale. But I find other things as well."

He shrugged.

"I'll bet you did."

"Finally I go back to Chambéry and I go to see Monsieur Sainte-Verde. He is surprised to see me, but he is pleasant, but not so pleasant that he offers me a drink. 'Monsieur Sainte-Verde,' I say, 'I have come to arrest you for the murder of Colonel Thery.'

" 'Very interesting,' he says. 'Perhaps you will explain a little more? Why me and not one of the other members of the club?' " Pluvet leaned forward and filled my coffee cup. "It is a reasonable question, eh?"

"Come on, you old so-and-so," I said. "How did you know to pick on Sainte-Verde? It might have been any of the others."

"Ha, yes. You see each member of the club paid in his turn for the dinner at the end of the day's expedition. The Sunday the Colonel was murdered it was Sainte-Verde's turn. It was he, in fact, who telephoned to this inn from Boisne, ordering the dinner. He was a terribly mean man, and he knew that he was going to murder the Colonel that day. His meanness got the better of his common sense. He ordered dinner for four only—because he knew the Colonel wouldn't arrive. If he'd ordered for five they would have had to put a third duck on and, although none of it would have been eaten, he would have been charged with it. As I say, *mon ami*, a duck is too much for one, but just right when shared with another person."